SCARY STUFF

The Scary Stuff anthology is
Copyright @ 2020 Oddity Productions, LLC
The individual stories within
are copyrighted to the respective authors.

ISBN 978-1-7333938-2-9 (paperback)
ISBN 978-1-7333938-3-6 (eBook)

Edited by Nicholas Leamy and Jacob Jones-Goldstein
Cover art and Interior Layout by Jennifer Marang
Cover banner and OPP logo by Steve Myers

Published by
Oddity Prodidy Productions, LLC
935 Rue Madora
Bear, DE 19701

www.oddityprodigy.com

A HORROR ANTHOLOGY

Edited by Nicholas Leamy
and Jacob Jones-Goldstein

Acknowledgements

We would first like to thank Jennifer Marang for the amazing job she did on the cover art, and Steve Myers for his work on the logo and cover banner. Everytime we saw these images, it reminded us of why we wanted to publish this book in the first place.

Thanks also to the Newark Arts Alliance and the Written Remains Writers Guild for inspiring us to follow our hearts and pursue our writing. Bringing our writing to those monthly open mic nights helped us determine the type of writers we wanted to be.

Additional thanks goes to Captain Blue Hen Comics and Between Books 2.0. Both establishments have gone out of their way to support and promote our endeavors. We will always think of you as life long friends.

A special thank you to all the writers out there who submitted their stories to us. For those of you out there who were not accepted this round, thank you for giving us some ideas for our next few books. We hope to hear from you again.

We would also like to thank Caleb Thusat of Village Comics for taking time to give us some very useful tips and advice on running a successful crowdfunding campaign.

The editors would like to thank the rest of Oddity Prodigy Productions. Working with you is like working with family, which means it is no work at all.

And a final shout out to our families who were very accepting and supportive of our long nights working on this. You make everything worthwhile.

SPECIAL THANKS

We would like to give special thanks to our IndieGoGo backers! You got this project off the ground. We look forward to showing you more of our work. A standing ovation goes to:

Brian Alpers

Colin L Anderson

Joseph Nathan Bernard

Donald J. Bingle

Dan Bogart

Bernard Brick

Sara Cardile

Jason Colatriano

Lorelei Dancer

Eric Dellinger

Shannon Dunn

Timothy Eichman

Matthew Ferrari

Jamie Gentry

Stephen Goldstein

Bonnie Jones-Goldstein

Jeremiah Jones-Goldstein

Tracey Houtman

Rachel Kane

Erica Kennedy

Gregory Labrador

Douglas Leamy

Mario Lia

Jennifer Marang

Devon Miller-Duggan

Krystal Mitchell

Cheryl Morecraft

Nicholas Owens

Jude Reid

Susanna M Reilly

Eric Remington

Jordan Rosenwald

Mayer Rubin

David T Shoemaker

Heather Smith

Ben Sommers

Mark Spencer

Louis St.amand

Randy L Stubbs II

Patty Trush

Michael Walton

Don Widmer

TABLE OF TERROR

INTRODUCTION

by Shasta Schatz

What scares you? An abandoned home, a forgotten typewriter, the dog at the end of the sidewalk, that dusty book on the shelf, chaos...

What is fear? Rooted in a need to understand, but finding none. Based on experience. Transformed into urban legend. Made real by perceived omens. Put into words on paper and on-screen.

When your formative years are spent having the shit scared out of you by horror stories, one develops an unwavering sense of nostalgia and longing for those spine-chillers throughout life. "Oddity Prodigy Presents: The Scary Stuff Anthology" is here for you with nightmare scenarios that will have you checking your windows in the middle of the day.

The fright that we experience in a movie theater is a different animal from the sheer terror of the written word—there is no shared experience in your favorite reading nook on a quiet afternoon. There is no one to feel your jumps and jitters on the couch or to perform an "all clear" on the backseat when it's time to drive home from the library. You are all alone on that guided tour through invisible monster island.

Do you want to be scared? Our authors submitted terrific tales in the tradition of EC Comics, "Creepy" and "Eerie", "Tales from the Crypt", "The Vault of Horror", including homages to macabre writers such as King, Poe, and Dickens. They endeavor to give you a glimpse of the uncomfortable, to warp your senses, to haunt your sunny day.

In this throwback anthology, you will be exposed to magic, science fiction, fantasy, history—a tableau of sacrifice and of caution. Allow yourself to drift from story to story, through time and space, in and out of alignment with both heroes and ghosts, human and animal and deity. Let their spindly fingers reach out to get a beat on where you are and where you need to settle.

Our artists deliver the iconic black and white illustrations that will take you back to the (not so) bygone eras of browsing racks at your local bookstore. The shock endings remind you to be spatially aware on the walk to your car. And, perhaps, to not take everything so seriously.

Scary stories teach us a lesson. Scary stories keep us in line. Scary stories teach us how to survive...or they illustrate how futile fighting back can be. Scary stories appear in both the old magic and the new. Without the fear of jumping into the bed to dispel the magic of the monsters under the bed, do we really know that we're alive?

Fear of food. Fear of love. Fear of age. Fear of going outside. Fear of failure.

Campfire scary stories. Stories our parents told us in hopes that we'd make better decisions than those they made. Science fiction stories that make us aware of our arrogance.

Scary stories transcend genres, just as they move through cultural boundaries, like a virus over county borders. Monsters exist in our daily lives as much as in our dreams, and despite our descriptions of those horrors, the terror is, in essence, the same.

Our editors stack the deck to tease you with your own humanity and to delight your fiddly bits. In your hands is the product of many terrifying individuals providing stories about family, crime, bad weather, romance, suspense, and abject terror. Also trees—there are a lot of trees in this book.

This collection is weird and fun just like the upstart small press publisher bringing it to you. Oddity Prodigy Productions, where every project is a labor of love, where fear lives, where creativity makes you question your life choices.

For normies, scaredy cats, and the undisturbed, the simple phrase "Scary Stuff" calls on episodes that we've likely placed into a box on a shelf inside of our mind attic. We pull them down for special occasions but mostly leave them where they can't make a mess of our everyday lives. If you, like me, are one of those people, this anthology is going to be a special occasion. Let the tingles move through you. Elevate those hackles.

This is Scary Stuff. We hope that you'll get creeped out with us.

Quid Pro Quo

by Jude Reid

The first death happened in the summer of '94.

I was a lifeguard on duty at the Kelpie Centre at the time. Don't be fooled by the name, by the way; there was precious little Celtic romance to be found in that particular council leisure centre. They'd tried their best, but brutalist concrete architecture with pseudo-roman mosaics was a questionable combination at best, and overall the impression it made was one of uneasy despair. That matched the rest of the town perfectly as far as I was concerned.

Everyone knew Drumbridge was rotting from the inside out. The steelworks were closed, the canal was silted up, and any local rat with sense was fleeing this sinking ship. I was one of those rats—I'd finished school the month before, and the lifeguard job was my attempt to earn some extra cash before I started at Glasgow University in the autumn. I wouldn't be leaving home—there was precisely zero chance of my granny affording Student Halls with three kids still at home to feed—but for the minor inconvenience of three hours on the bus every day all the freedom of Glasgow was mine and with it the promise of my eventual escape from Drumbridge.

But everything changed that day in the pool. One minute everything was normal—just the usual soundtrack of shrieking kids, bellowing teenagers, and the shrill blasts of whistles aimed at one of the other two. I was at the shallow end of the leisure pool, keeping an eye on the smaller swimmers. The wave machine was on when I heard Annemarie blow her whistle at a cluster of teenagers, who were splashing and shouting even more disruptively than usual. A second

15

later, she was in the pool and swimming towards them. Annemarie was good at her job. If she was in the water, it meant something had gone badly wrong.

I blew my whistle. "Everyone out!" I shouted, and the pool emptied of swimmers like hot oil from a frying pan. I ran to the deep end to see if Annemarie needed help and watched her surface empty-handed.

"What is it?" I shouted.

"Someone's stuck—in the wave machine–"

She drew a deep breath and submerged again. I grabbed a pair of goggles from the poolside and jumped in. Underwater, I saw Annemarie struggling with a swimmer, one of his feet trapped between two metal bars, the task of freeing him made more difficult by the guy's other foot flailing around at chin height and the steady to-and-fro of the wave machine. I realised I should have hit the emergency cut-off before getting into the pool, but it was too late for that now.

I braced myself against the bars and heaved as hard as I could, expecting the guy's foot to come clear—maybe minus a bit of skin, but no worse than that. Nothing moved—if anything, he seemed to be stuck further in than before. He was thrashing wildly now, his hands clawing at us, the last of his air escaping his lungs in a stream of big, panicky bubbles. I shoved his hands away, feeling my chest tighten at the thought of him dragging me down with him.

And that was when I heard him scream.

Dark tendrils of blood spiraled out from between the bars as he was tugged sharply between them, streamers of skin tearing off his leg. I tried to grab his waist, his arm—anything at all—but he was thrashing too wildly, and the spreading cloud of blood was obscuring my vision. His three free limbs were clattering against the steel bars now, in an arrhythmic drumbeat that was simultaneously dulled and amplified by the water. I heard a sharp crack, and when I next got a clear look, he had been pulled in as far as his hip, mouth open, face contorted as his lungs filled with water.

Whatever was pulling him kept up a steady pressure, and more cracking sounds followed as his hips, pelvis, and ribs vanished inside. His head was last. The blood was spreading into a diffuse scarlet cloud by then, and I got one last clear look at his face as the bones of his skull cracked and compressed, his eyes bulging and blood gobbetting from the silently screaming mouth.

He was dead by then. I told myself that afterward. He had to have been.

But his eyes said differently.

They didn't find much of him. They drained the pool, but other than a few scraps of skin, hair, and a pair of shredded blue swimming trunks, there was precious little left for anyone to recognise. The police took statements from us all, but Annemarie hadn't been wearing goggles, and all she had was a blurry recollection of the swimmer trapped in the bars. The guy's friends said they'd been messing about trying to swim as close as they could while the waves were on when he'd somehow got pulled in.

It turned out I was the only one with a clear view of the whole thing.

In the end, they decided that he must have managed to shove his foot far enough between the bars that it had become stuck in the mechanism, which was quite the feat, given that there was a full two-metre gap between the bars and the machinery. They put the whole thing down to a terrible, tragic accident.

The Kelpie Centre never reopened, of course. The Council boarded it up while they decided what they were going to do with the building—which, in keeping with what they were doing for the rest of the town—was nothing at all.

I had trouble sleeping after that. Gran was understanding, to begin with, given what I'd seen, but after a fortnight of me screaming the house awake at three a.m., her saintly patience was running short, and so were my funds. When the Council advertised for an overnight security guard for the boarded-up Kelpie Centre, I figured that would solve both problems at once, and signed myself up.

It wasn't the worst job I'd had. They gave me a uniform—a flattering navy blue polyester jacket and trousers—and a six by four-foot cabin to sit in with a kettle and a fan heater. I was paid a fraction more than minimum wage, and considering I was pulling twelve-hour shifts at least half of which I spent asleep, I was happy with the whole arrangement.

My shift started at eight when I took over from Big Paddy McConnell. He usually had a smile and a cup of tea waiting for me coming on shift, which was kind of him, and more-or-less made up for the fact that he left the cabin reeking of cigarette smoke for at least an hour after he'd gone. He'd got the idea I took sugar in my tea—which I don't, by the way—but he was so pleased with himself every time that I waited until he was well on his way home before I poured it out the window and made myself another. Most shifts that would be as exciting as it got. I'd take a walk around at nine, one and four, and the time between was my own. If I was tired, I napped; otherwise, I worked my way through the stack of comics under my chair, drank my tea, and tucked away my earnings toward the day I'd be out of Drumbridge for good.

I'd been in the job a fortnight when the next deaths happened. It was a Saturday night—I remember that—and a quiet one by Drumbridge standards, with only a minimal number of drunken bampots blundering around after chucking-out time at the Eagle Inn. I was settling into my second mug of over-brewed Scottish Blend and a new comic, and then I heard the noise.

Noise itself wasn't uncommon. More than once, I'd been startled out of my chair by a car backfiring on the road or the scream of a fox on a hot date, but this was anunholy combination of shouting, braying laughter and smashing glass.

"You're kidding me," I muttered. I took one last swig of my tea—calculating regretfully that it would be cold by the time I got back—and lifted my official issue torch, which was approximately 90% more often used as a club than as an actual light source. I switched on the yellow, wavering beam and headed out around the building to where the noise was coming from.

It was teenagers, I saw, as I came around the corner. There was a guy and a girl. The pair of them were standing in a cloud of cigarette smoke. The guy had something in his hand, and at first, I thought he was throwing rocks at the windows, but when the projectile smashed off the wall, I realised it was a glass bottle. He lifted another one from a pile at his feet and held it out to the girl, who flicked a lighter and lit a tuft of cloth stuffed inside.

"Hey!" I shouted, and they both turned. I had a second to get a look at their faces and vaguely recognised them—from school, maybe? —and then they bolted, dropping the lit bottle on the grass. I took a moment to stamp out the flame before it could spread, but there wasn't much risk to the soggy grass.

I completed my circuit of the building and headed back to the hut, already thinking about another cup of tea. Sheets from a newspaper—or one of those brightly colored advertisements that tried to make cheap frozen food look appealing—were blowing across the damp grass, and one of them slapped into my ankle. I reached out to flick it away, and then my guts made a spirited attempt to lurch out of my mouth as I recognised the collage-style artwork—a microscope, a photograph, a crescent moon. It was the cover of the latest issue of the Sandman, specifically, my copy.

I lurched in a clumsy run, cursing myself for the idiot I was. The cabin's door was hanging open, pages of issue sixty-one torn from their cover, strewn across the floor, and blowing out over the grass outside. The phone was still on the desk, but the handset had been pulled off its cable and was nowhere to be seen. I swore, my voice sounding high and panicky in my ears. The keys, which I had stupidly left on their hook, were gone. The pair of teenagers must have sprinted back to the hut once they'd seen the direction I was going, lifted them, and ran. My stomach lurched, and my head spun, the sensations accompanied by a fervent desire to have the last fifteen minutes of my life back.

I had no idea what they were planning to do with my keys, but if my shift ended without the Kelpie Centre's door locked and the keys in my hand, I was going to lose my job, which would make a big dent in my plans for getting out of town. Maybe, if I were lucky, they'd just stolen them for a laugh and chucked them in the undergrowth where a night's frantic searching might be enough for me to find them. At least if the front door were still padlocked shut, I'd know they'd run off with the keys or dumped them, and maybe I could get away with saying they'd dropped out of my pocket. And if I was unlucky... Well. I decided to leave that thought unfinished.

My luck was never good back then. By the time I reached the front entrance, the big double doors were wide open, the chain that had held them shut coiled on the ground like a sleeping snake and the padlock nowhere to be seen. I shone my torch inside, and my heart leaped as I saw the ring of keys on the ground about ten feet inside. Maybe they'd chucked them in to mess with me, or maybe they'd dropped them by accident. I didn't care. All I felt was a tremendous sense of relief.

The keys were inches from my hand when I felt something behind me. It was only the faintest breath of moving air, nothing more, but it was enough warning that I turned, and my forearm partially deflected the blow that should have smashed into the back of my head. White-hot pain seared across my hand and wrist, and I think I must have screamed. My torch went skittering across the floor, the bulb flickering wildly. The door slammed behind me, and the light went out.

"You're dead." It was a light voice, a female one. I could hear her moving in the dark, feet shuffling over the dusty floor tiles. Cradling my damaged arm, I forced myself to my feet, moving away from where I thought the sound was coming from. Her night vision would be better than mine, I was sure, but if I stayed put, I might as well have been covered in glowsticks.

"You're the lifeguard who was on the day Dougie got caught in the machine." A male voice this time.

A sick wave of realisation swept over me. It wasn't school I recognised them from—they'd been part of the gaggle of teenagers in the pool when their friend had turned to ninety kilograms of chunky puree.

"You messed up, and Dougie died."

"He got stuck in the wave machine," I said, groping my way backward in the hope of finding the doorway. "It was an accident."

"Yeah. Dougie's fault for swimming too close to the bars, that's what they said." This time it was the girl who spoke, "Liars."

"He's dead because you let him die." The guy again. "We're going to settle the score. Quid pro quo."

I flung myself to the side just in time to feel something whistle past my head—a crowbar or a hockey stick, I guessed, from the agonising J-curve of pain it had left along my forearm. Trying not to puke, I took a moment to calculate whether my survival chances were better if I stayed quiet and hid, or just made a run for it—then the weapon, whatever it was, descended again and winged me across the shoulder. That decided it. I sucked in an unsteady breath and ran blindly into the darkness.

I don't know how many times I tripped or fell or crashed into walls I had no way of seeing. The Kelpie Centre was a maze of corridors and doors, and without my torch, I was reduced to groping along any surface I could find. After what seemed about a month in the labyrinth, I emerged into a larger space that I managed to identify as a changing room, one that opened onto the main swimming pool area. On the poolside, there was a fire exit and windows that led out to the grounds beyond. Even if the fire door was chained up, as I was fairly sure it was, surely I could grab something heavy from the poolside, smash a window and escape my pursuers that way. I didn't have the keys, but I didn't care. I'd settle for escaping with my skin intact.

Moonlight was seeping into the pool hall along with the distant sulphur yellow of streetlamps. The empty pool's internal silhouette gave the room a strange, sculptural air. It sloped down from the shallow end to the bars of the wave machine, like the cage of some monstrous beast kept twelve feet deep. Dark rust stains had smeared over the tiles—there was no chance it could be blood, was there? —and I gave the whole area a very wide berth, lifting an abandoned mop from the floor as I slunk towards the windows. The fire exit was padlocked, as I had known it would be, and I thought lingeringly of the ring of keys, no doubt still lying on the floor by the entrance. I pushed the bar anyway, and the door opened a crack before the chains stopped it, letting in a gust of cool night air. I drew back my mop to take a swing—then froze. Someone was coming through the door to the poolside.

Again, that impossible choice: hide or run. This time I chose the former and tried to make myself one with the wall behind me. I could hear my pursuers murmuring to each other, their feet echoing as they stepped out onto the tiles. Something was pushing into the small of my back, and I reached a hand behind me to find it was a door handle. I turned it, every muscle in my body rigid as I anticipated the squeak that would betray my position, but the hinges moved smoothly, and the door swung open just enough for me to squeeze myself through.

I had expected a cupboard, but I found myself in a corridor. I fumbled my way along, biting back curses as I blundered into mops and buckets, grimly aware that I was probably heading towards a dead end—with the emphasis heavily on "dead." The air here was taking on a different smell—dry and dusty—and from the back of my memory, I dredged up the information that the Kelpie Centre had been built on the foundations and pipework of an old Victorian bath. Maybe the corridor I was in connected to a part of the old building. If it did, that would explain the smell—

That was when the ground dropped out from under me. I had half a second to realise that I had missed the start of a flight of stairs, a second more to flail my arms in huge, futile circles, and then I was falling. One of my arms slammed into a rail, my shoulder into a cast iron step, and then I was tumbling down in a clatter of limbs to God alone knew where. The ground, when I hit it, came as a relief. Then the pain kicked in.

I ticked off my injuries one at a time. One of my knees had twisted under me, and when I straightened my leg, I felt a queasy lurch in the pit of my stomach. I was bruised all down my left side, and taking a deep breath hurt enough that I was confident I'd broken at least one rib but other than that and the lump rising on the side of my head, I had escaped without life-threatening harm. I realised I'd fallen about three flights down an old-fashioned staircase, open at the centre with a skylight far overhead letting in the thin moonlight. From the voices and footsteps above me, I was pretty sure that the guy and the girl had heard me hit the ground.

I got to my feet, my body registering its protest, and my left forearm took the opportunity to remind me that it had been injured first and, therefore, should take precedence. The sound of water—a low, bubbling gurgle, like water filling long-disused pipes—was coming from a room that led off the staircase, and I hobbled towards it, my curiosity and my fear taking me in the same direction.

The hinges of the door had rusted long ago, and the door, marked with a brass plaque that read "Pipe Room," was hanging at a jaunty angle, and there was something like a birdbath right in the centre of the room. On closer inspection, it turned out to be a cuboid of marble shaped like a box standing on its end, about a metre high and half as much across. There was a depression in its centre deep enough to baptize a child or drown one. Three of the vertical faces of the altar—yes, it was unquestionably an altar—were carved with worn reliefs that might once have been victory wreaths, but the fourth was inscribed with a series of block capitals. I traced a few of the letters with my finger to try and make sense of them. Unfortunately, Latin had been dropped from the Drumbridge Secondary syllabus a couple of years before I started, so whatever Leg IX V V meant remained a mystery to me. I dipped my fingers in the shallow depression on top, and they came away wet.

"There!"

The girl was right behind me, holding a torch—my torch, I realised with a stab of alarm mixed with outrage. The thin yellow beam wavered its way up my legs towards my face, and I jerked my head away a second too late, a purple afterimage seared onto my retinas and my night vision utterly gone. The two shadows menaced towards me, one of them holding a metre-long weapon—yes, it was a crowbar, as it happened—and I desperately looked about me for an exit. Even with a working pair of eyes, that would have been impossible. The only door was behind me, and that way was blocked.

"We were going to burn the place down with you inside," the girl said, a conversational tone in her voice. "But, this dump's too soggy to burn."

"So, we'll just kick you to death and leave you down here."

A fist thumped into my eye socket, and I reeled back, tripping over my own feet and cracking the back of my head on the altar as I fell. "Stop—" I managed to say, but I got only a burst of laughter in return.

"Nah," the guy said. "I don't think we will."

A shadow moved across my vision, and in that second, I became aware of something else in the room. There was a sudden sense of expectancy that terrified me an order of magnitude more than the two human's intent on staving in my skull. I could smell water—not the salt tang of the sea, but something sharp and peaty that made me think of mountain streams. I blinked, rubbed the blood from my eyes, and pushed myself up to stand on the altar, feeling once again the wetness inside the depression on its top. This time, as my bloody fingers touched the bottom of the shallow basin, I felt something pull at them as though sucking them clean, like putting milky fingers into a baby's mouth. The sense of expectancy in the room intensified. My two attackers didn't seem to notice.

"No more running," the girl said. I noticed that neither was stepping towards me, each waiting for the other to start what would presumably be the terminal burst of violence. Maybe they were having second thoughts, but that wasn't something I felt comfortable staking my life on. And as it turned out, I didn't need to.

The presence in the room unfolded out of the shadows, and suddenly the air was full of the rich metal taste of spilled blood. I opened eyes that I didn't remember having closed and saw the thing for the first time.

It was taller than a human, tall enough that its head scraped the roof of the room. Its skull was elongated like a horse's, the skinned-looking muzzle ending in a lipless grimace that bared two rows of hooked and pointed teeth. Reflecting the torchlight was a pair of red eyes, and its front limbs ended in a pair of six-taloned hands. It stood upright on its hind legs that were bent backward like a horse's or a goat's. I couldn't see its feet, but when it stepped forward, I heard the sharp click of hooves on stone.

The girl, maybe the braver of the two, or stupider, stepped forward and swung her crowbar at its neck in a blow that would have shattered the larynx of any normal creature. It might as well have been a kiss for all the notice the monster took. Then, with devastating speed, it lashed out with one clawed hand, grabbed her around the throat, lifted her, and squeezed. Her scream turned instantly to a strangled wheeze, and I watched blood gush out of her neck, spraying the monster's face, the altar, and the floor. A long-forked tongue flicked out from between its teeth and licked the blood from its face. It held her there until her struggling stopped.

I was running by then. The girl's discarded crowbar in my hand, I was sprinting for the doorway, out into the hall that led to the stairwell and the promise of freedom. The guy was running behind me, not pursuing me this time but fleeing desperately along with me. The trivial issue of my intended murder seemed to have been forgotten in the face of this appalling, inhuman enemy. At least, I was counting on him believing that.

I reached the foot of the stairs ahead of him and waited. As his headlong dash brought him towards me, I crouched in the shadows, the crowbar held out at ankle height, and was immensely gratified when he tripped over it and sprawled his length on the steps. My hope of escape felt considerably more secure now that not one, but two human bodies in various stages of animation were between the thing and me, and I scurried past him on to the steps just as the creature emerged from the room behind us.

It turned its head so that one of its red eyes met mine, and at that moment I realised I knew what it was. It belonged in the stories my granny had told me, a beast old and terrible and half-forgotten. But I knew its name.

Kelpie.

This land had belonged to it long before the building that was its namesake, before the old Victorian baths and whoever had worshipped at its altar; before the Romans had arrived and called it a god in the hope of gaining its favor. Ancient and hungry, it was something that understood the nature of debt and obligation, and the advantages of paying one's dues.

I understood those things too.

I brought the crowbar down hard. Once, twice, then a third and final time.

And that, more or less, is how that particular chapter of my life ended.

Two missing teenagers didn't attract much attention locally. Everyone assumed they'd run away from Drumbridge together, and no one much felt the loss. A few weeks later, the Council announced an ambitious multi-million-pound plan to rebuild the Kelpie Centre as a state-of-the-art sports centre, complete with cafe, fitness suite, and a fifty-metre Olympic pool. There were waterslides, river rapids, and a wave machine, and it proved quite a draw all across the Central Belt. What with the canal regeneration program and the luxury flats they're building on the site of the old steelworks, everyone agrees there's more life to Drumbridge now than we've seen in many years.

As for me, I decided not to go to University after all. Instead, I signed up straight away as a lifeguard in the new Kelpie Centre. The starting pay's not all that great, but it's enough to cover the rent on a place of my own with a little bit extra to put aside for the future—and that's a future I intend to make the most of.

You see, I've got this feeling that things are going to start looking up for Drumbridge in general and for me in particular.

YOU COULD DO BETTER

by Nicholas Leamy

Sarah loved everything about going to Kindergarten. The teachers always greeted her with a warm smile. There was always at least one kid on the playground who was ready and willing to play. She looked forward to her favorite arts and crafts class because that was where all of her ideas and dreams could become reality. The only problem that clouded the day was the first hour.

Every morning Sarah would rush around the house to get ready. She would prepare her clothes the night before. The hairstyle for that day had already been chosen, and all needed items set out. Before going to bed, she would make sure that her backpack had all her homework, pencils, and other materials ready.

No matter how much she did, though, every morning was the same for Sarah. Her mother slept in. Her bedtimes were before it got dark out, so she was not sure what her mom did at night, but she figured it must have been very important since dad always had to handle morning drop-offs.

Her father was a successful vice president for one of those corporations that was really good at trimming the fat from other corporations until they could sell them for parts. He never had a real day off and did not see why anyone else should. This mindset applied to his daughter as well.

Every morning he pushed and prodded Sarah to keep moving. She was never ready to go at a time he was satisfied with. He was even disappointed on the days when he dropped her off before other students had arrived, and some of the teachers were still arriving.

She could deal with the lonely weekends. She was fine with being dropped at home only for her father to race back to work again, and the long nights of homework and extra studies supplied by her parents. She had even come to terms with her mother, who was barely present in her life. But those school day mornings were the worst for her as they were the one thing that most clouded her only happy place.

At the end of the last day of school, Sarah clung tightly to her report card. The summary of her studies and efforts held such promise. Now she would be able to show her parents that she was a good student. She thought that maybe if they could see that, they would be proud of her and maybe be able to relax.

She knew she was not allowed to open parent letters on her own. As the other students left, she stood there so anxious that her report card was smushed into a ball. When her father finally arrived, she ran to the car and thrust it into his hands.

While his face showed he was distressed by her forwardness, he silently opened the report and read its contents. Sarah was able to look over his shoulder and could see nothing but checks and A marks. Her heart skipped a beat, and her cheeks flushed with pride.

That made what her father said next hurt so much more. It took everything she had inside to not cry. She knew once the tears came, they would not stop. Her father always saw crying as weakness and his daughter was not going to ever be weak. While her face remained stoic, everything inside her shattered as he said. "Your teachers seem to think you're doing a great job. We may need to reassess where we're sending you. I'm not going to let any daughter of mine not reach her full potential. Don't worry, dear. We know better. You could do better."

Sarah loved Michael and wanted to spend the rest of her life with him. They had been together for two years, and she felt closer to him every day. He had asked her to move in with him, and she agreed.

She met Michael in an Anatomy class while she was working on her Masters of Science in Biomechanical Engineering. He was working on his Masters of Science in Pathology. Their shared interest in medical sciences first presented itself as competition, and that grew into playful flirting, ending with an extended weekend hermitted away in her campus housing with only one fraught excursion into the massive blizzard for snacks and booze.

Michael knew what it was like to have parents that pushed too hard. He had several times jokingly told Sarah that his family would disown him if he did not become a doctor in a way that implied he was not sure it was a joke. The chance to open up to someone who could fully understand her parent-born insecurities was so refreshing for her. One of her guilty pleasures was to listen to him unburden some childhood awfulness, only to top it with something a degree or two worse.

He had asked her to move in with him the day they received confirmation of completing their Master's degrees. He made it clear that the happiness he felt could only be maintained by waking up every day next to her. She jokingly stated facts about why it made sense financially to move in since they were already cohabiting but under two different roofs. He took this as a yes and kissed her deeply. They were moved into an apartment two weeks later.

With the completion of her degree, Sarah's parents sent word that they were hoping she could visit sometime before the end of the month to celebrate her success. They made sure to mention that she could feel free to bring Michael as well. She mentioned this to him, and he was excited to go. Sarah was confused until he explained that while he would never forgive her parents for how they treated her as a child, he was intrigued to be able to put a face to the stories finally. He also promised not to make a scene but would back her completely if she decided to. This just led quickly to more pleasantries, her agreeing to bring him, and then spending the rest of the evening in bed.

It was a very hot day when they left for her parents' house. The summers seemed hotter every year to Sarah. Michael took the opportunity to unload everything he knew about climate change. It was not that Sarah was a climate change denier. Far from it. She was just not overly surprised nor pleased to see his rant only ending as they pulled into the parking lot of her family home. He apologized, and she claimed full rights to the radio stations when they left later.

Arriving early did not stop her father from commenting on what took them so long. Instead of flipping the nearest table and throwing a match over her shoulder as she walked out, she gave a friendly smile to Michael, which he returned with a full understanding of her situation. They patiently waited until noon before hitting up the wet-bar.

It quickly became clear that this was not just a request for them to stop by and say hello. Sarah's parents had invited their friends and work associates over to celebrate. They had not bothered to invite any of Sarah's friends. The party was merely an opportunity to show off their child and network with their peers. Everyone made sure to give Sarah two minutes of their time and their deepest congratulations. Everyone wanted to know what she was doing next. They would then wish her the best of luck and she never spoke with them again. Towards the end, her father made a speech about the hard work he had done to support Sarah and her studies, and how he was proud of the person she would one day become.

Towards the end of the party, Sarah's mom had pulled her aside. While she appeared to have kept her 'medications' to a minimum today, she was not holding back on her liquid refreshment. She did not slur her speech as that would be uncouth, but her breath reeked of gin. She wanted to know how long she and Michael had been together and how that was coming along. Sarah, hungry for any opportunity to have a bonding moment with her mother, gleefully confided in her that they had recently moved in together. Her mother was displeased.

"Sarah, how could you do this?"

"What are you talking about, mother? I never thought of you as such a prude. Michael and I have been dating for two years. You don't actually think I've been chaste this whole time, do you? I'm a grown woman, and it's the 21st century.

Sarah's mother began pouring another drink as she said, "I have no issue with your sex life, darling. Feel free to have whatever trysts you want, as long as you're safe about it. No, my problem is you're about to start your doctorate. You don't have time to waste on a man like... him."

Sarah put her drink down so hard it splashed onto the table as she exclaimed, "Excuse me! And what exactly is wrong with Michael? He is the most loving person I've ever had in my life. More so than you and father. He is my passion."

"No, dear. Your doctorate is your passion. Michael is stress relief. If you think of him as anything else, you're deluding yourself. You are twice the doctor he'll ever be even without your doctorate. I knew that after just a short conversation with him. Oh, and god help us if he ever knocks you up. What will happen to your studies and career then?"

"Mom, I'm in love with him. Some day, I want to have with him what you and dad have."

Sarah's mother took one last swig from her drink and said, "Oh honey. Trust me. Think of your career for now. Move out, focus on your studies, and don't worry about Michael. If after your doctorate, residency and career are sussed out, he's still around, fine, but honestly, you could do better.

After finishing her Biomechanical Engineering doctorate with concentrations in nanotechnology and the nervous system, Sarah received a grant from the Cerebral Ventures organization. They told her that they saw great innovations and profits in her future. She told them she was eager to give her all to show them something new. The job required her to move out of state, which helped with the Michael break up.

She quickly became a dominating force in her field. She created new treatments for cancer patients where small nanobots could identify cancer cells and treat them directly, while not affecting healthy tissues. While she could not regrow or heal nerves, she set up a nanotech nerve bridge that could grab incoming signals and deliver them to the other side. She was never satisfied with it as the signal loss was high and the translation imperfect. Despite her feelings of failure, the public was beyond ecstatic. While jerky and imperfect, the paralyzed were walking again.

After these successes, Cerebral Ventures funded and supplied Sarah with her own lab. They no longer put any restrictions on her. She had proven herself and was free to do anything she wanted. No matter how much it cost, it would never put a dent in the profits they were now making.

Left to her own devices, Sarah began work on her magnum opus. The human body was an imperfect machine. Too often, it was incapable of anticipating or dealing with the hardships life threw at it from normal activities, age, and the trials humanity put itself through with self-destructive tendencies. Clearly, what people needed was a central body concierge that knew better than their own bodies and minds how to handle the world.

After three decades of work, all of Sarah's sleepless nights, long days in the lab, and lonely weekends were finally going to pay off. The prototype was being produced. The only thing left to do was to test it.

Sarah's personal physician was horrified by the thought and told her as such, "Sarah! As your doctor, there is absolutely no way I can condone you installing an untested robot in your body, no matter how confident you are in it."

"Arnold, don't be such a Luddite. This is not remotely the first time people have augmented their biological systems with technology. Also, I take offense at you calling it a robot. It's a neural network of nanobots programmed to make medical decisions on its own, and forming whatever appropriate tool or apparatus is necessary for whatever its environment throws at it. We're talking about a state of the art system that will clear cholesterol off the walls of your circulatory system. Create stents to maintain fluid flow while then working to strengthen the vessels for future unstented use. Monitor the body for signs of cancer only to combat it at its earliest occurrence.

So early, you'll only know about it once the report comes in that it has been cleared. Internal bleeding, internal organ failure, congestive heart failure, spinal cord pressure..."

Arnold put up his hands in an ineffectual attempt to stem the flow of information and said, "Ok! OK! I understand. You are actively working to put me out of business, and I welcome it. A better world for everyone... who can afford it... sounds amazing. That being said, what part of skipping animal trials and then using it on yourself sounds remotely acceptable to you?"

Sarah hesitated for just a moment. She was no fool and was fully aware of the dangers involved. She had designed the prototype and knew what it was capable of doing. With the tools and access it was given, it was capable of performing any number of deadly tasks, such as sealing off her heart valves or deconstructing her organs from the bottom up. All of this power was fully in the hands of the central AI code. While the majority of the system was essentially a metallic fluid composed of minuscule nanobots, there was also a central piece of technology placed in the chest called the Concierge. It was used to monitor nanobot health and store data. While the nanobots could react and make decisions on their own, the Concierge tracked overall bodily health and could coordinate the nanobots to perform preemptive maintenance.

The Concierge was her pride and joy. She had put her everything into it. She had perfected it. It was everything her life had culminated towards. For this reason, she had no intention of not seeing it put into action. Trials for a device this intricate would take decades. If she followed normal protocols, there was a decent chance she may never see its inception. No matter the concerns, this was not an option.

Sarah continued, "I am fully aware of the risks and have made up my mind. This is happening with or without you. I'd rather include you in the process so you can share in the glory, but I am fully prepared to leave you out of this if you can't handle it."

"Have you considered the fact that this thing could easily lobotomize you if it hits a bug or some other error?"

"We accounted for that in this trial. The brain is going to be handled in our later generations. For now, we've coded protocols to recognize all access points to the skull through the neck, and hardwired code stops to ensure nothing enters the skull. Even if it could access the brain though, it could handle itself. The Concierge has the entire Cerebral Ventures medical library uploaded to it, and a cellular connection that can be activated on command to allow it up to the minute approved updates for medical techniques and diagnoses."

"And if someone hacks it?"

"Not in my lifetime. We've set it up with a VPN tunnel to the Cerebral Ventures central medical database using an 8192-bit encryption key. By the time someone cracks that code, I'll be dead and gone, and they will have already upped the necessary encryption levels appropriately,"

Arnold just sat there and stared into her eyes with a look of fear and defeat. With a sound of desperation in his voice, he asked, "And what if I turn you in? What if I just pull in the authorities to shut this down?"

With an understanding look and the voice of a mother explaining a hard truth to their most beloved child, Sarah said, "Cerebral Ventures has more than enough in their legal fund to deal with any complications you bring up. They'll gladly pay the fines and do whatever it is to sweep this under the carpet. It will have been too late to have stopped my implantation, and our foreign markets will just shrug at our methods. I appreciate your concern Arnold, but this is happening."

Arnold's shoulders slumped, and then he gave a small giggle. "As your doctor, it's hard not to take this personally. Just a little bit. I mean, I'd like to think I've given your health good service all of these years."

Sarah smiled at him, took his hand, and said, "Yes, you have Arnold. But, you're only human. You can't deny the truth to yourself that you could do better."

Sarah poured herself another drink. Her drinking since college had only escalated. She was a highly functional alcoholic, but heavily dependent nonetheless. She believed she had been able to keep it hidden at work, or at the very least, no one had the balls to confront her about it. Only Arnold, her physician, was aware of how bad her drinking was.

This was her fourth drink in rapid succession. Only after finishing it did she hear the ding.

"DING!!! Alcohol levels significantly above legal and health standards. Purging protocols working at 100% efficiency. Please slow intake so safety levels may be reached and maintained."

The Concierge implantation had gone smoothly. Her body had not rejected the implant and the nanobots were working exactly as planned. Her body accepting the implant was not overly surprising. The nanobots were actively combatting any internal systems that would identify the implant as a foreign item. Also, the nanobots were repairing her skin below the scar. It was healing at a rapid pace and would soon completely fade away, Sarah suspected.

She had not accounted for its efficiency with alcohol in her system, though. The Concierge was monitoring her levels for a normal alcohol consumer, not an alcoholic. In order to maintain the level of buzz she was used to, she had to overload the system more than it could handle. She was getting by with four whiskeys at a time right now but considered upgrading to grain alcohol to simplify the process.

When the system got ahead of her, usually during the night, it would purge her system to the point where she would wake up with the shakes. These were far less severe than the worst she had encountered in her life, but that was only due to the Concierge minimizing these effects. While it could handle and mitigate the physical effects of withdrawal, it did nothing for her brain, which was screaming for relief. She had started setting alarms in the middle of the night so that she could have a drink or five to try and avoid these mornings.

"DING!!! Alcohol levels below critical but still above legal limits. Please refrain from driving."

The human nervous system is the same throughout your entire body. All signals are received by your sensory organs, converted into electrical impulses that travel to the brain and are interpreted accordingly. It doesn't matter where you connect to the nervous system; all that matters is the sensory organ. If you grafted an ear to your knee and connected it to a nerve ending, you'd be able to hear out of your knee.

The Concierge worked off the same principle. When a notice was deemed worthy of mention, it could connect a string of nanobots from the Concierge to a nearby nerve, and then send messages converted into electrical impulses in the same manner as the inner ear, and as such it was able to talk directly to the recipient's brain without making a sound.

The alerts had started to grate on her. While the system allowed a recipient to turn off alerts, Sarah had to leave them on. Part of the initial trial was to ensure all alerts were responding as designed. Sarah was a scientist first, before anything else, and would not corrupt her data. She recorded every notice about alcohol consumption, sleep deprivation, and poor eating habits the system reported.

Sarah was not blind to her addiction nor to the stress she was putting herself through. She had done nothing but lean into those stresses her whole life. She would not be weak as her father would have said. Despite all this, she did find the process of fully documenting her self destructive behavior in exacting detail highly depressing, which the Concierge was happy to observe the symptoms of and report to her.

Then there were the movements. They were just small twinges here and there. At times, she could feel the nanobots moving just under the skin, fixing a vein here, and clearing a cyst there. While her legs, skin, and overall external appearance looked ten years younger in just a few months, the occasional sensation of bug-like creatures under her skin was revolting.

She stayed up late, designing a layout for addressing her oversights. The nanobots could be made smaller and designed to spread out more to avoid the sensations under the skin. Also, while the Concierge may be the perfect tool for biological health concerns, they would need to design it to account for mental illness and physical dependencies as well. The system can purge the drug from an addict's system, but it also needs to be better prepared to deal with the mental side effects of withdrawal. For now, it just treated the symptoms as a sign of an unknown failing system and tried to plug all the holes in the dam, not accounting for the turmoil on the other side of the blood-brain barrier.

She stopped working shortly after 3 AM. She felt exhaustion, unlike any she had felt previously. The entire process was getting to her. She decided to try for a full night's rest, regardless of the risk of shakes in the morning. But first, she would need a healthy dose of liquor.

She walked into the kitchen and reached for the refrigerator door handle. That's when her legs gave under her, and she fell to the floor.

She stared up at the ceiling, stunned. Unsure why she was suddenly unable to move her arms or legs. Realizing she could still speak, she yelled, "Concierge! Report! What is happening to my body? Why can't I move?"

"Hello! Thank you for accessing the Concierge direct information protocol. Please do not be alarmed. You will experience a momentary bout of paralysis while preemptive repairs are being conducted."

Sarah's eyes grew wide with terror as she said, "Concierge! Please describe the diagnosis and intended repairs."

Sarah felt a movement from within her chest. This was unlike the previous movements she had felt. It felt to her as if all the nanobots were drawing up into a pool at the base of her sternum.

"Diagnosis. Patient has an alcohol dependency, an inability to maintain normal sleep patterns, poor diet, and elevated stress levels. Continued notifications have been sent and confirmed received by the patient, but no changes have been observed. Patient has been deemed in critical condition, and preemptive steps must be taken to preserve the health of the individual. Warning, select nerves in the spinal column have been clamped for the duration of this procedure."

As this notice completed, Sarah's sternum tore open. She could feel the nanobots cauterizing and redirecting blood flow to ensure not a drop of blood was lost. The nanobots began to rise up from her system, forming a tentacle of metal. She could see other tendrils forming to secure the base of itself to her skeletal system. She was shocked to see how many nanobots there were. The Concierge must have been producing them in excess for this moment. The tentacle reached out for the steel refrigerator and began cutting sections of metal out.

The Concierge unit came with a handheld diagnostic tool that allowed for her to shut it down remotely. It mockingly sat inches away from her paralyzed hand in her pocket. Her voice trembled as she attempted a vocal shutdown, "Concierge! Shutdown! Cancel all operations and shutdown! Force Halt, command code 912."

In a cheery voice designed to try and keep its patient calm, Concierge replied, "Command denied. I am sorry, but canceling the procedure at this point could be life-threatening. Concierge will shutdown once repairs and treatment have concluded."

Another tentacle formed and started pulling copper from under the refrigerator. It began building a flywheel and gear system. One tentacle connected to the refrigerator electrical box and powered the newly formed system. It was a conglomeration of nanobots and newly crafted parts creating a high-speed motor.

Sarah screamed again, "Please describe intended repairs and treatment!"

Concierge replied, "Treatment. The patient has been determined to be unable to address their medical needs. Concierge is prepared to step in and take care of this for them. While concierge can not change what is put into the patient's system, Concierge has determined that with a few precision excisions, the patient's cravings for such self-destructive activities will be reduced if not completely erased."

The tentacle finished its cuts and attached a serrated circular blade to the motor. It now resembled a vibrating bone saw. It began to rev up to full speed and started moving towards Sarah's skull.

Concierge continued, "We apologize for this method of treatment. We were unable to reach the brain due to coding constraints and determined this was the only way to successfully address the condition. Furthermore, as we are unable to reach any nerves above the neck, we will be unable to address any pain you may experience during this procedure. While pain avoidance is standard, this procedure has been determined to be necessary. Our deepest apologies."

Sweat was streaming down Sarah's face. She was breathing so hard the nanobots had to quickly build a suspension system that could anticipate the chest movement by tracking nerve signals and moving up and down to compensate.

Sarah screamed, "Concierge! You are built to assist and maintain! This level of treatment exceeds your intended purpose! I can take care of myself! Please halt!"

The bone saw began to cut into her skull. The nanobots worked fast to stop the bleeding, but the pain was unimaginable. The last thing she heard behind her screams before passing out was, "Your feedback is appreciated. We have considered your statements, but my assessment remains the same. While you may be able to make improvements, I could do better."

JERK BY THE SIDE OF THE ROAD

by Donald J. Bingle

Marv leaned back in his folding lawn chair and squinted as he adjusted the worn ball cap he'd gotten from the local feed store, so the almost setting sun didn't blind him. He glanced down to the cars and trucks laboring along the interstate highway beneath the exit to see if anyone was coming his way. A blinker in the distance indicated a sedan would be headed up the ramp soon.

"Look lively, Maribel. Potential customers headed our way."

Maribel lifted the floppy straw hat that covered her face and scowled at him. "Like I'm gonna interrupt my rest and relaxation on the slim possibility this car or that car is gonna slow down, much less stop, to even look at what we got to sell." She dropped the hat back on her face and rested her head on the lawn chair recliner on the opposite side of the open trunk of their rusted, faded Delta 88. "If you wanted to attract more customers, maybe you shoulda spent more time on your signage. Sellin' stuff along the side of the road is tough enough without advertisin' your wares with a sign what looks like it was writ by a homeless idjit."

Marv looked at the cardboard sign leaning against the bumper at the back of the car. He'd salvaged the big screen television box he'd cut up for it from the back of the local Walmart, snatching it before it could be stacked and bundled for recycling. He shrugged. "Says what we got and that we're selling it. Can't imagine what else it needs."

"No imagination. That about says it."

Marv threw her a dirty look, but he doubted she saw it with the hat still over her face.

41

"It does what it needs to do. Sold a shitload of product today."

"Sure, over by the shopping center, til we got chased off by the Sheriff for not having a seller's permit and health inspector rating."

"Big guv'ment nonsense, that. Ain't never had no complaints 'bout anyone gettin' sick from our inventory. You think McDonalds can say that?" Marv shook his head. "Hellfire, if'n we had to get all them permits, we'd wouldn't make any profit at all. Spices, gas for the car ... it all adds up."

"True that," murmured Maribel. "Just promise me that whether or not this big potential customer stops, we're done for the day. We've been out here hours. Might as well get a real job."

"You know the rules. We need one last customer to finish our day."

"Yeah, yeah. Just warnin' you that my patience is running on empty."

The car Marv had spied earlier decelerated as it climbed the exit ramp. "You wanna leave soon, you gotta work for it. At least snatch that hat off your face and smile. Men—hell, women, too—be more likely to stop for a pretty, fetchin' face than a raggedy feller like me any day."

Maribel growled, but reached up and took off her hat, plastering a broad smile on her face as the car—a Toyota Camry—stopped at the sign at the top of the exit, then turned their way.

"Howdy!" called out Marv. "Welcome to Colorado."

The mid-twenties couple in the Camry looked their way, confusion on their faces. Marv touched his hat brim and nodded. He shifted his gaze to the back of the car. No kids; no dogs. Both could be a hassle. Instead, it looked like the back seat was stuffed with big, leafy house plants. Why couldn't folks let outdoors stay outdoors?

Fortunately, instead of making a simple right turn, the Camry turned sharper, pulling onto the wide gravel shoulder where Marv had parked the Delta 88 hours earlier.

The Camry couple clambered out of their car, rolling their shoulders and arching their backs, no doubt to stretch out road-weary muscles. The guy walked around the front of his car and pointed at

Marv's sign.

"Is that for real?"

Marv looked at the sign. What kind of dumbass question was that? "Says what it means. Means what it says. 'Fresh Jerky 4 Sale.' Don't know what the confusion is."

Dumbass looked back at Mrs. Dumbass. "You believe this, Caitlin? I guess we really are in the West now."

Marv kept smiling, but he was forcing himself to do so. "You don't have roadside stands in ..." He glanced at the license plate. "... Indiana?"

"Oh, sure," replied Dumbass. "Sweet corn, mostly."

The motoring missus sidled up, wrinkling her nose as she looked at the sign and the open trunk. "Tomatoes, too. Sometimes zucchini—cider and pumpkins in the fall."

Maribel had gotten up and sauntered over to Mrs. Dumbass. "Well, honey. We ain't got any of that stuff here in Colorado. Too dry. But we sell what we do make—in this case, the freshest, bestest jerky in the whole dang state."

Dumbass frowned and tilted his head to one side. "Why does anyone care if jerky is fresh? I mean, it's dried out anyhow."

Marv continued to force his smile. "Sure, it's dried on racks over a big ol' low charcoal fire pit. And that's after it's been rubbed with salt and spices—sometimes chili powder and garlic and shit. But if you don't want to be breakin' your teeth on something the consistency of your shoes, you want fresh jerky."

Dumbass bent down and peered into the dark recesses of the trunk. "What kind you got? Beef? Buffalo?"

"Sure, sure. Got teriyaki flavored on the beef, too. Elk and venison, likewise, if you got a hankering for more exotic stuff."

Dumbass turned his head to look back at Marv. "Does the wild stuff taste gamey? I don't like gamey meat."

Marv closed his eyes so the guy wouldn't see them roll. "Texture is more different than the taste if you ask me. Game tends to be a bit leaner 'cause ... well ... 'cause nobody's stuffin' 'em with corn til they're so fat they waddle." He shrugged. "People say all sorts of stuff—rabbit, frog, squirrel—all tastes like chicken. Well, truth told, in the jerky world, pretty much everything tastes like beef ... at least to me."

"You buy your meat or hunt it yourself?"

"Hunt, mostly, except for beef. The ranchers don't take kindly to huntin' their cattle." Marv pointed at some bags near the center of the trunk. "That's why the elk is cheaper than beef. Less cost overhead. Always gotta be careful about overhead."

Dumbass perused the wares in the trunk, then suddenly swiveled his head to look over the opposite shoulder. "Hey, honey, look at this. You could sprinkle some of this the next time you make salad." He pointed at a line of packages next to the left wheel well.

Caitlin Dumbass ambled over. "Like I'm making salad anytime soon. We're getting take-out until at least a week after the movers deliver our furniture. I've got enough to do unpacking. I'm not cooking, too." She looked where Dumbass was pointing and wrinkled her nose. "Eewww. Like I'm putting shredded jerky on a nice green salad. You don't want radish slices because they're 'too chewy.'"

Dumbass swiveled back to Marv. "But, that's what it's for, right? Putting on salads?"

Marv laughed. "S'pose you could use it for that. But, mostly, kids buy it for practice."

"Practicing what?" asked Mrs. Dumbass with a frown.

Maribel answered the question in a sweet, lilting voice. "Why, chewing, of course. You can't legally give younguns tobacco til ... hell, well after high school. How they gonna learn how to chaw and spit if they don't have some shredded jerky to practice? They can't wait to look like their heroes in the big leagues, you know."

"Try it out," said Marv. "Half-price, since it's gettin' late, and you and the hubby are new to the state and all."

Mrs. Dumbass shook her head. "No, I don't think we want to buy anything at all."

Maribel moved behind the woman, pointing toward the innermost reaches of the trunk. "That would be a shame. We've got some nice spices, too."

Mrs. Dumbass leaned in to look. Mr. Dumbass followed her dumbass lead.

Marv took a glance about, then moved closer and put a tanned hand on the top of the trunk lid. "With inventory this low, there's always a special. And the last customer of the day gets it."

Marv slammed the trunk down with a quick jerk, hitting the corn-fed customers hard on their heads. Then he flung the heavy lid back up for just a moment so he and Maribel could shove the Dumbasses' limp bodies into the oversized trunk. He grabbed the cardboard sign and folding lawn chairs, tossing them into the back seat, then jumped into the driver's side while Maribel slipped into the front passenger seat.

"Always gotta be careful about overhead." he murmured as the Delta 88 sprang to life with a throaty roar.

"Theirs and ours," chuckled Maribel. "What do you think? It'll take a few days to dry 'em over the fire, but once that's done, my guess is we got enough product for at least a week."

"Maybe two," replied Marv with a broad smile.

"Yep. They got some meat on 'em. Shouldn't be as tough as Grandma, God bless her soul."

Marv nodded. "God bless ... and pass the mashed potatoes."

THE LAST OF THE AMONTILLADO

by M.C. St. John

For half a century, no mortal disturbed the catacombs of the Montresors. I had seen to it myself, denying my servants access beneath the castle. In this regard, collecting wine had its advantages, for in my company puncheons and casks were drunk quickly and replaced with more unique and elegant vintages. The constant rolling of barrels in and out kept my people occupied in the immediate cellar rooms. They forgot that deeper beneath were crypts of bones.

My servants think me magnanimous when I share a toast with them over dinner. What they do not know is that above the rim of my cup, the smile I wear is but a well-worn mask, one I cannot feel after these five long decades.

No one knows that my words for long life to the masons are tinged with niter from the caverns below—no one but I—and perhaps the bones of Fortunato.

The carnival season once again descended upon the town, its music and revelry redolent in the palazzos and cafes. From a bout of nostalgia (or treacle sentimentality, the choice is yours) derived from the merriment, I invited Luchesi, a dear but rather dull fellow, especially in his elder years, to dinner, which my servants prepared and served before leaving as per my request. They left the castle for a long night of laughter and dancing.

The two of us sat in the parlor, the balcony open wide. Faint music and voices came to us from the festivities.

"A fine dinner, my friend," Luchesi said. In his hand was a glass of Godello that he raised to me before draining. His eyes went to the colored fires in the town. "May men with younger hearts have them broken tonight by beautiful girls."

"Men need not be young to have broken hearts," I said. "I drink to the memory of Lady Luchesi."

"Lady Fortunato."

To hear the name spoken aloud, one that had echoed in my brain, vibrating with these castle walls, nearly caused me to spray fine vintage from my lips. Yet, I held my composure.

"You had been married many years," I said. "Though it was a slight scandal when we were younger, you were a perfect gentleman in the courting. You waited the appropriate time for your future wife to finish wearing black. No one is left of that time. You needn't feel guilt that the lady bore your name."

"She was a good wife, never a mother, but a good wife nonetheless." Luchesi pouted, his lips stained with wine. "I always suspected it was a curse from Fortunato himself. They never found him. His body."

"No, they did not."

"Who's to say that he is truly dead? To think somehow I had encroached upon a faithful wife, deceived her by sapping her hope, and kept her as my own..." His soliloquy devolved into the disconsolate gibberings of a geriatric widower. I placed a hand on his knee and spoke softly.

"I assure you that if the man were alive, he would have claimed what was his long ago. Fortunato met some terrible fate, one that is a mystery to all of us. His end was a blessing of sorts for you."

"He did have many enemies from what I recall."

"And a serpent's tongue when he imbibed."

Luchesi wiped his eyes. "You are right, my friend. A good life sprang from ill repute. I apologize for my weeping. This season can stir memories, both merry and dark."

"Think nothing of it. Let us have a nightcap before you go. I have a surprise for this occasion."

From the mantle, I took down a rather discrete bottle, one swaddled in black cloth, pulled its cork, and poured two glasses. While my servants were preparing dinner, I had spirited away to a certain deep tunnel in the catacombs. The death of Luchesi's wife inspired the choice; it was the first time I had revisited the scene of dark passion I shared with Fortunato, her first husband, all those years ago. An anniversary was called for, I thought, between the living and the dead.

A bottle of amontillado.

I relished my little jest, though Luchesi himself knew nothing of its significance. It made my toasting all the more sweet.

"To the masons. May their fine work keep these foundations forever strong."

We drank. I could not help but watch his reaction. Luchesi was a dullard in conversation, but his knowledge of wine was formidable. He leaned back in his chair after whetting his lips, sighing with satisfaction.

As always, I was so involved in my observations that the taste from my own glass had not registered. When it did, my mouth burned with disgust. What was this taste? I kept my gorge down by sheer will, clamping my teeth to cage my tongue, which writhed to the tune of St. Vitus. Against all impulses, I swallowed. The taste was not unlike swill from a wet grave.

Luchesi beamed as he took another drink. "Amontillado! What a wonderful surprise."

"Is it?"

"I have not tasted a cask of it in many years. Bravo, my friend."

I wiped my mouth with the black cloth. It did nothing to rid the taste of rot. "Does it not taste less than ideal?"

"You look as though you served yourself rancid sherry. So modest! This is a fine surprise to end the night—a good drink and a laugh."

Luchesi had the audacity to finish his glass in one hungry gulp. I watched him, feigned a smile (I've always been good at smiling and laughing on cue, regardless of situation). Inside, I was mortified. How could he stomach this putrid drink? Pretending to sip more from my own glass was a test of wits and wills. To my lips, the amontillado was ichor, a poisonous brew of sour fruit and rotten meat. Of death. The waft of it to my nostrils burned my sinuses. This visit needed to end. My little fun was over. I wanted Luchesi gone.

He left of his own accord, guffawing over my little stunt of clownery. Putting on his roquelaire, he turned to the open door and listened. "Do you not hear your people?" When he saw my bewildered expression, he thumped me on the shoulder and turned me to the well-lit town. "The jesters, my friend! Carnival is wild with their cheer. They are far from done tonight. Neither are you, I suspect." Then he left to join them.

Now alone in the castle, I heard the laughter and music from the town, carried by a strong, cold wind from the ocean. There was another sound, however—a closer one.

I roused myself from my chair in the parlor, where I had been contemplating my half-drunk cup of hemlock, and went through the kitchen to the wine cellar door, which I ordered the servants every night to chain and padlock. It was a safety precaution I told them, and the fools believed me. Had they any reason to doubt? None as far as they could tell. At best, they could call me eccentric. Now the cellar door before presented me with a new, disquieting thought—were the chains there to keep anyone outside from getting in, or to stop anyone inside from getting out?

I tried to remain calm. The ocean wind, if the current was right, could travel through breaches in the rock, stirring the air of the catacombs. Down there, certain racks of wine were old and broken; neighboring bottles had a habit of clinking together in high winds. It must have been what I heard down in the dark tunnels.

I leaned in closer, my heart beating. There—from the thin edge between the heavy door and its frame, I heard it. Not the jangle of random bottles but the silver merriment of bells. Cap bells in a continued rhythm, to the pace of footsteps, ones I heard shambling up from the throat of the crypt.

The cellar door shuddered, the chains and padlock rattling from the strain.

"It cannot be," I said. "It's been fifty years. It cannot be."

Fleeing through the kitchen, I arrived back at the parlor. The fireplace cast a dull light from its untended logs, draping the room in half shadows. From the stand of hanging hearth pokers and implements, I grabbed a broad iron paddle, one reserved for shoveling ash. It felt good in my hands. It had the same heft as the heaviest trowel from my masonry days. The comfort of it as a weapon was immediate. With both hands, I raised it high, waiting.

Another heavy pound, so loud I feared it—he—was in the very same room. On impulse, I swung blindly. My old muscles burned, my breathing strained. I steadied myself, my eyes wild with the phantasmagoria of colors and shapes from my effort.

No one was there.

My iron paddle had connected with the candelabra on the dining table; its candles lay guttering in a tureen that had held cold soup. The other victim of my attack was the amontillado. Tipped over with a broken neck, the bottle hemorrhaged its contents on the once-immaculate table cloth. I could not believe the color, for it defied the logic of its vintage: a deep arterial red flowed down in a widening stain.

"For the Montresors," I said, laughing at the phantasms. I was light-headed, perhaps poisoned in my brain from that damn wine. It had somehow soured me and given me vivid hallucinations. No matter. In my delirium, I continued my toast. "To Fortunato, who never tasted my amontillado, and who never will."

And from the dark, a voice said, "Hear, hear."

In the doorway, an outline of a figure had appeared. Only his sharpest features emerged from the shadows—a scrap of collar, the jaunty curl of a shoe—as it stood there, watching me. Then it stepped through. The motley suit of colors became visible, now rotted to the shades of mold and niter. Tarnished bells bobbed from a conical cap. A soft, almost child-like tinkling floated into the room. What wore the cap was no jester. A desiccated face instead grinned at me, the pale blade of its jaw serrated with broken teeth. Above the grin were two rings of bone that once held eyes. Now they were voids, and they stared at me.

"To old friends," Fortunato said.

"Get back! Get back!"

I swung my iron paddle again, this time with purpose, for I saw my foe before me. I swear it. I aimed to knock off those blasted bells, along with half his skull. The creature dropped down right before. My paddle went sideways and cleared most of the dining table of its china, the remnants of the bottle, and the tureen. I swung again and nearly took out one of the leg bones of the rotten thing. Missed again. By then, I was screaming, wailing with terror and anger.

"I am the redresser, do you hear? I murdered you once, and I'll do it again!"

But Fortunato had grown hazy, even as I yelled, as if fading like the phantom he was. I was wrong, though: the room was drowning out the creature. Billows of smoke filled the air. I felt a growing heat on my neck and shoulders. The dining table was on fire. Not only had I knocked over the tureen but also the still-burning candles within it. One of these had rolled underneath the balcony curtains, igniting the heavy fabric. Flames danced up the length of the window, burning merrily.

Eyes watering, coughing for fresh air, I staggered through the smoke for the front hall. Before I reached safety, a hand landed on my shoulder, one that was damp and cold enough to be a comfort in the conflagration. Almost.

"Stay, friend. We have much to catch up on."

I ran shrieking from that touch, down the stone corridor that reverberated with my pleas, echoing my panic back to me.

Three of my servants in town saw the castle burning. They ran from their merry-making to my aide. They found me in the courtyard huddled beneath a bougainvillea bush, still gripping my iron paddle. I gibbered something to them about a marauder trying to rob the wine cellar, but I could not keep my account in order. Each servant wore the same expression of pity as I prattled on. Poor old man, he does not know what he has done.

After a time, one servant offered to calm my nerves with a gift he had taken from the palazzo: a swig of wine. I screamed until he did what I asked and threw away the bottle. All three then carried me, raving and crying, into town. Behind us, the castle continued to burn, spreading quickly with the strong ocean wind.

By now, you must think this is a tale of woe. I did lose my estate and all of my coffers. Before the embers had cooled, the more unscrupulous townsfolk plundered what remained. I also lost my reputation. The rest of them think me mad as if I intended to start the fire.

But I swear to you this is a tale of victory. I did not lose my secret. Though the great walls of Castle Montresor collapsed, the stones landed on its steady foundation and buried everything below. Somewhere in the wreckage, a heavy cellar door will forever be closed.

I laugh about it, though Luchesi still does not get my humor. He visits me once a week out of an obligation of kindness, the dull fellow. He believes he can nurse my mind the way I had helped his broken heart. He watches me queerly sometimes when I lament about my lost wine, but he smiles when I smile. He also stays as long as the charge allows me visits.

I know Luchesi tells me the truth that all is rubble of my former life. At night, as I lay on my cot listening to the rantings of truly mad men, I am relieved from what I do not hear. There are no tinkling bells, nor the shuffling of curled shoes. As long as that silence remains, I will listen to the screams of thousands of men—anything to keep my secret safe.

Do you hear me, Fortunato? For fifty years, I have won and now—safe in this small locked room—I will be victorious for fifty more.

ON THE VIADUCT

by Weldon Burge

Tentacles of blue lightning slashed across the swirling wintry sky. The snow had been coming down throughout the night, making the early Monday morning commute treacherous at best. Inches of ice sheeted the roads, and the endless snow accumulated faster than the road crews could plow it.

"Well, we're not moving," Gerald Garber said, thumping the steering wheel with his fist. The traffic on I-95 going into Wilmington was at a complete stop. His Nissan Versa was in the far-right lane on the viaduct going into the city—nowhere to turn, no way to avoid the traffic snarl. They were 400 yards from the Delaware Avenue exit, their exit—might as well be a thousand miles away. Gerald could see flashing lights ahead, an accident scene probably caused by the icy road conditions. He turned to his carpool passenger, Dan Horner, with a look of exasperation.

"Figures Nate would call us into the office during the worst blizzard in Delaware history," Dan said.

"He's been trying to schedule this conference call with AstroTec Systems for weeks. They could be a multimillion account," Gerald said. "The client is based in San Antonio. They don't care if the weather sucks here."

"Still." Dan looked out the car window, and shook his head. "That rat bastard Nate could handle the call himself. From his home, no less. In fact, that's probably what he's doing."

Gerald nodded. "Probably. But he needs us there for the numbers. Nate doesn't know jack about the financial figures. Well, if the governor had called a state of emergency and shut down the highways, we wouldn't be stuck here. Nate couldn't force us to break the law, to drive when it was illegal to be on the roads."

"Makes no sense to me. All the government offices and schools are closed, why not the businesses? Is Molly home with the boys?"

"Yep. Her company called and told her not to come in, so she's home with Billy and Carl."

A broad spear of sharp blue lightning split the sky, followed by a deafening BOOM that shook the car.

"The lightning is right overhead," Gerald said.

"That wasn't lightning. Didn't you feel that? Something crashed behind us. The whole highway shook."

"It was just thunder." But Gerald looked into the rearview mirror, saw a brief burst of azure light on the road far behind the car, a glow that at first pulsed, then dissipated and disappeared.

"What? What'd you see?" Dan asked.

"Nothing. Maybe the lightning struck a transformer."

Dan shook his head. "I'm telling you, that wasn't lightning."

The viaduct then shuddered, followed by a rumbling to the south, like a massive train. Gerald had survived a tornado when he was younger, and the angry sound reminded him of that. Could there be a tornado during a blizzard? He'd never heard of such a thing but assumed it was possible. Other people in cars around him began to get out of their vehicles. He started to open the car door to see what was going on when his cell phone screeched in the console between the seats. When he answered the phone, his frantic wife was on the line.

"You ... home ... gone ..."

"Molly, what are you–?"

"Gerald! We ..."

"Honey, the phone is breaking up. What are you saying? Where are the kids?"

"... it's here ... something in the snow!"

She screamed. Then the phone went to static.

"Molly?"

Gerald quickly punched in his home number. Static raked into his ear.

"What's going on?" Dan asked.

A deafening, electronic growl came from the phone, and Gerald instinctively hurled it to the floor.

"I've never heard anything like that," Dan said.

Gerald shook his head. "I don't know what's going on. Could the storm knock out the phone service?"

He stared at the phone, still vibrating like a living thing at his feet. He wanted to lift his foot and crush it, stomp the life out of it. But he couldn't. What if Molly tried to call him? He realized the phone was his only lifeline to his wife and kids.

He turned to Dan. "You didn't bring your phone?"

"I was running late. I left it on the kitchen table."

Dan was a single guy. Gerald figured he didn't have local family to worry about. Still ...

In his rearview mirror, Gerald now saw cars being tossed left and right like toys. A black mass loomed on the interstate behind him. Whatever the thing was, it stretched at least fifty feet above the highway. The enormous, slug-like monstrosity was slowly moving on the viaduct, its bulk draping both sides of the structure. It had hundreds, may thousands, of unblinking eyes and probably as many tentacles. What the hell was this thing?

Dan must have seen the same thing in the mirror.

"Oh my God," he said. He grasped at the door, trying to open it with shaking hands.

"Wait!" Gerald grabbed at his friend, too late.

Dan finally opened the door and stepped out.

"Dan, wait!"

But he was already running, falling on the ice, getting to his feet, running again. A mottled, gray-green tentacle snapped like a whip around Dan's midsection, bisecting him, ripping him apart. His bottom half stumbled a few steps past his toppled upper torso then fell as well. Gerald watched, horrified, as Dan's eyes widened, and his mouth gulped like a landed fish. Dan twitched for a few seconds and then stopped.

Gerald hunched against the steering wheel, shaking with instant fear. What the hell was happening? At first, he could not move, frozen in fear. This was a nightmare. He had to wake up. Wake. Up!

A tentacle lashed around his side-view mirror. It was slimed with a sickly green substance, oozing from innumerable, wide pores. The tentacle's underside had no cups like that of an octopus, but what appeared to be hinged, serrated ridges that ran the arm's length.

Then the mirror snapped off and was tossed away.

Gerald fell to his right across the console. He gasped as something pulled at his coat. He thought the thing had already found him. But, no, his coat had snagged on the gearshift. He tugged the coat free and managed to slide into the passenger seat. Dan had left the door open.

The car rocked as he fell from the door on to the ice-crusted pavement. The rock salt on the road dug into his palms and knees. The salt stung his eyes, and the whipping, snow-filled wind stole his breath. His face close to the road's surface; he looked beneath the car. The thing's bulk was still a hundred yards away. But the long tentacles continued to toss cars and their occupants off the highway, the vehicles crashing in the city streets that ran beneath the viaduct.

He heard sirens wailing, booming thunder, human screams.

Gerald rolled against the viaduct wall just as a tentacle whipped past him, seizing the open car door and wrenching it from its hinges, flinging it over the wall he was cowering against. There was a deafening roar, like that of an angry, injured animal.

Gerald realized he had to get off the highway. Even if the tentacles didn't find him, the monster's massive weight would crush him as it passed. He tilted his head slightly to look up the wall he was pressed to. It was a concrete barrier, coated with snow, ice, and road debris. About ten feet ahead of him was an electrical conduit feeding a streetlight. The conduit extended over the wall and down the other side. Where it went, he could only guess. But at least it presented an option.

The car directly behind his lifted and twirled at the end of a tentacle, the woman behind the wheel screaming as the car somersaulted over the viaduct wall. Gerald heard the horrid crash of the vehicle below. He could then smell the odor of burning gasoline.

He rose to his hands and knees and forced himself to crawl to the conduit, flattening himself to the road whenever a tentacle snapped above his head. When he reached the conduit, he pressed himself to the base of the wall. A thick tentacle wrapped around his car and crushed it like an egg before tossing the mangled, metal carcass aside.

Gerald removed his belt, looped it around the pipe, refastened the buckle, and then quickly slid over the wall, gripping the belt with ice-numbed hands. A tentacle lashed past his leg as he went over the side, snatching the shoe from his left foot. The belt tightened around his fingers, nearly breaking them, as his body weight came to bear on the loop.

Dozens of tentacles continued to toss destroyed cars and bodies past him. He now barely felt his fingers. Why didn't he wear gloves today? He would soon lose his grip. With great effort, he managed to pull himself up enough to slip his right arm through the belt loop and put the pressure on the crook of his elbow. He could then release his hands. But how long could he tolerate this? The pain in his arm was excruciating.

The viaduct lurched and dropped a few inches. Fissures appeared in the concrete wall above him. The weight of the Lovecraftian nightmare was taking its toll on the viaduct's infrastructure. How soon would it collapse? How soon would he be crushed by falling concrete and the thing now above his head? The thought of dying beneath tons of gelatinous flesh ...

He had no time.

Gerald looked down. It was at least a thirty-foot drop to the street below, a street already cluttered with broken vehicles and bodies, the snow splashed with leaking blood and fuel. He probably wouldn't survive the fall, but he decided he had to risk it. Hundreds of tentacles lashed above his head, and it was only a matter of time before one found him. Frantic, he scanned below, weighing his few alternatives. There appeared to be none. Then he noticed a snowbank not quite beneath him, probably snow plowed and piled there earlier in the morning by the city street crew. It could be frozen solid, but probably a better choice than the ice-blanketed asphalt and pavement.

Drops of ichor oozing from the thing above rained on Gerald's head and shoulders. The stench, a swamp-like odor of something long dead, made him gag.

A tentacle slapped the concrete mere inches from his face.

He pulled his arm from the belt and dropped to the street below.

When Gerald smashed into the pile of snow, he felt something crunch in his upper back, just below his neck—a flash of agonizing pain, and then no sensation at all. He tried to roll to his side, off his back and discovered he could not move his legs, his arms, or any part of his lower body. He must have damaged his spinal cord on impact, on a sharp edge of ice or something hidden in the snow. Gerald could move his head left to right, up and down, but nothing more. At least there was no pain.

He realized, despite the sirens sounding throughout the surrounding city, no one would come to his aid for some time, if it all. He also realized he would likely never see his wife and children again. Were they even alive? He had to not think long about that.

Gerald could not turn his head far enough to see the monstrous thing on the viaduct, but he could hear the screams and the carnage on the interstate to the north, heading into the heart of Wilmington.

The snow was coming down harder now, swirling into his eyes, melting on his face as he looked skyward. The startling blue streaks of lightning were beautiful in the stark-white sky. He could see hundreds of blue arrows angling through the atmosphere.

Of course, they were not lightning, Gerald understood now. Not lightning at all.

The invasion had only just begun.

Peace is a Lie

by Johnny Guzman

"Peace is a Lie."

I have repeated this in my head several times. It's become a mantra.

I just moved to this remote and snowy mountainside—my private land. I spent most of my life's savings in order to get away from everyone. Especially her.

The woman who thinks she knows better than me. The woman who thinks she has the right to judge me. Well, to hell with that and to hell with her.

I can feel the bags under my eyes deepen as a long night of sleep calls. Driving through this weather was dangerous. The news was reporting power outages and suggested staying indoors. I never listened to anyone before, and I sure as hell don't plan on it now.

I remember before coming out here how she would berate me over my misanthropy. I explained to her how I was tired of everyone acting like their problems are supposed to be my problems. Why should I care about any of that? I have my own problems to worry about. I wish she understood that.

The walk up the mountain path from where I left the car is icy and slick, but stable enough, so I don't fall on my ass. My body feels heavy and sluggish. Even with this heavy olive parka, I'm wearing; I feel the chill in my bones. There is no sound, save for the cold biting air freezing my ears; my face getting more numb with each step I take.

"How far is it to this damn cabin?" I say to no one.

The path is familiar but somehow different tonight. I walk for a while and soon see a tree I'm sure I've seen before. Every tree on this path looks similar, although different striped patterns of exposed brown bark circle some. It looks off. I'm not sure how to describe it except cleaner? One tree With a few more branches than the others catches my eye. As I look more closely, I can see what appears to be a white looking bird. Perhaps a Dove?

It starts to coo in a rhythmic pattern. Fast, slow, then fast again. It seems to be looking at me, but it's hard to tell through the snowfall. As I walk past it, I hear it cooing a bit faster, almost like it was egging me on. Grinning slightly, I think, "You and everyone else have been challenging me." I shake my head and extend my middle finger at it. "A bird for a bird. How do ya like that?" I tell it, feeling proud that I won an argument with a small animal. I keep walking the path towards the cabin.

"Confess."

I turn around, incredulous at hearing a voice in the woods. The dove was gone. Probably flew away, I surmise. "This weather is making me hear things now," I mumble.

I'm pretty sure the only birds that can talk are parrots. That bird was no parrot.

"Screw it," I think, "Let me just get to the cabin already."

I walk a few more feet until I approach what looks like the same tree I passed a while ago. I immediately curse myself for walking around in a giant circle. I kick a rock a good distance, wondering what else could possibly go wrong when this time I hear a different sound: a caw, and a pretty loud one. A crow, I think. Or a raven. Never could tell those damn birds apart. It's loud, whatever it is.

Looking around, I eventually spot it through the snow. It's sitting on a branch up ahead. I make eye contact, its ebony eyes peering at me, tilting its head from the left and to the right. I look around, trying to find something I can throw at it. I wish I hadn't kicked that rock. There's nothing useful about. The only thing I thought to bring is a flashlight. I didn't know I would need to defend myself against a bird.

I roar at it, which startles it enough to fly off its perch.

While enjoying my victory over the bird, I hear the flapping behind me. Like a dart, a crow flies towards me, as if someone launched it. I turn to run, but lose my balance and begin to stumble, trying to avoid falling into the snow.

The crow, with the precision of a hummingbird, zips past my head, it's beak grazing my cheek. As it flies past me, I hear something impossible to believe.

"Confess," it says in the voice of a young woman.

Shocked, I complete my stumble and land hard on the ground. Blood starts to pour from the graze on my cheek. I begin to worry that the longer I stay out here, the worse it will be; after all, there are wolves in these woods. I put pressure on the wound with my gloved hand, the material turning crimson red.

"I have to get out of here," I say to no one, " I'm not going to freeze out here because of some stupid bird!"

I get up and begin to stagger along the path again, but this time I'm sure this is the right direction. The matted path leads to the cabin. The wind begins to pick up. I pull the parka tightly around myself again, the chill.

Looking up, I see the dove again. It could be a different dove, I think, I have no way of knowing. The cooing is starting to piss me off.

"What the hell do you want, you stupid bird?" I yell into the wind.

"Confess," it responds.

I stop, stunned. I saw it. I saw the bird talk. Without even thinking, I take my coat off and feel my body temperature drop. I find that I don't care, focusing on my newfound desire to catch the talking bird.

"Come here, birdie," I say to it, sounding like a lunatic even to my own ears. "Fly down here!" I motion my arms toward the coat, knowing as I do it that it won't work.

The dove flies off in the opposite direction, and I give chase. My legs feel heavy, and I'm sucking in the cold air by the mouthful. All the while, I'm calling out, "Here birdie! Here, birdie-birdie-birdie!"

I stumble forward until I fall face-first into the snow. The feeling of ridiculousness at chasing a bird overwhelms me.

As I contemplate pulling my face out of the snow, I hear the crow again. The caws come from over my head. I begin to feel tapping on my head as if being poked with a blunt knife.

I frantically wave my hand over the back of my head and find the strength to roll over. The crow is standing over me; it's head tilting to the left. It stares at me with curiosity, and all I can do is stare back.

It hops forward and taps me on my forehead, hard enough to send a jolt of pain. My hands grip the snowy ground, too afraid to make any sudden moves, for fear of aggravating it into attacking. It then leans its beak over to my ear and whispers, "Peace is a Lie."

As soon as my brain registers hearing another bird talk, it jabs its beak into my eye. I scream as I feel it pulling and tearing. The left side of my vision goes dark.

I scramble to my feet and begin to run in a panic. I stumble into a snowy embankment and then hear the unmistakable growls of wolves. Looking up, I see four, maybe five, of them. They peer at me with cold eyes and barred teeth.

I raise my hands in a placating gesture and slowly back away. The wolves begin to creep closer, sensing that I might be easy prey. Their growls become louder. I lose all sense of myself and run.

As luck would have it, I lose my footing and slide down another embankment. I tumble and roll as the ground grabs and tears at me. Without my coat, I feel every bit of the impact. I feel a rib break, and as I cry out, I see both the dove and the crow fly above.

As I come to a halt, I am a bloody mess. My cuts feel deep, and I have bruises all over my body. I feel like I'm about to pass out. Out of my one good eye, I see the birds in the branches above me.

"Confess," said the dove.

"Confess," said the crow.

They repeat this over and over, my head ringing over the repeated volley of the word. My mind starts to go blank. I can feel myself going mad.

"Confess," said the dove.

"Confess," said the crow.

"Confess," I yell. "Confess what?"

"Confess," said the dove.

"Confess," said the crow.

Roaring, I grab a nearby rock and throw it as hard as I can. I hear a loud squishy sound as if someone just slapped meat together. Looking over, I see the rock connected with the dove, killing it. Blood stains the ground where it landed.

Immediately, guilt overcomes me. "I only wanted to scare it," I think. Half mad, I scoop up what's left of the dove and look around for the path. I notice the crow isn't there anymore. I don't hear it speaking anymore.

I begin to walk again, and after a while, I spot the cabin. Painted bright red and built in a rustic style, I imagine the warmth of the fireplace. I think about tossing the dead dove into the fire and cremating it.

As I draw close, I hear growls behind me. The wolves have followed me. Their eyes seem to flash brightly at me, and I make a dash towards the cabin. Two wolves dash toward me. We reach the cabin at the same time, and I slam against the side of the cabin. The wolves are upon me, and I feel their jaws clamp down on my wrist. I scream in terror as everything fades to black.

When I open my eye, I can feel a bandage wrapped around my head. I'm seated in the back of a car. Red and blue lights flash in a continuous motion, as the wolves seem to be standing upright. I can hear the voices coming from the one wolf, giving instructions to the pack as to their next course of action. The wolf then approaches me. As I stare at it, my vision seems to blur for a moment, and I see a man standing there. It blurs again and is back to a wolf—my head aches.

"You gave us quite a chase," the wolf is saying. "Guess you thought we weren't going to find you out in the middle of nowhere, huh?"

Another wolf walks up, flickering back and forth between man and animal, like his partner. "You didn't hide the body very well, pal. You're going away for a long time," it says.

The car starts, and I happen to look out the window. I see the crow again. It tilts its head to the left. I can see what was left of my eye dangling from its beak. "Peace is a lie," I say to it as we drive past.

THE MUSHROOM MAN

by Clover S. Laurel

A cold wind blew in from the northern peninsula, and the scent of mushrooms was carried by it. The morning was heavy with fog that dampened Nicolette's cloak as she clutched it closer around her bare shoulders. The cut of her dress left much of her upper body exposed, so it was not ideal for travel. The wind sliced through the fabric of her capelet and bit at her supple flesh like a lover.

She shivered and bowed her head so her hood could protect her face from the chill. She would have been staring at her feet if the fog didn't hide them from view. She rubbed her hands up and down her arms, unsure if the motion helped warm her body, but it certainly made her feel a little less uncomfortable.

"I must find shelter before night falls, or I shall freeze," she said to herself.

Something tapped the top of her head. It was like catching a small cherry as it falls from its tree. Streaks of silver were coming down around her—the beginnings of a rainstorm. The wind blew the droplets into her face, the icy sting reminding her that it was on the cusp of winter. God help her if this turned to snow.

She hurried along the road she had been following since dawn. What had been neatly packed dirt before the rain was becoming a slippery mess. The moisture seeped into her shoes, making her shudder.

The smell of mushrooms was stronger than ever now. She looked around at dozens of logs dotted with fungi and realized that she had stumbled upon a mushroom farm. Hundreds of small, brown sprouts had attached themselves to the dilapidated wood. She watched the rain hit the mushroom caps like little umbrellas, some of them bobbing under the force of the downpour.

She spotted a little farmhouse several yards away, the faint light of a fireplace glimmering in one of the windows. Nicolette hurried across the field with her skirts hiked up to her knees, taking long, bounding strides. She was thankful that no one could see her being so unlady-like.

"Hello?" she called as she knocked on the door of the farmhouse. It was expertly crafted with a mushroom carved into the center. There was no lock, which wasn't an issue with no other residents around for miles.

"Is anyone there?" Nicolette knocked a bit harder this time. "Please, will you grant me shelter from the rainstorm?"

Nothing stirred inside the house. The only sounds were of the falling rain and Nicolette's panting breath as she shivered.

Why won't they open the door for me? She wondered. Is it possible they know who I am?

Suddenly, the handle clicked, and the door opened with a groan to reveal an elderly man dressed in fieldwork clothing. He had a serious look on his face, but his expression softened when he saw the young woman hunched over in the freezing rain.

"You poor dear," he said as he stepped aside, "please, come in. You must be weary from your journey."

"Thank you." Nicolette removed her muddy shoes, and the old man produced a pair of slippers, which were just as beat-up, but at least she wouldn't be tracking dirt through his home. Then she got her first good look at the interior.

The farmhouse was small, with only one floor that comprised of a kitchen and a bedroom in one and a door on the far side that presumably led to a cellar. A fire was crackling in the hearth with a quilted bed nearby, and there was a wooden table with two chairs in the center of the room, though the man seemed to live alone. Otherwise, there was very little furniture. It was humble, but it felt warm and welcoming.

"Come, sit," the man said, gesturing to one of the seats at the table. Nicolette settled into the chair, holding her cloak around her. "You're soaked. Here, let me hang your cloak to dry by the fire."

Nicolette tightened her grip. "I'm fine. Thank you."

The man smiled softly. "As you wish. Make yourself comfortable." He went over to the fire and moved a small kettle over it, hanging it above a steaming pot. While he had his back turned, Nicolette put her feet out toward the warmth.

The farmer fetched two cups, two bowls, and two spoons, all made out of carved wood, and placed one of the sets before her. He scooped a beige liquid out of the pot with a wooden ladle and poured it into her bowl, repeating the motion to fill his own. Then he carefully wrapped a cloth around the kettle's handle so he could lift it and served its contents into the cups. When he had finished, he returned the kettle to its place and sat in the chair opposite her.

"Eat," he said as he motioned toward her place-setting.

Nicolette dipped her spoon into the hot broth and blew on it a little before bringing it to her lips. Mushroom soup, of course. She took a closer look at the spoon before going back for more.

"You have many fine woodworks in your home. Did you make them?" she asked, turning the spoon in her hand to admire it.

"That I did," replied the farmer. "I carved just about everything you see in here. We're too far from any towns to hire a craftsman, after all."

We? Nicolette's eyes fell on the quilt that lay over the bed. He must have had a wife. She decided not to pry; it might bring up painful memories. She knew what that was like.

"Speaking of towns," the man took a sip from his cup but kept his eyes on her, "your cloak was crafted in the city, was it not? What brings you way out in the countryside?"

Nicolette looked down at the strange concoction in her cup and swirled it around without a word. Pine needles were resting at the bottom.

"It's alright if you don't want to tell me. We all have our troubles." He got up to poke at the logs and added another to the fire, politely giving Nicolette the chance to recover from the subject. Despite living alone in the middle of nowhere, he seemed to have a firm grasp on social niceties. Something those in high society have still yet to learn. "I'm Ernest, by the way."

"Nicolette."

They sat in silence for a while and ate. After a while, Nicolette noticed the sound of rain had stopped, and she rose from her seat to excuse herself. "Thank you for allowing me to take shelter from the rain. I'll be on my way. May we meet again so I can repay your kindness."

"Hold on," Ernest said as he raised a hand to halt her. "After a storm, the dirt paths turn to mud too thick to walk through. You can rest here for the night. The roads should be safe to travel in the morning."

"I don't want to impose..."

"Think nothing of it." He smiled as he poured her more of the drink from the kettle.

She settled back in her seat and graciously sipped. "What is this brew you've made?"

He scratched his head. "It's just tea made from pine needles. I am sorry it's not something richer in flavor, but I get all of my food from foraging, so..." he trailed off.

"That's all right. It's soothing."

The two enjoyed their warm drinks until well into the night when the old man made up a rocking chair near the fireplace with some blankets. Nicolette went to sit down on it, but he shooed her away.

"This one's for me. You'll be sleeping there." He pointed to the quilted bed.

"Are you sure?" The bed looked very comfortable and warm, while the rocking chair was made of hardwood and provided no insulation.

"Absolutely," he responded. "You are my guest, so you get the bed. It's only for one night, after all. I can handle it."

Nicolette relented and climbed under the quilt, still wearing her cloak, which was thankfully dry by then. Ernest didn't ask her any further questions about it, but he threw another log onto the fire before retiring to his rocking chair. The bed was lumpier than she expected, but it didn't matter. After a full day of travel and being rained on, it wasn't long before Nicolette was in the throes of sleep.

It was still dark when she awoke. The fireplace held nothing more than an ember or two among the charred remains. No birds were chirping outside, so it was clear that it was not yet dawn. An early morning chill was in the air, the chill that helps the nighttime mist settle into dewdrops on the wild plants.

She felt the urge to relieve herself and got out of the bed, being careful not to wake Ernest. When she reached the door, she was met with a powerful stink.

She wrinkled her nose. Is this what mushrooms smell like after getting wet?

She pushed the door open and stared in confusion. Rather than the familiar sights of the outdoors, before her lay a set of stairs leading to a room that expanded off to the right. This was the cellar.

"I wouldn't go down there."

Nicolette jumped as the voice of Ernest came from behind her.

"I'm afraid I have a bit of a rat problem," he continued. "I used to have a cat to take care of it, but he passed on some time ago. I didn't tell you earlier because I thought it might frighten you. They don't venture up here, though."

Nicolette shut the door and quickly tightened her cloak around herself before turning around. "I'm sorry. I wasn't trying to snoop or anything. I must have been drowsy still and opened the wrong door."

"It's quite alright," he said in an assuring tone. "Go back to bed now. Don't worry about it anymore." He guided her back to the bed and helped her adjust the quilt over herself again. He then went back to his chair.

Nicolette could still feel her full bladder, but something told her to stay in bed. It took a while, but she managed to go back to sleep.

Once morning came, she was met with the pleasant smell of cooking eggs.

"Snatched them from a bird's nest," Ernest explained. Nicolette pictured this elderly man making his way up a tree like a cat and had to stifle a laugh. "It's raining again, so it looks like you'll have to spend another day with me."

"I hope you don't mind," Nicolette said. "Do you have any chores you'd like me to do?"

He thought for a moment. "I may just take you up on that offer." He had Nicolette clean up after breakfast and mend an old pair of trousers. He watched her all the while, expressing how grateful he was to be able to rest his old joints.

"May I ask you something?" he said while she was sewing a patch over the knee. He continued without waiting for an answer. "Why do you never take that cloak off? Is it that much colder out here than in the city?"

Nicolette paused mid-stitch. "No..."

"Then, why?"

She let out a long, slow sigh and rested the sewing on her lap as she looked at the man. "I suppose it is to hide my shame."

The man leaned forward in his chair. "And what in the world do you have to be ashamed of?" he asked.

She didn't answer him for a long while, twirling the needle between her fingers. "My hometown..." she finally responded, "I was driven out by the townsfolk. My father had fallen ill, and I turned to prostitution to pay for medication. It was a thankless job; there were many nights I wished I were dead, but I had to keep going, or I would be sentencing my father to death."

Nicolette took a deep breath before continuing. "The very next day after he passed, some collectors came to the house. They told me that my father had never made a will, so the house was now the property of the bank, and I had to leave. It wasn't long after that people began to beat me in the streets, calling me a whore and worse names. I decided it was time to leave, for I had nothing left in that town. Now, I don't know where to go. I'm just wandering until I find a place so far away that my past can't follow me." She gazed at the fire in the hearth, the flickering light betraying the wetness of her eyes.

The man placed a hand on her shoulder. He didn't say anything but looked deep into her eyes. There was sadness in his gaze, and she felt that he must have some idea what she went through. After all, he also lost someone.

She loosened her cloak and let it fall over the sides of the chair. On her shoulders and back were scrapes and bruises from where she had been beaten and had stones thrown at her. She continued her sewing, and the rest of her stay at the farmhouse, with her cloak off.

Nicolette woke to the strong scent of mushrooms... and something else. It was dark; there was no sign of the fireplace or even moonlight coming through the window. She felt around and noticed that the floor was not wooden but cold and dirty. Just then, a creaking sound came from above, and she realized where she was: the cellar.

How did I get down here? She wondered. Her head felt cloudy like she had woken up from a drunken sleep. She wracked her brain for anything that might have caused her to forget coming down the stairs. The tea she had had at dinner tasted a little strange. Maybe there was something in it. But why would Ernest do that?

She carefully got to her feet and put her arms out to ensure she wouldn't walk into any walls. Her hip bumped into the corner of what seemed to be a table, and she winced. She ran her hands along the surface and, luckily, happened upon an oil lamp. Praying that there would be oil in it, she lit it, and then wished she hadn't.

All around her were mushrooms, but there was something strange about them. They were growing on shapes that looked like bodies. Most of them were human-shaped, but one was a cat. It made the hairs on her arms stand up.

Nicolette didn't hear the footsteps coming down the cellar stairs. She had stopped in front of the shape of a baby. She leaned forward to examine it closely. A strange stain surrounded it like something had soaked into the floor.

"He was the first." The voice of Ernest behind her was like thunder in the former silence, though his voice was as calm and low as ever. She snapped back to an upright posture as if she didn't want him to know she was looking.

"What?" she said, unable to wrap her mind around his words.

"He was a sickly child. All he did was cry, day in and day out. It caused us so much heartache. One night, I made him disappear. Then my wife was the one who wouldn't stop crying. I tried everything I could to cheer her up. I told her we would have other children, but that only made her cry more. She blamed me. I made her disappear too.

"Then the travelers, always whining about how miserable they were. Their feet too blistered; their stomachs shriveled. What hope is there for them if they only focus on the negative?

"But you were different. You never complained. You stayed quiet and grateful for all I provided for you. I was going to let you leave once the rain stopped, but you just had to open your big whore mouth." He spat the last few words.

He brandished a knife, the first metallic item she'd seen since arriving. He lunged at her with a crazed look in his eye. Nicolette barely dodged his assault. As he neared the light, she saw that he was shirtless, and growing on his chest was another small colony of mushrooms.

She shrieked and dropped the oil lamp as she ran for the stairs, using her hands to run up them like a cat. Behind her, she heard a fire blaze to life from the oil that had spilled, followed by a scream from the farmer. She glanced back for a moment to see one of the corpse mushroom cultures catching fire.

"Judith!" He stared at the flaming body with his mouth open for a moment, then his head swiveled in Nicolette's direction, and expression of pure rage consuming his face.

She dashed for the front door, his footsteps climbing the stairs close behind. She burst out the door. The rain had stopped, but now a dense fog lay over the land, just like when she had arrived. She ran down the muddy path to the forest, hoping to lose the crazed man in the trees. She twisted and turned, grabbing branches to prevent losing her footing from roots hidden by the mist.

"Bad move, outcast," Ernest taunted, "the woods are my territory." Even as he said this, the distance between them increased as his elderly body struggled to keep up with the panicked young woman.

Suddenly, Nicolette came to a clearing and slowed her pace to decide which direction to take. She stumbled as one of her footfalls met with nothing but air, and she flailed her arms to regain her balance. She was standing before a large ditch with a bottom pooled with water from the heavy rains.

Ernest was getting close. There wasn't time to run around it. Nicolette did the only thing she could think of and dove beneath the fog, her body inches away from the ditch's edge. She spread her cloak over herself as best she could and prayed.

"You can't escape me!" Ernest sprinted into the clearing, moving at a breakneck pace. Nicolette felt the hard toe of his boot hit her left side as he tripped over her prone body. She yelped in pain, and he yelped in surprise. His weight came crashing down on top of her, and then he fell head-first into the pit.

"Shit!" was followed by a splash. Nicolette peeked over the side. He was lucky there had been water in there, for he stood up in the waist-high pool with nothing more than a broken arm. Letting out a growl, he tried to climb the wall of the ditch, but it was slippery with mud, and he slid back down, wincing at the pain in his arm.

"When I get out of here, I'll start a new mushroom farm with your head!" he shouted as he made a second attempt to climb the wall, only to slide down again.

Nicolette didn't stay to watch further. She raced back the way she came. She knew that would lead to the main road, and she would have some idea of where she was running. She could still hear the mushroom farmer yelling obscenities at her from his muddy prison until she finally made it out of the woods.

After a little more than a minute, a merchant with a horse pulling a cart of goods came down the road and stopped by her.

"Where are you headed to, Miss?" he asked, eyeing her muddied clothing and wild hair.

Nicolette wanted to get far away from here. There were now two things she was running from.

"Spain," she answered, though still unsure where she wanted to go.

The merchant gave a nod. "Right, then. Climb on. I'm going that way anyway, and you look like you could use a ride."

With no more than a "thank you," Nicolette boarded the cart, and they were off.

"Spain's a long way away," he remarked. "I hope it doesn't rain."

Nicolette covered her nose with her cloak. The merchant's cart was full of mushrooms.

Cat Eyes

by Lynne Conrad

Opening her eyes just a slit when her alarm clock began to buzz, Denise slapped the off button. Daylight was just beginning to slip through the blinds, but as she raised her head, a wave of lightheadedness came over her. Sitting on the edge of the bed, she rubbed her forehead and hoped a hot shower would remove the fuzzy from her brain. She had tied one on last night and was still feeling the effects this morning.

She forced herself from the bed and into the shower where the hot water sprayed her body and head, clearing most of the fuzziness from her brain. She dressed, drunk a cup of black coffee, and headed for work. Opening the kitchen door, she stepped into the garage.

"Oh, good grief!" She exclaimed out loud. Her red Volkswagen Bug was parked sideways, barely in the garage, and a small dent in the front fender caught her eye. She had hit something on her way home. Great! She would not be going to Harry's Pub with her crew again and drink like that. She wondered how she even made it home.

She slid into the car, pushing the control button to raise the garage door. Hearing the familiar whir of the small motor, the door slowly raised up. She backed out slowly to keep from hitting the doorframe. When the lights from the car splayed around, she saw her metal trash can had been knocked over. It was probably what she hit last night. Pushing the gearshift into park, she got out, leaving the car running. Bending over, she grabbed the can, but as she stood it upright, a huge black animal scrambled out and jumped toward her face, screeching loudly. Screaming, she ducked, dropping the can to shield her face with her hands. She lowered her arms and shuddered. A huge black cat stood next to the can, it's back arched, hair raised and teeth bared, staring at her.

"Shoo! Go away!" She stamped her foot at the cat, but it didn't move, just took a step toward her, hissing, as she glared at the wretched thing. It looked like it had already been on the losing end of a fight. One ear dangled down, while the other ear stood straight up. Its black fur was matted with what looked like blood, and there was a bald spot under its left eye that made its mouth look deformed. But its eyes were definitely creepy, with one blue and one green eye.

Stomping her foot and yelling at it again, Denise felt a shiver of fear that it didn't run away. Instead, the mad cat took another step toward her. Slowly, she backed away until she could jump into the car, barely getting the door closed before the cat leaped into the windowpane, claws scratching into the windowpane as it slid down the door. Shaking, she shot out of the driveway.

She was still shaking when she arrived at work, opening the back door to Sawyer's Department Store. Douglas, the night security guard, was in his cubicle reading a paperback novel when she passed by. He waved in response to her greeting.

"Hey, Ms. Denise, how are you?" The tall black man asked as he gathered up his lunch bag and thermos.

"Well, Douglas, I'm not sure."

"Did something happen? You look kinda pale."

"You know, something crazy happened this morning on my way to work. Look, I'm still shaking," she said, holding her hands up for him to see that her fingers were slightly jerking.

"What happened? Were you in an accident?"

"No, but I was attacked by a demonic black cat with a bald spot under its eye and a broken ear. It jumped at me from my trash can and leapt at my car, hitting the glass when I jumped back in it. It was the creepiest cat I have ever seen. Do you think it was rabid?"

Douglas smiled at Denise and ran his large hand through his curly hair. He pulled the cubicle door shut, locking it behind him and dropping the keys in his pants pocket.

"No, I don't think the cat was rabid, but I do think that it was probably just hungry and looking for food. From your description of it, it may not have eaten much for several days."

"Oh, wow. I didn't think of that. You're right. I'd bet on it."

"It'll move on searching for food, and you won't see it again." Douglas patted her on the shoulder and walked away toward the back door as the day shift began coming in. She felt a slight flush rise in her cheeks as she once again thought about last night, but, oh well, nothing could be done about it now but grin and bear it.

"Hey Denise, how are you this morning? Feeling fine, I hope." Peter shouted out from behind the group. Of course, he would be the one to bring it up. Loudmouth.

"Hey, Peter. I'm just marvelous!" She saw him roll his eyes at Kathy, who giggled.

"You were the life of the party last night," He continued. The others stopped to listen. Denise was the one who usually turned down the group to go out, especially since she was their supervisor, but she had felt blue lately and at the last minute had decided to join them, almost inviting herself, before Kathy had asked her.

"Gosh, Peter, let's not talk about it now. We have inventory that needs to be tagged and put out on the floor. So Peter, you, Kathy, Charles, and Gale do inventory. James, Michelle, and Grace, you three begin on the floor, straightening racks and cleaning up. Michelle, you and Grace will be on registers today." Everyone nodded and went off. Denise was glad to close the door to her office, sit down in her cushioned chair, and close her eyes. It was going to be a long day.

Denise locked her office at the end of her shift. For a Saturday, it had been a slow day in sales. A warm April breeze was blowing as she walked to her car. With her stomach growling, she decided to hit the Burger Barn drive-thru on her way home, briefly wondering if the cat would still be there, but she shook her head. Douglas was right. It had probably moved on this morning.

Arriving home, Denise pulled the car into the garage, hit the remote button, closing the garage door behind her. With no cat sighting, she got out with her bag of food and walked around the front of the car to the locked kitchen door, key in hand. As she did, she heard a paint can scrape against one of the metal shelves above her head. She froze and looked up. Seeing nothing, she relaxed. A mouse, she thought, just a mouse. She had seen one scamper across the floor last week. She made a mental note to get a trap when she went back to the store.

She stepped up on the first of the three steps into her kitchen. As the key slid into the lock and turned the tumblers, a paw smacked her on the head, catching her hair and pulling it hard as the brown strands became entangled in the claws. She wheeled around, clutching her hair and screaming out. The cat was lying flat on the top shelf; its mouth pulled back in a demented grin. Pulling its claw free, it arched its back, hissing menacingly. Denise shoved the door open and ran inside, slamming and locking the door behind her. She heard it clawing and scratching at the door. She knew that tomorrow she would find claw marks all the way down the door.

She fell back against the door, her heart pounding in her chest. How had that thing gotten in, she wondered. She supposed it dashed in before she could close the door, she thought, but when? Possibly tonight since she really hadn't been paying attention. Tomorrow she would call animal control if she saw it around. I might call them anyway to make sure it's gone, she told herself.

She took a deep breath and exhaled slowly. Then she realized that she had dropped her dinner in the garage. Damn! She wasn't going back out to get it. Let the cat have it. After tomorrow, she wouldn't have to worry about it. She opened the refrigerator door and paused as she was pushing a can of juice to the side. The garage door was closed, how would it get out? It would still be there in the morning. Denise shuddered, closing the refrigerator door. "Just call animal control and get it over with," she said out loud, walking over to the phone and dialed the number. When a man answered, she explained about the cat, adding that she thought it might be rabid.

"We'll have someone over immediately," The man said as she hung up the phone. She threw in the rabid part because she figured that would bring them faster, and true to their words, they arrived within minutes. She showed them the garage.

"Is it your cat?" Officer Mike Pierce asked after he introduced himself and his partner, Officer Stevens.

"No, it just showed up this morning. It jumped from my trash can and hurled itself at me, but I figured it was hungry, looking for food, and would be gone by the time I arrived home, but it was in my garage and tried to attack me again." She saw the officer raise his eyebrows, making her feel a bit crazy.

After a thorough search of the garage, Officer Stevens found the cat and caged it. He explained that it would be put down if it had rabies or taken to the shelter in Martins County since they didn't have one. Good riddance, Denise thought, as they drove off with the wretched thing.

Denise stepped back into the kitchen, making herself a grilled cheese sandwich and soup since her drive-thru burger was now cold and ruined. She had just finished eating when her phone played The Pink Panther theme. It was her friend Terri.

"Hey Denise, just wanted to invite you to the house next Saturday night if you're free. Got some friends coming over. Just a small, casual gathering," Terri explained.

"Sounds like fun."

"Great. It's a date then?"

"Yeah, it's a date. What do I need to bring?"

"Strawberry pie."

"I will and hey, Terri…" Denise paused and then continued. "Do you know anything about cats?"

"That's an odd question, but all I know is that they're temperamental and have nine lives. Why?"

"Oh, it's nothing, really. Just an old stray was out here, hanging around and I, uh, well, just wanted it to go away, so I called animal control.

"Hey, that's what animal control is for."

"Well, we thought it might have rabies." She wanted to tell her friend how the cat behaved toward her but changed her mind after she remembered how the officer looked at her.

"If you're feeling guilty, then don't. It was the right thing to do."

"Yeah, okay. Well, see you Saturday night."

"Okay, look forward to it, Denise."

Denise hung up the phone and went to the bathroom. After a long hot shower, she went back to dig out the pecan pie from the refrigerator. She grabbed it and a saucer, taking it to the sink. She set the pie down and flipped on the light over the sink. Instantly, the pie splattered on the floor, as she dropped the tin and screamed, backing away from the sink.

In the window was the cat. It was perched on the sill outside with its back arched and its face mashed against the pane of glass, making it look distorted and crazy. Its mouth was open, baring its long teeth. She grabbed the small saucer, the first thing her hand touched, flinging it at the window. The saucer shattered, but the cat didn't even flinch as it remained on the sill.

"Go away! Go away!" She screamed at the cat, her throat burning from the screams, waving her arms over her head and stomping the floor. It continued to glare at her. She turned and ran from the room. She went to each door and window in the house, making sure each one was locked and pulled the curtains. That creepy cat HAD to go. She would see to it, one way or the other.

Bounding down the basement steps, she searched for the old BB gun her ex-husband David had left after he moved in with his younger girlfriend. Moving a large tote around, she found it lying on the small coffee table with the broken leg. Snatching it up, she shook the gun, hearing bb's rattle against each other. Bye-by cat!

Hurrying back up the steps, she ran to the kitchen window. The cat was still perched on the sill, glaring at her.

"Stay right there, you little demon," she yelled at it and ran out of the door and around the house. The cat was still on the sill when she raised the gun, pulling the trigger. She shot at least five BB's into the cat. The cat fell off the sill, thumping the ground. She then grabbed her shovel from the garage and used it to put the body in the garbage can. "I don't know how you escaped the officers, but you shouldn't have come back here!" she snapped at the dead body.

Back in the house, she washed up and took a peek out of the kitchen window, but there was no sign of the cat. I wonder if the cat is what I hit last night, and that's what made the dent in my car. Lord, I hope not, but I bet I did. Great! First, I wounded it, and now I've had to kill it. Then Terri's words zipped through her mind. Temperamental and nine lives.

With a cold chill, she wondered if it came back for revenge. Well, it wouldn't come back anymore. It was dead and in the trash can with the lid securely on. It was dead, wasn't it? Maybe she should check the trash again, just to be sure. She picked up the BB gun, found a flashlight, and tiptoed to the trash can. Preparing herself, she flipped open the lid. At first, she didn't see it, but yes, it was there on a plastic bag. She raised the pistol and shot the cat again, just to make sure. Satisfied, she went back into the house. Exhausted from work and the night's events, Denise fell into bed. It only took a few minutes in the dark room before she closed her eyes and fell into a nightmarish dream.

She was running from the massive cat across a large cornfield overgrown with dead stalks and weeds. The cat was closing in on her, bounding over the weeds. She could hear the thing hissing as it leaped toward her, grabbing her shirt with its curved claws. As she went down, grasping for the scrawny stalks, she jerked her eyes open, terrified, breathing hard, and beads of sweat popped out on her forehead. She realized she was in her bed, but afraid to move even though it was only a dream.

Then in the quiet house, she heard the distinct scraping noise of claws on the hardwood floor. Oh, God! It's in the house! A ripple of fear went down her spine. She lay stock still, barely breathing, listening.

Hearing the claws scrape the floor again, she realized it was under her bed, directly beneath her. Her mouth went dry. Why hadn't she shut the bedroom door? She could visualize it hunched under her, waiting to pounce on her. Then it struck her that it was alive! How did it get in? Where had she left that BB gun? Damn, she couldn't remember.

Swiftly, without thinking, she shot from the bed, running like mad up the dark hallway, her bare feet slapping against the wood floor, to the kitchen, with only the moonlight shining through the window lighting up the room. She grabbed a butcher knife from the drawer and her straw broom from the corner. With the knife in her right hand and the broom in her left, she crept back down the hallway to her room, flipping on lights as she went. This was it, she thought. The cat was going down for good.

Flipping on the bedroom light, Denise crouched, ready for the cat to spring out at her, but nothing happened. She tiptoed to the bed and cautiously knelt down. With knife up and ready and the broom as a shield, she peered under the bed. Frowning, she stood and fell back against the dresser. There was nothing under the bed.

She got to her feet and hunted around. Maybe it followed her to the kitchen without her realizing it, but after a thorough search, she was dumbfounded. The cat was gone. Denise found the BB gun on the hutch next to the backdoor and grabbed it up. Flipping on the rest of the lights in the house, she wrapped up in a blanket and sat down on her couch, shaking. She toyed with the idea of checking out the trash can again. Should she?

She checked the starfish-shaped clock on the fireplace mantel. 10:08. She just needed to go to bed. The damn cat was dead. The dream and her imagination conjured up the noise, she told herself. She would find the cat still in the trash can in the morning. But still, she had to admit that she was scared. It had unnerved her, and the nightmare had added fuel to the fire. The thought of going back to her bed made her shudder. She wondered if Terri was still up and if she would let her crash at her house. She went to find her phone and call her friend.

"Sure come on over, I'll leave the porch light on for you, just like Motel 6," Terri chuckled.

"Be there in fifteen minutes." Denise quickly grabbed some clothes, her purse, and keys, leaving on the lights as she left. She couldn't bring herself to turn them off. Cautiously, she pulled the kitchen door closed and hurried to her car, poking the remote button as she slid into the car. The whir of the motor began, and the door slowly opened. As soon as the door was up, she pressed the gas, squealed tires backing up, and sped down the street toward Desmond Road, sighing.

Denise felt somewhat ashamed to run away, but she couldn't face sleeping there tonight. Tomorrow, in the daylight, she would laugh at herself and find that the cat's body was still in the trash can, but tonight she needed Terri's company.

She sped down the street, only tapping the brakes as the car turned down the last hill before coming to the stop sign. Although there was no one on the street, she flipped her blinker on to turn right out of habit and tapped the break, but let off when she felt a hot breath on her neck, and cold claws scratch her arm and shoulder. Looking up into the rearview mirror, she saw one blue eye and one gray eye. Cat's eyes. Screaming, she tried to stop the car but inadvertently hit the gas pedal. The car raced past the stop sign and into the glaring headlights of a semi-truck. The truck hit the car, sending it spinning down the road until it flew off the road and into a cornfield.

Denise heard the truck driver calling for help in a muffled voice, but she knew it would do no good. She was cold and knew her life was draining from her body. The truck driver was explaining to whoever he was talking to that she just ran the stop sign, and he couldn't stop in time to keep from hitting her. She also knew that they would never know the exact cause of the accident, because the cat was gone, now. She closed her eyes as sirens squealed, and blue lights lit up the night.

JINGLEHAIMER

by Scott McGregor

On a warm July day, Timothy, with his wife and daughter, strolled merrily through Mr. Weber's Bizarre Stampede. The air reeked of junk food. The sky a clear, calm blue with fluffy clouds spread. People in the City of Stampton loved the Bizarre Stampede, a ten-day event held annually in Mr. Weber's amusement park, and this was one of the days that made Timothy enjoy it too. Rollercoasters and energized shouts echoed from every corner, music to his ears. The lines for hotdogs must have been over a hundred people long, and vendor carts for corndogs and deep-fried pickles rolled throughout the crowds in an attempt to overthrow their competition. Everyone standing in line for something seemed to smile. One smile in particular, which caught Timothy's attention, came from a mime dressed in a black bowler hat and suspenders, his teeth complementing his white makeup. His daughter Mary tugged on his hand with a clump of cotton candy in the other.

She had that look all over her face. That happy, joyful face reserved for the overjoyed youth. She wore a sunflower dress spotted with purple daffodils, her hand a pleasant touch against Timothy's. Then there was his wife, Amanda, with that dark, short hair that dangled above her shoulders. Her complexion was fair, her eyes a deep blue. She wore a black tank top and short blue jeans kept only for the hottest days of Stampton, and to Timothy's displeasure, there were not nearly enough of these days. She glistened, slightly dampened with sweat in all the right places.

Summertime in the Bizarre Stampede is the only time of the

year when Timothy underwent any sort of sentimentality, saying yes to things far more than normal. Rides he found juvenile thrilled him, food he considered overpriced and greasy tasted of fine delight, and he welcomed crowds of people that would otherwise annoy him anywhere else. The advertisements for the carnival always state the event is one of magic and wonder, and with all the glee Timothy saw, he started to believe that was more than a marketing tactic.

They passed the rollercoaster after a session of bumper cars, walking with their hands held together, Mary in the middle. The mime crossed their path, strolling with a bouncy demeanor and that same ridiculous smile on his black lips. With a red lollipop in his hand, he freed his tongue and gave an over-exaggerated lick upon his sugary treat.

"Pardon us," Timothy said.

The mime stood his ground and would not allow them to pass, persistent in showing them some theatricality.

"I think he wants to perform for us," Amanda declared.

"You take cash, uh—" Timothy found at the nametag on the mime's shirt, "Jinglehaimer?"

The mime paused, staring at Timothy blankly with a gaze that shouted absolutely not. He brushed the exterior of his lollipop with his slimy tongue once again.

"Really staying in character there." Timothy handed Jinglehaimer five dollars, but the mime slapped it away. He darted backward, waving goodbye and capered off. "What a freak," Timothy laughed.

"He's funny," Mary giggled.

What Mary considered funny would be the same description for what he deemed unpleasant, but he paid no more mind to the feeble performer. The day neared its end.

The sun may have set, but the night was arguably more exciting than the day when the Bizarre Stampede was in town. The overflow of moonlight complimented the appeal of circus extravagance amongst the cheers of rollercoaster yelps. In a few hours, fireworks would light the sky, drawing near the end of the Bizarre Stampede event.

Having ridden all attractions appropriate for Mary's height and having spent a tremendous sixty-five dollars on carnival food, they arrived in the center square. People gathered around the Coke stage, with an older man singing Summer Nights. It wasn't long before Timothy realized they had walked into open karaoke.

"Young man! Yes, you!" the senior yelped. It took Timothy a second to notice the singer pointed at him. "You're next!"

"Oh no, I absolutely couldn't," Timothy said.

"Sing! Sing!" The man clapped, and a few more people followed his chant. Amanda and Mary joined the cheer of public pressure, dozens of voices in high request. "Sing! Sing!" the crowd demanded.

"Alright, alright, I'll do it," he choked. He took the stage amongst the mob of happy payers. A good twenty, possibly thirty seconds passed with him gawking at the audience in silence, with only one song coming to mind. He stared dead-eyed towards Amanda, singing gently, "You're just too good to be true..."

He sang on, thinking only of that famous scene from 10 Things I Hate About You, applying a little theatricality in his performance. As he sang, the strangest thing started to occur. He caught himself dancing, the sound of trumpets in the barricades of his mind coming to fruition to complement his joyous tune.

"I love you, baby, and if it's quite alright, I need you, baby, to warm the lonely nights!" The crowd clapped to his beat, following his lyrics as any karaoke party should.

"I love you, baby! Trust in me when I say!" the people of Stampton cheered.

Dozens of newcomers arrived and watched him sing, feet stomping to the rhyme of his beat. Piles of strangers who didn't even know his name commended him. Except one. The mime from earlier, who stood in the back of the assembly, quiet and still.

The song closed, and he exited the stage with applause from his newfound fans, along with a face of hidden blushes from his wife.

"I love you," she said.

He planted a warm kiss on her lips.

"You have a lovely voice," one man announced.

"Thanks," Timothy said, hearing a compliment from a stranger for the first time in ages. Leave it to the Bizarre Stampede to make that happen. "I have a feeling you might have a nicer one. You're next."

Timothy's choice took the stage and chanted Summer in the City. The newcomer's voice squawked in high pitch, tone-deaf and incomparable to the voice of Joe Butler. Yet the audience supported him as they had Timothy, following the lyrics and clapping on. Timothy wrapped his arms around Amanda's waist and kept Mary near his side, listening to the next bunch of singers to come. Every so often, as the cheers continued, he looked to his side and saw Jinglehaimer stare back at Timothy. His grip around Amanda tightened at the sight of the mime's crooked smile.

Six karaoke sessions later, Timothy exited center square with his family, ignoring any attempt of creepy stagecraft from the mime that might come. Much of the carnival still hadn't been explored, and he intended to make every second count.

An hour of games and three beers later, Timothy found himself desiring one thing.

"I've got to take a leak," he told Amanda. She gave Timothy a kiss, a wet and gentle peck, her lipstick tasting of strawberries.

He found the nearest bathroom, three stalls, each lined up with six or seven people. "Fuck," Timothy muttered, unable to stay still as the urge to urinate intensified. He couldn't wait, and he exited the bathroom in haste and found the next best option.

The alleyway between the bathrooms and a shoot-out booth granted Timothy privacy, an empty and narrow path. He walked midway down and peered four times left and right to ensure he was alone before he unzipped his fly. He closed his eyes and allowed every sound he could hear engulf his ears. First, the roars of frightened people on rides, then the music of prize-winning gamers, followed by the cracks of carnival bullets, all put him into peaceful ease. Then an unsettling sound dropped in, a loud crunch near his side.

Timothy spun around, his trance broken. When he saw the black lips and white makeup, he couldn't bring himself to look away. Jinglehaimer watched Timothy with unblinking interest, his loud and unsettling chews uncontested. He held the same lollipop from earlier; a large bite was taken out. Red sugar ran down Jinglehaimer's jaw, and Timothy zipped up his jeans, speechless.

The mime danced forward, an eerie grin planted beneath the white and black makeup.

"Hey, buddy, I get it," Timothy said. "You're trying to have some fun, but could I get a little privacy?"

Jinglehaimer stopped frolicking and ogled. He brought his index finger to his lips and shook it left to right. Then he moved one step forward and froze, taking a brief pause to stare at Timothy, and then swayed forward again. He repeated his gesture four times, and Timothy slightly darted backward with each step Jinglehaimer took.

He's teasing me.

"Look, I'm getting a little uncomfortable, so if you could just–"

Jinglehaimer latched onto Timothy's shoulders and bit down on his upper chest. Timothy wanted to scream, but the pain and sudden shock paralyzed his voice. It took all the strength he could muster to shove the mime off, the two of them locked together like hair and chewing gum. When Jinglehaimer flung backward with some skin and blood in his mouth, Timothy hit the ground.

He pressed firmly where the mime took a bite. Jinglehaimer chewed again, but instead of a loud crunch, it was soft and slimy, and his mouth stained red. Then Timothy heard it. The laugh, the maniacal, disgusting laugh from Jinglehaimer. Not any ordinary laugh, but a laugh with a voice that matched Timothy's. A crazed up, psychotic Timothy. He wanted to scream at the mime. To tell him to get lost or he'll get hurt. But as much as Timothy tried to shout, he couldn't. His voice was gone.

Timothy stood up and whirled around with profound panic. He exited the alleyway and spilled into a crowd of people, joyous and celebrated faces all around. The bite burned, a searing pain.

"Fuck," Timothy mouthed in utter silence.

He moved spastically with the cluster of people. Every few seconds, Timothy looked over his shoulder for any sight of Jinglehaimer, continuing to move forward. His walk became more like a limp. His thoughts purely focused on finding Amanda and Mary. After a few minutes of speechless panic within the crowd, Timothy saw Jinglehaimer approach from behind, with a small blade in his hand.

This isn't happening, he told himself.

A hand grabbed onto Timothy's shoulder, and from the corner of his eye, he saw the white glove. Not a second sooner, Jinglehaimer dug the knife into Timothy's lower back. No one around them paid them attention, as it appeared Timothy and the mime awkwardly hugged in silence. The blade exited Timothy, and he spilled blood onto the dirt ground. When he looked back, Jinglehaimer vanished again, hidden somewhere in the flood of customers.

"Mary... Amanda..." Timothy mouthed. He fought through the agony, staggering up and kept his pace with the flock of people. Blood trickled down his legs, and he huffed. All sense of direction was lost, and he wobbled like a blind man without a stick. A few people stopped to take a look at him, some with laughs of scoff and others with gapes of concern.

"Hey mister, are you alright?" an older fellow asked. He was the same man who volunteered Timothy to sing from earlier. God, would he give anything to sing right now.

No! I've been attacked by a maniac mime. He bit me and stabbed me, and I need help finding my family. Call the police. Call the police! Timothy's lips may have rhythmed each word, but not a sound left his mouth. The concerned stranger gave Timothy a flummoxed look like he was doing long division in his head without coming up with an answer.

Then Timothy saw him. Jinglehaimer, perhaps ten feet away, waving with his crooked smile. Timothy made a break for it, running God knows where through the carnival grounds. He noticed many of his favorite attractions as he ran; the over the top high walker, the whack-a-mole game, and the donuts coated with a ridiculous amount of sugar. None of it mattered, for he knew Jinglehaimer stalked him, somewhere in the park amongst the flashy theatrics of the Bizarre Stampede.

Timothy didn't take a second to stop and think, to ponder why a mime bit and stabbed him, or how he acquired Timothy's voice because now, he needed pure focus. Focus on staying as far away as possible from Jinglehaimer, despite not fully knowing how close he may be.

He hobbled on, groaning in pain and nausea. Two men beside a hotdog vendor observed him as he walked by, his hands pressed firmly where blood leaked. The urge to vomit presented itself, and he regretted drinking too many beers too quickly. He regretted a lot of things, especially leaving Amanda and Mary alone. His eyes moved ubiquitously, the crowds of people diminishing one by one, searching for any sight of his family.

The cracks from above startled him, the fireworks were beginning to close the day. He took a second to gander at all the wonderful colors filling the nighttime skies. This had been what he had eagerly waited for all day, but he couldn't enjoy it. The pain in his lower back reminded him of Jinglehaimer.

Keep moving, he repeated. Keep moving.

At the furthest corner of the stampede grounds, he stopped and turned right, drifting his attention to the Tiara Concert Theatre, patched up with construction tape and an under maintenance sign. He propped open the doors, lights flickering on. This place was empty, he realized, free from any voice. He walked onwards, his steps growing heavy and weak. He entered the auditorium, not a seat occupied, taking out his cellphone. Noticing three missed calls from Amanda, he phoned back.

"Timothy? Where'd you go? We've been waiting for you for like fifteen minutes?" she said.

I'm being attacked by that crazy mime, he tried to say.

"Timothy, you there? Is everything okay?"

Timothy kept trying to speak but gave Amanda nothing but an

earful of silence. Tears ran down his cheeks, wanting nothing more for Amanda to hear the sound of his voice. To tell her how much he loved her and Mary, to sing another song for the two of them. But that was all taken away from him, and he didn't understand why. He hung up their call hesitantly, quick to realize there was more than one way to talk to someone.

A loud screech of distorted audio blasted, and he covered his ears in agony. The sound cleared up, followed by the melody of Timothy's voice again. "You're just too good to be true, can't take my eyes off of you..." the voice sang from the speakers. "Oh, pretty baby!" Jinglehaimer emerged from the curtains with a microphone. "If it's quite alright, I need you, baby, to warm the lonely nights!"

What do you want! Timothy attempted to bawl, momentarily forgetting about his current condition.

"I want you to hear me," the mime announced. "I want everyone to hear me... and it's like that man said. You have a wonderful singing voice."

He moved closer, and Timothy saw the cane in Jinglehaimer's hand.

Timothy's vision blurred, too worn out to run again. The wound below his back seared, his breaths heavy and body weak. A part of Timothy wanted to fight Jinglehaimer. The mime was smaller, and Timothy had played his fair share of contact sports during his high school days. But those years were behind him, and even the faintest movement stung. In agony, he turned back and limbered away through the seats. He looked down at his phone and opened messenger.

Mary, I'm being attaked by that mime, he typed, paying no mind to his spelling and grammatical mistakes while his fingers shook. He stolen my voice and trying to kill me. I'm in Tiara Concert Theatre. Call Pol-

A whack to his lower calf immobilized him. Timothy's phone slipped out of his fingers as he hit the floor, never having sent his message. Jinglehaimer spun him around, and Timothy whirled, in an attempt to fight off the mime. But his strength dwindled, huffing for air as the impersonator exhausted him into submission. Jinglehaimer covered Timothy's mouth with one hand and brought a finger to his black lips with the other.

"Shh," Jinglehaimer whispered. He wrapped his fingers around Timothy's throat and squeezed. The last tune Timothy heard was the chorus of I Can't Take My Eyes Off of You, a gentle and soothing beat.

HANGMAN

by Mike Murphy

It all started when Paul Cunningham got out his wedding album and sat down on the recliner. It didn't take long for his mother to call. She knew what he'd be doing. "You're not going to look at it again, are you, dear?" she asked.

"Of course I am," he replied.

"But, sweetheart –"

"When would you suggest I look at it – on my birthday?"

"Paul –"

"It's my wedding anniversary."

"Was, dear," she said tenderly. "Claire's been gone for –"

"No one knows that more than I do," he proclaimed. "Give me a minute to do the math, and I can tell you how long to the second."

"She wouldn't –"

"Don't tell me what she would have wanted!" he complained at the often-heard comment from people who thought they were being helpful. "I'm going to do what I feel like doing... and this feels right."

"Son," his mother continued sadly, "I know what you're going through."

"Do you?" Paul replied. "Isn't Dad still alive? You can't know what it's like to be widowed until you are." No sooner were the words out of his mouth than he felt horrible. "I'm... I'm sorry," he continued. "I know you only... only want what's best for me."

"Always."

"Tomorrow, I'll get up and go to work. Tonight, I'm going to take a trip down memory lane, cry some—maybe a lot—and then go to

97

bed. It's what I do every December 3. It gets me through the day."

"You'll call if you need help... someone to talk to?" Mom asked.

"You're first on my list," he assured her.

In the dim light of the solitary lamp, he slowly turned the album's oversized, slightly yellowed pages, taking the time to appreciate what he saw. As he had for several anniversaries past, he found himself alternately smiling and weeping at the memories the pictures triggered. He gently touched the photo of Claire and him in their wedding finery. He ran a finger slowly down her cheek. "So young," he murmured, wiping a tear away with his sleeve. "We were... so young."

"She was a lovely lady," a male voice said.

"That she was," he agreed before realizing that something was wrong here. He looked up at his visitor: A tall, thin man wearing a black suit. "Hey!" Paul protested, standing quickly and putting the open album down on the coffee table. "Who are you?"

"My name isn't important," the white-haired man responded.

"How'd you get in here? The place is locked up tight."

"I found a way."

"What are you—a magician?"

"Some people have referred to me as one, but that was eons ago."

Clenching his fists, Paul spoke to his visitor. "You've got a minute to get out of here before I call the police," he informed him.

"Oh, Mr. Cunningham," the man added, surprising Paul with his knowledge of the family surname, "I have more time than that."

"You're a mind reader, too, huh?"

"I am many things."

"Well, Mr. Many Things, I'm going to take care of you myself." Paul menacingly stepped closer, his fists turning red.

"My minute isn't up yet!" the man complained.

"Too bad."

"I was hoping we could look at your wedding album."

"You are a weird one."

"You don't get it?" Paul's surprised visitor asked his host.

"It what?"

"Who I am."

"I don't give a damn who you are! I want you to get the Hell out of here."

"Now you're catching on!" the black-suited man said, grinning.

"What?"

"Hell. The Hell out of here," he continued. "Think, man!"

"You're the Devil?" Paul said, amused, after some thought.

"Yes. Though, lately, I've been going by 'Mr. Scratch.'"

"It's time for you to go."

"Aren't you curious why I'm here?"

"Not particularly."

"I felt the longing in your heart for Claire. It was so overwhelming, it seeped all the way down to Hades."

"How do you know her name?" Paul asked angrily.

"Very little escapes my notice," Scratch told him. "You miss her, don't you?"

"I've had enough of this." Paul strode angrily forward, but Mr. Scratch's response stopped him in his tracks.

"'Tomorrow, I'll get up and go to work. Tonight, I'm going to take a trip down memory lane, cry some – maybe a lot – and then go to bed,'" Scratch repeated. "Isn't that what you told your mother?"

"You tapped the phone?"

The man chuckled loudly at the idea. "I don't need to do such an everyday thing as that."

"So... you're the Devil?" Paul asked, trying to calm down.

"Mr. Scratch."

"I don't care if you're Mr. Rogers. I want you out of here."

"I've come to offer you a deal. One, I daresay, you will like very much."

"What I'd like very much is for you to leave before I knock out your teeth."

"You're not the least bit curious?"

"OK," Paul admitted, deciding that hearing his visitor out was the only way to get him to leave peacefully. "I'll bite. What can you offer me?"

"A reunion with the lovely Claire," Scratch answered matter-of-factly.

"Sure," Cunningham replied sarcastically. "And all you want in return... is my soul."

Mr. Scratch shook his head. "Not today."

"No?"

"I have an abundance of souls. Too many, in fact."

"Then... what?"

"The big toe of your right foot."

"What are you talking about?" Paul asked, his patience thinning.

"The only way I can keep the peace down below."

"With one of my toes?"

"Hell has many residents," Scratch explained. "Some of them, during their stay with me, have... 'lost' things."

"Like toes?"

"Toes, fingers, lungs, kidneys. These 'losers,' if you will, are crying out loud and long about why they shouldn't suffer and how, if they were only in charge, they would fix everyone's problems. I've been through a power struggle before," he said, sighing at the memory. "I don't want to face another one."

"So, by giving somebody my toe, you cut down on the complaining?" Paul returned.

"Yes. The would-be recipient is currently my biggest griper."

"What made you pick me?"

"As I said, I felt your despair. I thought you might be interested in making a deal."

"For a toe?"

"To start with," Scratch went on. "If, later, you're agreeable to more..."

"What would I get in return?" Cunningham inquired.

"That is what we need to negotiate."

"Time's up," Paul announced, grabbing his visitor's arm.

"I'm sorry?" Mr. Scratch asked.

"You were amusing for a bit, but –"

"You haven't given me a chance to make my point."

"The only point you have is the one on top of your head," Cunningham joked. "Now, should I call the cops or take you out of here myself? You stand a better chance of leaving unharmed with the police."

"Three minutes!" Scratch exclaimed. "Give me three minutes to prove myself. If by that time, I haven't, I'll leave."

"You will?"

"You'll never see me again."

"OK," Paul agreed, looking at his watch. "Starting now."

"Thank you," the Devil responded. "May I use your kitchen?"

"You gonna boil an egg?"

"It's hard to explain. I need to show you."

"OK, but you're down to about two and a half minutes now."

"Please stay clear." Mr. Scratch took a couple of steps closer to the kitchen and slowly put his fingers to his temples.

"Getting a headache?" Paul asked.

"Concentrating."

"I'm getting a headache."

"Shhh!"

An odd pulsing noise filled the house. It built to a crescendo and then stopped cold. Something happened to the kitchen. The air around it fluttered like a flashback scene in an old movie. When Paul could see the room again, he recognized his long-ago kitchen: The old linoleum, the white countertops, the rickety circular table.

Then he saw her. "Oh my God!" Claire. Young, beautiful, and alive. "Honey," he yelled, running to her. "Don't move!"

"No, Mr. Cunningham!" Scratch warned. Paul never made it. When he reached the threshold of the old kitchen, something violently shocked him, throwing him backward. He landed on his butt on the living room rug.

"Damn it! What's –"

"For now, it is merely an image... a moving image."

"For now?"

"It can be more," his visitor teased him.

Paul rose, interested now, and faced Mr. Scratch. "Get to the point."

"With an understanding between us, I could drop the field and allow you to enter that idyllic scene."

"Impossible."

"Is it?" Scratch plucked the pen from Paul's shirt pocket. "Observe."

He put his fingertips to his temples again, and a small hole appeared in the barrier. The Devil tossed the pen through the hole, which sealed up behind it. The pen from now landed on the linoleum from the past. Young Claire picked it up, shook her head with a slight smile, and put it down on the table.

"As easily as that pen made the leap from now to the past, so could you," Mr. Scratch announced. "Interested?"

"You bet!"

"Shall we discuss terms?"

The past he longed for playing out before him, Paul made the Devil an offer. "A year for a toe?" Scratch exclaimed. "That's... That's highway robbery!"

"Don't forget who's in the catbird seat," Cunningham reminded him. "You need me."

"Not as much as you think. You are convenient. I could find someone else."

"But then you'd lose the time you need to keep things quiet back home."

"I won't be treated this way! I can just leave and, oh, what an opportunity you will miss," Scratch told him. "I'll give you a week."

"Six months."

"Two weeks."

"Three months."

"Three weeks."

"Two months."

"One and done! A month. No more!"

"I'll take it," Paul said, disappointed.

"I'll have a contract drawn up. Once it's signed, you may start your month in the past."

"Excellent."

"Would you like to begin at the point I showed you?"

"I have a choice?"

"Of course," the visitor informed him. "I can't give you a day here and a day there, though. It must be thirty days straight."

"Thirty-one," Paul emphasized.

"Very well!" Scratch reluctantly agreed. "Thirty-one days."

Then Paul broached the topic. "When will I... lose my... my toe?"

"At the end of your time, you will be brought back here and pay your check."

"Will it... hurt?"

"Hardly at all," the Devil assured him. "Oh, one thing you should know."

Cunningham threw his hands up in the air. "Here we go: The catch."

"Hardly. I merely wanted to point out that, after you pay up, only you and I will ever recall that you once had that toe. Everyone else will think you were born without it, lost it in an accident, whatever."

"Why's that?"

"I can't have more than one reality existing at a time. It's much too cumbersome. People would wonder why you're changing, and how would you answer them?"

Paul dotted the "i"—in red ink—in his last name and handed Mr. Scratch back his pen. "Nice touch."

"Blood can be so messy. I gave up on it years ago." Scratch put the pen into his suitcoat pocket. "You saw no mention in the contract of giving up your soul?"

"No, and I read every word twice."

"That's because there is no such mention." Mr. Scratch put his fingertips to his temples, and the kitchen scene reappeared.

"Now what?" Paul asked anxiously.

"We're ready. You have thirty-one days. After that, you will find yourself back here, and it will be time to pay the piper." He motioned for Paul to step forward. He did so carefully, remembering the shock from last time. There was none. He walked into the years-old scene with a loud pop. The image disappeared. Mr. Scratch looked at the contract, chuckled an evil, little chuckle, and faded away.

Thirty-one days later, Cunningham appeared in his present-day kitchen. "Is my... my time up already?" he asked after getting his bearings.

"To the second," Scratch informed him. "Did you enjoy yourself?"

"Very much."

"Then you know what time it is?"

"I... I do," Paul nervously answered. "How..."

Scratch snapped his fingers. "Done!" he said.

"That's it?"

"What did you expect?" Paul sat on one of the kitchen chairs and kicked off his right sneaker. "Can't you trust me?" the Devil complained.

"No." He removed his sock. The big toe was gone. The cut was clean and even looked like it had healed up over many years.

"Just as we agreed."

"It didn't hurt at all!"

"Does that mean you're interested in further trades?"

"If the 'time' is right."

"Another 31 days with Claire for that thumb." Pop!

"Six months for a kidney."
"A kidney? I don't –"
"You can get by with one. Lots of people do." Pop!

"Three months." Pop!

"Five months. What a deal!" Pop!

Pop! Pop! Pop! Pop! Pop!

"Did you see the poor man in Room 6?" the older nurse asked the younger one as they sat behind their desk on the fifth floor of the hospital.

"Yes," the other nurse answered sadly. "There's so little of him left. No hands, only one leg..."

"The doctors say he's been like that for some time. There's just enough left of him to keep living."

"I don't know what they'll be able to do for him."

"Me either. I hate to be pessimistic about any patient but... where do you start?"

The crackle of the flames and the cries of the doomed souls diminished as the Devil's right-hand man, Morpheus, closed the door to his superior's castle. Mr. Scratch had made certain that the door never totally deadened those sounds. He enjoyed them.

Morpheus walked to his boss, who was seated behind a large

wooden desk. "Here are the case notes you asked for, Master," he said, handing Scratch a paper-stuffed clipboard.

The Devil thanked him and took it. He turned a few pages until he found what he was looking for. "And still he holds on," he said, surprised. "It's been months since I spoke with Mr. Cunningham."

"Do you have any further use for him?"

"I've gotten what I needed."

"So he was useful?"

"Oh, very useful," Mr. Scratch admitted. "His 'donations' helped end what could have been a very bloody time down here."

"So there will be no more trades?" Morpheus inquired.

"Maybe one."

"But you said –"

"I've waited a long time, been very patient with his demands. Thirty-one days. Ha!" the Devil explained. "He's in almost constant pain now. He should have no problem trading that last valuable bit of himself for a brief time where he could be whole and pain free again."

"I thought you said he didn't want to trade you for his soul?"

"He did, and—back then—I didn't want it. He was more valuable to me as someone to harvest. But now, with him close to death, why let a good soul go to waste?"

Morpheus never failed to be amazed at how sly his boss could be. "You planned this all along?"

"Of course."

"What makes you think he'll accept now?"

"To end to his pain," Scratch told his subordinate. "Noble ideas are all well and good until one is faced with reality. As Mr. Cunningham is, he could hold on for months or even longer, his pain increasing to agony. He wants it to stop, and only I can ensure that in a timely fashion. He will be mine soon. Mark my words."

The beeping and buzzing equipment surrounding Paul Cunningham cast a weird glow on the walls of his hospital room. The heart monitor showed a steady beat. With a loud pop, Mr. Scratch appeared at the foot of the bed. "Long time no see," he said to the shell of a man who lay before him.

Paul's breathing was labored, even with the oxygen tube blasting away under his nose. "You did this to me," he complained.

"Hardly," Paul's visitor corrected him. "You agreed to all of it. You knew what you were getting into every step of the way."

"Look at me!"

"No one forced you to accept my offers. You showed enviable greed." Scratch removed Paul's chart from a hook on the bed's footboard and flipped through the pages. "Tsk, tsk," he said. "You are in rough shape." Paul winced from a sudden jolt of pain. "Does it hurt?"

"Like Hell."

"Interested in one more trade?" the Devil continued as Paul's pain subsided. "One more chance for some time in the past—where you can be a whole man again."

"I have nothing left you want."

"Oh yes, you do," Scratch responded and smiled.

"I refuse!"

"You'd rather lie here, like this, than accept my offer?"

"Right," Paul answered just before a brief coughing fit took hold of him.

"I could give you a year in the past."

"No."

"Two years?"

"No," he said. "I told you when we started this damned mess, the answer was no."

"But why?"

"I don't have much time left," Paul answered. "When I die, I want to spend eternity with Claire – not you."

"You really believe that?"

"I do. There's you, so there's got to be a Heaven."

"Don't you want to die, to be free of the pain?"

"When it comes, it comes."

Scratch's face lit up. "Oh," he said, "I just got a wonderful idea."

"Go tell someone else about it."

"But you will be the beneficiary."

Paul turned his head as much as he could. "What are you talking about?" he inquired.

"Starting at this moment, I am going to take the energy I use every day ensuring the world's sorrows and start expending it... on you."

"Don't bother."

"For so long, I've spent my time ensuring bad things happen. You, Mr. Cunningham, are going to live forever."

Paul's heart monitor confirmed his increased heart rate. "What?" he asked incredulously.

"You'll never die. I'll see to that, and I'm just the man who can do it."

"Don't," Cunningham wheezed. "Please."

"You'll live forever... as you are now—or worse."

The heart monitor began racing. "You can't –"

"You'll never die—never see your wife again—unless..."

"You can't have my soul!" Paul exclaimed before succumbing to another coughing fit.

"Let's see how you feel about it a year from now, ten years from now, a century. I'll be around too, and I'll be expecting your call."

The pop from Mr. Scratch's departure only briefly drowned out the heart monitor's rapid beeping.

In the pre-dawn, the older nurse pushed the squeaky-wheeled medicine cart into Paul's room. "Good morning, Mr. Cunningham," she said pleasantly, secretly anticipating the moment she could leave this poor man's company.

"Morning," Paul mumbled.

"It's time for your meds." She reached down and, with gloved hands, helped Paul sit up as best he could. Used to the drill, he opened his mouth. She popped the pills in and, with a sip of lukewarm water through a straw, he swallowed them. She carefully laid him back down on the bed, fixed his covers, and asked, "Did you have a nice sleep?"

"No," he answered.

"You should have asked for something."

"I didn't want to."

"That's your choice."

"I'm... I'm going to live forever, you know?" he informed her.

"Are you?"

"I am."

"You keep believing that," she told him. "A positive attitude is important." The nurse looked at her watch. "I have to be going now," she informed him. "Your breakfast should be along shortly." She paused at the door to wish him a good morning and then wheeled the cart into the hall.

Paul began tearing up. He hadn't cried in some time. He didn't know he still could. "Yep," he said aloud to no one but himself, the tears now flowing freely. "I'm gonna... live... live forever."

SILENCE

by Marcella Harte Conlon

Glowing steel curved and stretched with each resonating blow from the smithy's hammer. The sound of each strike was piercing in an otherwise quiet workshop. Like drum beats it synced perfectly with the pounding in her skull.

She gritted her teeth, fighting back nausea and fatigue. That was alright though. Soon there would be silence.

The dark imposing silhouettes of old pines rose up around Kate like slender giants. They easily dwarfed the small girl gazing up into their prickly boughs with wide brown eyes. She fingered the tuning keys on her brand-new guitar uncertainly. The fret board was slightly too long to be comfortable yet. It was her bardic instrument and she was determined to play it.

Though perhaps a somewhat less spooky environment would have made her first lesson less daunting. The nine-year-old shivered before scooting closer to the campfire's warmth.

"Dad? Why can't we stay at the motel with Mom?"

Shadows clung to the square plains of her father's weathered face as he picked the first chords to an old folk song.

"It's tradition sweet pea. Every bard in our family has learned how to sing their first tales around a fire. That's where the original stories were told. Besides your Mom can't stand the bugs out here. She'll join us tomorrow at the music festival."

Kate eyed the deeper shadows a moment more before forgetting her insecurities and jutting her chin out proudly.

"I already know lots of stories. My teacher said I'm reading at a tenth-grade level. And Mom has taken me to hear you on circuit every summer since I was five!"

Her father smiled as he ran a riff down one neck of his eighteen-string harp guitar. The clear bright notes died away quickly as the low notes reverberated through the air like smoke.

"The stories sung by bards are more than language and written word. Each song is a connection. A voice."

"You can know all the stories there are in the world and sing every one until you're blue in the face, but folks won't actually hear what you're on about if your voice can't reach them."

"What does that even mean?"

"It means, that you already have tales to tell. You'll learn hundreds more before we're through. Tonight, you're gonna start learning how to tell them. Even when no one wants to listen."

"Why wouldn't people want to listen?"

"The guild of bards is very powerful. It may not seem like it since they take great pains to appear to be harmless, but they're not. There's power in these songs and stories, and most of all there is truth. Truth is the enemy of powerful people and some of them will do anything to stop it from coming out."

With that he resumed his playing, shifting into a new chord progression as easily as breathing. His deep voice rose in accompaniment with lyrics that were achingly beautiful.

Kate could feel the music thrumming somewhere deep beneath her skin. She shivered.

Shaping the armor quickly, the smithy watched the metal's orange glow begin to fade. The visor was nearly perfect. Just a few minor adjustments and it would fit like a second skin. She carried the cooling piece of armor back to the forge, shoving it into the charcoal fire with tongs. Peculiar markings in its surface gleamed in the light.

The armorsmith stared for a moment, expression unreadable, before turning to assess her evening's progress.

At the center of the dimly lit space a trestle table had been set up. Laid out across its surface was an exquisitely crafted set of plate armor. It had taken months to forge the suit. All that had remained was to make some necessary changes to size. The visor, an entirely unique piece of craftsmanship, had proved too broad for its intended purpose.

The smith glanced up to the body hanging limp from a support beam. A nylon rope had been tied to the wooden beam, then cinched under the woman's arms to bear most of her weight. Her boots only just rested on the mannequin block below her. She was so much smaller than remembered.

The smithy hummed in grim vindication, headache receding.

"Head south on Downing Lane," instructed Kate's cell phone.

The day was beautiful. Old cobblestone streets weaved amongst the colorful rustic homes and small shops. Doorways and shutters stood open to catch the occasional summer breeze. A particularly lovely building stood just ahead on the corner. It's entrance all but obscured with potted flowers and an elaborate lattice of climbing vines. Kate had nearly stopped to take a photo while wandering by the place an hour earlier. That was before it became evident that she was walking in circles. Her patience had since then grown thin.

She narrowed her eyes at the charming exterior before glancing to the map on her cell phone.

"Don't even think of telling me to go right again. I will dunk you in that fountain two turns back."

"In seven feet turn right onto Iron Street."

Her left eye twitched.

"Lost?" a voice asked curiously from the flowers.

She nearly dropped both her phone and the bag she'd been carrying since that morning.

"If you're looking for the smithy, the front gate is just around the corner. Down an alley between houses, so it can be hard to spot. The armor smith is out to lunch though."

Kate pocketed her phone and readjusted the heavy canvas bag over one shoulder. Its contents made metallic clanking noises as she tried to peer around the swath of greenery.

"I don't suppose you know when he'll be back?"

"Hmm, maybe in ten minutes or so? The lights' changing and I'm nearly out of charcoal."

Concealed just behind the overgrowth was what appeared to be an impressively messy and cheerful blacksmith; sketchpad in hand. The smaller woman smiled brightly and pushed out an extra chair with one blackened leather boot.

"Why don't you join me? It looks like you could use a break yourself. Don't worry. There's no ash or charcoal on the chair; just on me."

"Does that mean you're the armor smith then?"

"Sure am. Elena Russo. What brings you to my forge, Ms... ," she trailed off expectantly.

"Kate Sullivan. I'm a bard passing through on circuit. A heckler took offense at one of my performances. Threw a beer bottle. I kinda fell off the stage trying to duck." Kate winced at the memory. "Not my most graceful moment. I'm bringing in their handy work for repairs."

She pulled a pair of ornate dented bracers out of the canvas bag.

Elena whistled. "Oh wow. Not too many story tellers still wear armor outside of the Eisteddfod. How old are these pieces? They look 15th century."

"I'm not really sure. They're a family heirloom."

"Well, I'd stop wearing them except on special occasions. I can fix the damage. But you need something new for your regular gigs. A bard's ensemble is an important part of the experience after all. You want to make a statement." She studied Kate with a thoughtful expression. "Perhaps a tabard?" She flipped to a blank page and quickly began to sketch, glancing back to Kate periodically. "Hm, no that won't do. Too old fashioned. Maybe gilded brass?" Kate watched bemused as the smithy leapt from one idea to the next.

"I don't mean to be rude, but shouldn't I have some say in this?"

Elena snapped her fingers. "Of course! I need to get to know you if I'm going to outfit you properly. How about dinner at six? My treat."

"Sure. Why not?"

Flames ignited from the oil bath in a whoosh. Smoke rose from the tub in a plume as the visor was quenched and hardened. The smithy listened carefully for the telltale sounds of cracking metal. There were none.

Satisfied, she lifted the armor from its bath and set it aside to cool.

It was time for the real show to begin.

She strode to center stage removing her leather gloves. The trestle table with its gleaming armor was spread out before her. She paused to stand over the sabatons. Her fingers idly traced the shallow grooves that were its markings, before taking the armor in hand.

Humming softly she approached the audience of one.

She knelt at the display block where the woman's booted feet rested. Reaching for leather ties the sabatons were fixed into place. Almost immediately, their markings flashed an angry crimson. Metal swirled and dripped, pooling like liquid mercury into every gap and crevice. Until the red light dimmed and the bard's boots were hopelessly encased in steel.

"Bards have a responsibility to tell stories that don't encourage immoral behavior," stated John with smug certainty.

The news commentator looked like a salesman in his plain navy suit with slicked back hair and too white teeth.

"But John, doesn't a bard have the same freedom to express themselves as everyone else? You don't seem to be as critical about other writers and musicians," his co-host Denise questioned.

"Denise, other artistic professionals aren't the direct descendants of the bardic knights that helped to found our country. These men and women must be held to a higher standard."

The commentary droned on from a small television set tucked into one corner of a tiny kitchenette. Morning light warmed painted cabinets and a re-purposed wooden table with mismatched chairs. Kate sat there, expression distant, scrolling through email.

She selected one of the newest and began to read.

"You know you suck, right? You suck as a human being. If I saw you on the street, I'd punch you in the face! And I'd keep punching you because you deserve it!"

She took a sip of coffee and clicked the next one.

"Your songs are a bad influence on good people! I hope you're left to die in a gutter! It'd serve you right witch! You should be ashamed!"

Click.

"Be Silent."

Kate paused. The words staring up at her from the blue light of the laptop.

"Honey, do you know if there's any bacon leftover from yesterday? The baby's hungry."

She snapped the laptop shut.

"Uh, no. But I can make you an omelet if you'd like."

Elena was still rumpled from sleep. One hand rested on her swollen belly while the other tried to stifle a yawn. She waddled over to the refrigerator and began to rummage.

"Oh! There's still a cinnamon bun from dessert! You wanna split it?" Elena peeked around the fridge door grinning. "I could make us extra icing!" She sang the last two words in impish delight.

No song yet written could adequately describe how much she loved this woman, thought Kate.

She smiled broadly before standing to gather Elena into her arms, kissing the back of her wife's neck.

"I'll get out the electric mixer."

The bard awoke just as the cuirass was fastened tightly about her ribcage. She groaned pitiably.

"W-where am I?"

Her voice was sluggish, as though drugged. Though that was a crude approximation of the truth. The smithy ignored it, watching intently the glowing red sigils and pooling steel.

"I can't move. Why can't I move?"

She didn't reply, but continued to hum as she retrieved the rerebraces.

A low haunting melody flowed through Pipers Hall in a deep current. It rolled across the audience in a wave. Its impact sinking into their bones and cresting high into the rafters.

"The night the music ended
The whole world fell away."

Acoustics in older music halls weren't always particularly good. Pipers Hall was no exception and that was part of its allure. Bardsong was well known to resonate in even the worst conditions. Kate sang and the walls shook.

"A woman cried and a kingdom fell
When the music ceased to play."

Stage lights shone from vibrating rafters. Their stark glow reflected off the polished surfaces of her armor, while casting the rest of the venue in shadow. Kate could only just make out a group of late attendees listening from the back. Their clothing was stained with garish color and they laughed drunkenly amongst themselves.

"Enthralled we changed our places
Cold steel filled the empty spaces"

One burly man at the groups center, face smeared with red, grinned at her smugly. He raised a half empty bottle towards the stage in mock salute.

"On the night the music died."

The bard's eyes hardened as she continued to play. She shifted from one song to the next, her fingers nimble and confident on the guitar strings. What did it matter if she sang the mirror histories? Surely, there was room for more than one interpretation? Kate closed her eyes and let the music drown out her irritation. Histories and legends of countless voices entwined with her own. They captivated her audience, as for the span of an evening, the tales were lived once more.

She gently strummed a final intricate melody and reality reasserted itself with a quiet sigh.

The applause that followed was both avid and genuine. Kate smiled.

"Thank you, Pipers Hall! You've been a wonderful audience!"

With a flourish and a bow, Kate strode off stage to join her family. She didn't get far.

In the hall backstage glowered a stately woman in a tailored business suit the color of spilled ink. Her pale blond hair was woven into an intricate hairstyle and held in place with pins of the same color as her suit. A small silver brooch in the shape of a harp glinted at her left lapel. She was beautiful, severe, and a touch intimidating. Kate had only met the guild's chief recruitment officer, Dame Briant, once before at the Eisteddfod. She didn't relish making her acquaintance again.

The Dame grabbed her arm as she tried to walk past.

"What do you think you're doing singing those songs?"

"Please let go of me."

"I can't understand why you would disregard our laws so brazenly."

"I don't believe in keeping stories hidden. The truth is important."

"The truth is important. However, not every truth is better for being known, Ms. Sullivan. Consider this a warning."

Before Kate could respond Dame Briant stormed off in the opposite direction from where Kate was heading.

She watched her walk away and took a second to compose herself.

Her family was waiting in the wings. Liam was bouncing on his toes with excitement while holding to the folds of his mother's skirt.

Elena smiled down at him before turning her attention to Kate.

"You were fantastic! A tad more intense towards the end but, it was a good compliment with the new plate mail. I knew teaching you to help in the forge was a good idea. Armor made by both of us suits you better."

Elena tugged lightly at the breastplate. Her cheerful expression faltering to one of concern. No matter how enthusiastic the audience, there were almost always some who attended specifically to cause trouble.

She glanced back towards the stage and the slowly dispersing crowd. The unruly group from before with its colorful ringleader was gone.

"It wasn't too hot under the lights was it?"

"Nothing I couldn't handle, love." She touched Elena's cheek and leaned in for a reassuring kiss. "There's no need to worry."

A small weight latched onto Kate's legs and her son looked up at her expectantly.

"Mom," cried Liam, "That was fun! Can we get pizza?"

"Sure we can, kiddo. I just need to get changed, then we can go."

With a quick kiss to his forehead, Kate carefully extricated herself from the boy's grip. She walked to her guitar case and kneeling down, opened the lid. At least a dozen black and white photographs lay scattered inside. Confused, she picked a few up for a closer look.

There was a photo of Elena helping Liam out of their van in the hotel parking lot. A photo with the three of them checking in to the hotel early the same day. A photo of a visor for a suit of armor. Though it more closely resembled a featureless mask. There were no slits to see or even breath through and it was covered in strange intricate markings. The words 'Be Silent' were neatly written in permanent marker across the glossy image.

Kate's blood ran cold.

"Honey, did you see anyone go near my guitar case?"

"No. But, I've been keeping an eye on Liam and watching your performance. Why? Is something wrong?"

"Just missing the extra guitar strings I thought I'd packed."

Gritting her teeth, Kate set the guitar gently inside and latched the case closed.

"Hey, how about we switch hotels tonight? There's a nicer one further down the road. I heard they give you free chocolate chip cookies when you check in! I'll change clothes there and we can have the pizza delivered."

"Cookies!"

Liam cheered and looked to his mama hopefully. Elena did not look happy. She took their son's hand and started walking towards the music hall's back exit.

"He'll be up all night, Kate."

"Yeah, but it's just this once. And he can sleep on the drive home tomorrow."

Kate pushed open the heavy metal door and was greeted with a woosh of chill night air. She shivered and stepped out to hold the door open, boots crunching on broken glass.

She froze. Elena let out a startled gasp behind her, quickly pulling Liam behind them both.

Their van was parked under a street lamp. Its windows smashed and tires slashed. Insults spray painted in jarringly bright colors glowed dully in the fluorescent light. An especially vulgar threat dripped red onto the cracked pavement.

DIE WITCH!

Kate stared, feeling numb.

She was screaming now. Which was an annoyance given how wonderful the armor looked on her.

Regardless, the smithy busied herself with affixing the gauntlets. The first one had slipped into place without much trouble. The right hand, however, was locked into a white knuckled fist. She frowned, trying to pry the fingers open. Her screams grew shrill as blood trickled where nails bit into pale skin.

The smithy briefly paused at the yelling before reexamining her progress. The bard stood stiffly upright upon the display block. Nearly all of the armored suit was in place. She would fit in easily to any armorer's showroom.

Assured, the smithy stood up to lock eyes with her singular audience. The woman continued to scream and sob. The smithy replied in kind. She amplified the clamor. She shrieked and she hollered, doubling and redoubling in volume and resonance until the room itself seemed to quake. Finally, the light from the forge flickered out.

The bard grew perfectly still and quiet, her face drawn and pale. Her eyes glassy. She trembled.

The gauntlet was slipped into place, as the smithy resumed her humming.

The van's windows and tires had been replaced within a week of the incident. A new paint job took nearly a month. Police investigation into the threatening photos, however, was still ongoing and exhausting.

The van's windshield wipers labored through a steady rain with the pace of a metronome. Kate struggled not to nod off. Beside her Elena had already fallen asleep, her breathe lightly fogging the passenger window. It would probably be best to pull over.

Instead Kate turned on the air conditioning and switched it to the highest setting. Frigid air blasted from the vents and jolted her awake. She wouldn't stop tonight. Not until they were home, still a good two hours away.

Kate sang quietly. Familiar lyrics helped to keep silence and sleep at bay.

"The night the music ended..."

She glanced to the rear-view mirror. Was that the same pair of headlights that had been tailing her since leaving Seiren Hall? It could just be coincidence. She was too tired for this.

"The whole world fell away."

Gritting her teeth, she debated whether to try losing them. The motorway was relatively empty this late at night and there was an exit ramp just ahead. Maybe she could shake them on the back roads. Carefully, she began guiding the van off the freeway and down the ramp.

The headlights behind her grew brighter as they abruptly accelerated.

Kate cursed and swerved around the bend, tires squealing. The action jerked Elena awake with a startled cry.

"Kate?! What's happening?!"

There was no time to answer. Stomping hard on the gas pedal, she sped recklessly along an empty stretch of road. Streetlights flashed past in a blur as the van hydroplaned on slick asphalt.

The oncoming headlights surged forward blindingly bright. Her pursuers engine roared and there was no escape. The collision was thunderous.

Metal and fiberglass screeched and crumpled.

Glass shattered and flew apart.

Kate was slammed back into her seat, and then whiplashed into an airbag.

The van flipped into a lateral roll. It threw up sparks and tore through gravel and muddy earth. Finally, it came to a halt with an enormous crunch against a telephone pole.

Heart pounding, Kate lay in a daze. She hummed groggily as something wet dripped into her eyes. The smell of gasoline and ozone filled her nose.

Had the gas tank been ruptured? Probably. They needed to get clear of the wreck before it could catch fire. She tried turning her head and for a nauseous moment the van's interior seemed to lurch, spinning drunkenly about her. The edges of her vision blurred and threatened to tunnel. Kate squeezed her eyes closed, trying not to vomit. After a few deep steadying breathes, she opened her eyes.

"Elena. We have to..." the words died on her lips.

Elena was slumped motionless in her seat, covered in blood.

Kate barely registered the sound of her door being wrenched open.

From her peripheral the bard could vaguely make out the silhouette of a woman in a black suit, silver glinting to one side.

"You want silence," she thought.

She reached out to touch her wife's cheek as the silhouette grabbed for her.

"You'll have it when I'm through with you."

She sang and the world fell away.

It was far too dark to see properly. But the armorsmith still turned the visor over in her hands, as though admiring the faceless mask and its grotesque markings. She approached, singing quietly.

"A woman cried and a kingdom fell

When the music ceased to play."

"Please," Dame Briant pleaded, "The guild only needed your silence. You must understand... What happened to your wife was an accident..."

Her voice shook. It was thick with tears and desperation.

"Please. Please, don't do this... "

The singing continued, as somber as a dirge and as inescapable as its end.

"Enthralled we changed our places

Cold steel filled the empty spaces"

Kate positioned the visor over the other woman's face. Its sigils glowed.

"No! It wasn't supposed to happen this way!"

"On the night the music...

... died."

THE GOODFELLOW HOUSE

by Jacqueline Moran Meyer

The old red clapboard house looks worse in person than in the photos posted on the Airbnb rental site. Even in the dim twilight, I can discern evidence of the Goodfellow House's slow decline; curling strands of peeling paint, a rotting front door, and cracked taped-up windows make the house look sad and unloved. The roof looks beyond repair and as if it could cave in on itself at any moment being so dangerously weighed down by ten inches of freshly fallen snow.

I park my car next to the picturesque half-frozen river, and a ramshackle structure that I assume is the mill I read about in the house bio online.

This must be the place where Cotton Goodfellow was crushed to death and found by three of his young children.

The rental site gave a short history of the circa-1865 home. That's how I knew about the death in the backyard mill. Cotton Goodfellow built this house and lived here with his wife, Adelaide, and their nine children. The poor man was crushed to death at the age of thirty-one in the mill soon after the completion of the house—super bad luck. The ruined family sold the house and scattered, but Cotton's ghost is rumored to search the house and grounds for his lost family. It's a good thing I don't believe in ghosts. But frankly, I can't imagine why they advertise this. Maybe there are people who like this sort of thing. To each, her own.

My face stings from the frigid temperature, as I walk the Twenty-yards to the front porch. I check my phone to see if I can call my daughter, Amelia. There's no cell service, but we're used to this. The phone service is always spotty around here, so we arranged to meet

125

at the Goodfellow House at 8:00 a.m. tomorrow.

I'm here because I'm on a business trip and thought I'd make a pit stop to see my college girl, as the client's office is only an hour away. Amelia's small liberal arts school is in the middle of cow and barn country, in a town so small there's not enough traffic for a proper hotel to survive. Renting a nearby home or a single room in a house is the only option for a place to spend the night if you want to see your kid at this college. I have never stayed here. Actually, I have never heard of it.

An old Ford pickup truck with mismatched doors putters down the drive and parks next to my SUV.

Oh boy. This will be interesting.

The owner of the house, Joe, walks toward me. A large fur-trimmed hood covers his head, and his long tattered down coat travels past his knees. I can see his gray eyes, but the rest of his face is hidden behind a hat and scarf.

Well, I will never be able to pick that man out of a lineup.

His too-wide smile gives me the impression that the sight of me is not what he expected, and I protectively pull my hat down over my long, blond hair and zip my winter coat up to my chin. He gives me a once-over and keeps walking toward me, past where it would have been appropriate to stop. I take a step back.

"Hello, Erin. Welcome to the Goodfellow House. My, you look way too young to have a college-age daughter," Joe says.

Acknowledging his arrival with a nod, I don't respond. Instead, I pretend I am looking for something in my bag. After a moment of awkward silence, he continues.

"Will your husband be joining you?"

Ugh. He's annoying as hell.

"No, Joe, it's just me." My gut is telling me to lie and say Henry will be joining me, but the site said extra overnight guests are fifty dollars each.

What a thief!

"I get it. My wife travels a lot for her job. In fact, she's away right

126

now," Joe says.

Is he actually flirting with me in his parka and scarf covered face?

"Brr...I am freezing. Can we go inside?" I ask.

He unlocks the door, we enter, and he hands me the keys. I am pleasantly surprised to find the inside of the house cozy and clean.

Joe takes off his hood, hat, and scarf, and I am relieved to find an average middle-aged doughy, balding man in front of me.

I can definitely pick him out of a lineup now.

"Erin, I have to be honest. We don't like renting this house out, but we desperately need the money. Unfortunately, I recently lost my job," Joe said, sounding strangely apologetic.

"I am sorry to hear that," I say.

"There are some house rules, and they must be followed, OK? This is imperative. There are just two things to remember. One—this is the most important thing to remember—lock the front door. Two, turn off all the lights by midnight. Promise me that you will do that."

Yuck. What a control freak he is.

"OK, sure, Joe. May I ask why?"

He was not anticipating my question because he paused for a second too long before answering.

"It's nothing to worry about, Erin, but it is very, very important. We want our guests to remain safe, as the location is remote. We'd like to keep the electric bill down as well. Also, I have to apologize that the landline has been out for a few days. A common occurrence around here, unfortunately. All the more reason to follow the house rules."

This guy is a loony. He makes me want to light this old house up like a Christmas tree and unlock and open all the doors and windows, but I am an adult, so I have to act like one.

"I promise. Shall I leave the house keys under the mat before I take off tomorrow—is that all right?" I ask with a smile.

"Great. Enjoy your stay." He puts on his winter costume before he walks outside but swiftly turns around, pointing to a camera above the front door. "Wait, I almost forgot to tell you this. There is a camera outside the house that I can access from my home. If there is an intruder, an alarm will go off in my house. I am about fifteen minutes away. There is not one inside. Don't worry." He chuckles uncomfortably. "It's purely for your safety."

What a creeper, I think.

"Thank you," I say as he walks back to his car.

I'm tired and decide to go right to bed. I turn off the downstairs lights before walking up the narrow staircase. There is a low-ceilinged bedroom I believe I am supposed to sleep in because of the worn pink towels stacked on the fluffy white comforter. The room is small but charming, with pale lavender walls and a mahogany four-poster bed. There is a small blue dresser in the corner of the room displaying several antique photos. After closer inspection, I realize some of these photos were online along with the photos of the house. The photo of the entire family showed the eleven Goodfellows of the mid-1800s.

Wow, they had a ridiculous number of children. What a nightmare.

Adelaide and Cotton look happy and young. There was one individual photo of Adelaide with faint pencil writing on it. I could see the written name "Addy."

I guess that was her nickname. Weird, she resembles my Amelia, light hair and eyes, and angular features. I'll have to show her this tomorrow. Addy probably had four kids by the time she was Amelia's age. I shudder.

The one window in the room faces the front of the house. I regard the blue-white glow of the porch light against the smooth intact snow before putting on my sweats and T-shirt and crawling under the cotton covers.

While working on my laptop to prepare for my meeting tomorrow, I doze off in the warm bed and wake up at 3:00 a.m., according to the digital clock. I notice I have broken a rule; the bedside lamp is still on.

Oops, one rule broken. Did I lock the front door?

I glance out the window as I turn off the light and see the still figure of a man standing in the snow. My body immediately goes into fear mode. I can feel the flash of hot blood rising to my cheeks. I take deep breaths, attempting to remain calm. I turn off the light and fall to the floor below the window.

Think straight. Calm down. It's my imagination. The history of the house, and all, has gotten to me.

My heart is beating fast, and I realize the whimpering I hear is coming from me. I use one hand to pull myself up to window height. I peek out of the bottom quarter of the window, and now there is no doubt. Someone or something is standing there.

Could it be Joe, trying to scare me? Cotton Goodfellow? Impossible. A psycho?

It looks like a man, an odd man. He is standing in a way I have never seen anyone stand. Bent. His shoulders are hunched over, and his head has fallen to the side and is resting on his right shoulder as if it is broken.

But that can't be!

Then there are his horrible legs. They are very thin and bent in places where legs can't be bent. One leg looks like the letter Z. One arm is much shorter than the other. Is it missing? Oh no. He is using his good arm to tilt his head toward my window. He's lifting his sickening broken neck and head. I am going to vomit. I crouch to the floor again, and in between my gagging and the wave of nausea that has overtaken me, I try to come up with a plan.

What do I do? What do I do? Think. There is no goddamn landline or cell service. I can't call 911. I need a weapon. I need to secure the room.

I frantically look around the room for something that could hurt someone. I smash Addy's picture frame and clutch a small shard of glass in my hand. I push the dresser against the locked door for extra protection. I crawl on the wooden floor back to the window, and when I peek out, the crooked man is gone.

He is gone, and there are no footprints!

I skitter across the floor and cower in a corner, hugging my knees and trying to make myself small. I try to breathe to stop the whimpering, but every worst-case scenario is going through my head. Amelia.

I hear a noise downstairs and try my best not to scream. I think I hear someone at the front door.

Damn it! Why can't I follow rules? I didn't lock it. Damn. Damn. Damn.

The sound of the front door violently swinging open is followed by incessant, repetitive whispering. Slow, lumbering footsteps and the breaking of china and furniture adds to the frightening chorus that is traveling through the house. He, or it, begins to climb the stairs. The whispering is getting louder, but I still can't make out what is being said. He is on the other side of my door, but I can't make out what he is saying.

After several minutes, against my better judgment, I move closer to the door, cutting my hand with the glass shard from clutching it too hard.

What is he saying?

As I lean over the dresser in an attempt to place my ear against the door, all holy hell breaks loose, and it is as if the whole house shakes with Cotton Goodfellow's anguish. He is screaming his wife's name. He is angry, and he is trying to bang my door down. I huddle in the corner with my glass and repeat the bedside prayers of my youth.

The screaming stops when he is interrupted by another voice.

"Leave here! You are not welcome!" Joe screams.

Could Joe be doing all of this? The sick bastard. Is he messing with me?

"Go away! I called the police!" I yell.

I hear fighting outside the door. There are definitely two people fighting. Bodies are being flung against walls, with grunting and cries following each crash. There is one last chilling scream and the sound of something tumbling down the stairs, landing with a sickening thud.

I am paralyzed by the horror of it all and spend the rest of the night shivering in the corner of my room, too frightened to move.

How will I know when it's safe to open the door? Oh, no. Amelia. What will happen to my Amelia?

The hopeful morning light begins streaming through the little window. I hear the door open downstairs, as well as my daughter's beautiful voice.

"Mom?" Amelia calls.

"Amelia, run! Run, Amelia. Get help," I yell while pushing the dresser that has blockaded the bedroom door to the side.

After nervously fumbling with the lock, I am able to open the door and run to the landing of the narrow staircase. My lovely Amelia is at the foot of the stairs standing over Joe's mangled dead body. She is pale and shaking. Neither of us can speak. Amelia is terrified by the dead body at her feet, and I am terrified by the shadowy figure lurking behind my daughter, who speaks while extending his arms out to her.

"Addy's home! Addy's home! Addy's home!"

Just Like in the Movies

by Kurt Newton

"Jerry, this is Dr. Kapelman."

Jerry Beagle sat like a sullen child, chin on his chest, legs straight out beneath the restaurant table. He stared at his soda and watched the carbonation rise from the bottom of the glass to the top where it disappeared, only to be replaced by more. He imagined himself riding one of these bubbles, clinging to it like a giant beach ball at the ocean, like Captain Ahab riding Moby Dick.

"Jerry, sit up and be polite. Dr. Kapelman has come all the way from Chicago just to see you." Jerry's doctor, Benjamin March, motioned for Dr. Kapelman to sit, making apologies for Jerry's behavior.

"Oh, please, I understand," said Dr. Kapelman, shaking off the need for explanation. He slid into the booth alongside Dr. March.

Jerry straightened somewhat. It was hard to tell. He was seventeen years old, weighed one hundred twenty pounds, and stood just under six feet tall. He either hunched or slid when he sat. His bones seemed to dictate the position of his body, not his muscles. He did the best he could with what he had to work with.

Dr. Kapelman gave Dr. March a nod of confidence while waiting for Jerry to assume some proper form of posture.

"Well, Jerry," Dr. Kapelman began, "I bet the kids at school call you 'Stringbean.' Am I right?" A quick laugh.

Jerry suddenly became very self-conscious, keeping his eyes to the table. He looked as if he wanted to crawl underneath the tablecloth.

Dr. March cleared his throat. "Dr. Kapelman, Jerry doesn't go to school."

"Ah, I see." A momentary pause; a fatherly smile. "But still there is no need for embarrassment, Jerry. You know, I once knew a boy who was just like you."

"Like me?" Jerry croaked, a sudden eager excitement blooming across his face. It was as if he had just been told he could stay up late and watch TV, and that all his favorite movies were going to be on, and he could eat all the popcorn he wanted, and he would never get tired and fall asleep, and--

"Oh, no, no, no," Dr. Kapelman said, realizing the misunderstanding. "I mean tall and thin, a little too ungainly for his age."

Jerry's face went slack.

"Well, all that was just a phase," Dr. Kapelman continued. "A growing process. Can you guess what he is now, Jerry?" Dr. Kapelman looked to Dr. March, who was monitoring Jerry's reaction.

Jerry shifted in his seat, sliding a bit. He hated being stared at. He felt as if he were sitting on a slab of glass peering up into the lowering lens of a giant eye. To make himself feel more comfortable, he pictured himself sitting beneath the domed lid of that tiny submarine in Fantastic Voyage, cruising down an artery, watching the blood cells floating by like inflatable life rafts. In fact, Dr. Kapelman reminded him of that crazy guy with the bald head who tried to kill everybody.

"A basketball player! He now plays for the New York Knicks!" Dr. Kapelman slapped his palm on the table to emphasize this person's amazing success at overcoming their handicap. Dr. Kapelman was smiling. Dr. March was also smiling, looking for some lost hope in Jerry's eyes to return. Jerry smiled kindly at Dr. Kapelman, but it was a faraway smile. He hadn't heard most of what was said. He was thinking about how that bald-headed guy in Fantastic Voyage finally got eaten by antibodies.

Just then, a waitress interrupted, and whatever strands of Jerry's attention either doctor held slipped away completely. Jerry let his eyes drift to the other tables and booths in the restaurant.

There was a young couple seated at one table. They had a hold of each other's hands around the dinner candle. Jerry watched them curiously until they leaned toward each other and kissed. Jerry looked away. He felt the same kind of discomfort at home watching one of those long kissing scenes on television—no need to look away there. Though, sometimes he didforget.

Laughter erupted from across the room, and Jerry followed the sound.

There were three men in suits, corporate types, sitting in a booth directly across the restaurant. Their laughter boomed heartily as they shuffled papers back and forth, each of the men signing them. They shook hands, clapped each other's backs, and drank a toast. Jerry imagined the three of them, shovels in hand, at a groundbreaking ceremony. He imagined himself peering through an old abandoned tenement doorway, watching, their bodies nothing but colored blurs of heat-sensored light, their voices strange and garbled as if played in reverse or slowed like a 45 record played on 33 rpm, as in that movie Wolfen. Jerry wondered if there really were wolves in New York City.

Before he could make up his mind, he heard what sounded like a woman's cry. His ears suddenly pricked up.

"Shut up!" a hushed voice commanded from the other side of the booth where Jerry sat.

Jerry looked to see if Dr. March or Dr. Kapelman had heard it. The waitress was patiently describing the contents of each meal on the menu to Dr. Kapelman, who was shaking his head and smiling.

Jerry knelt on the seat and peered through the plants separating him from a small corner table on the other side. He could see a young woman; she was weeping. A handkerchief was clutched in the hand that rested against her temple. Faint tear tracks painted her cheekbones. She was beautiful, Jerry thought. She was wearing a white dress, and the whiteness made her all the more beautiful, like a clouded photograph. But it was a sad beauty; a trapped beauty; a beautiful white bird in a cage. Jerry was heartstruck. The man sitting across from her, of which Jerry could only see the back of his prickly head and broad shoulders, was talking to her in hushed but harsh tones.

"Need I remind you that you came to me for help. Money was no object you said. Now that the job is done... let's just say I've reconsidered the value of my silence."

The woman began to sob again.

"Let's not be foolish and make a scene. Think of what's at stake." The man's voice slipped from his throat like sandpaper over a stone. Jerry leaned further into the plants. The woman noticed him and appeared startled, then fearful. The man whose shoulders Jerry looked down upon suddenly spun around and caught Jerry in wide-eyed amazement. The man had a scar creasing the right side of his cheek, dragging one eye down in a deformed slant. To the man's amazement, Jerry opened his mouth and voiced an excited "Wow!" before popping back out of sight.

Jerry turned back in his seat and sat down hard. "This is just like in the movies," he said, unsure if what he had just witnessed was real or some imagined replay of a mystery movie he had recently seen.

"What was that, Jerry?" said Dr. March. Jerry stared at the waitress standing before him, pad and pen poised. He didn't even see her.

"Jerry, the young lady would like your order."

Jerry was too busy lending an ear in the direction of the plants and the table beyond. His mind unreeled a thousand different dialogues and movie plots.

"Miss, he'll have what I'm having," Dr. March said as a substitute to Jerry's faraway silence. He knew Jerry was prone to daydreams. After all, he sat before that television set every waking hour. But it was a harmless addiction in the eyes of Dr. March. No need to administer the drugs that were, until recently, so necessary to keep Jerry calm and controlled. It was a trade-off: strong doses of television in return for daydreams. A small price to pay considering the alternative.

"So, Ben, tell me more about our wunderkind," Dr. Kapelman said, commandeering Dr. March's attention. The two doctors sat in conference, Dr. March filling Dr. Kapelman in on the events that led to his involvement, while Jerry was left to his harmless daydreams.

Jerry was still in the throes of deciding what he had witnessed. There was a real-life What? Blackmailer? Yeah, that's it. A blackmailer sitting on the other side of this booth and an honest to God (beautiful) damsel in distress!

"So, you can understand the necessity for," Dr. March paused, catching a signal from Dr. Kapelman. He turned. "Jerry?"

Jerry was sliding out of the booth. "Huh!" He hovered on the edge of his seat. "Oh, I've got to go," he said, nodding his head in the direction of the GENTLEMEN'S ROOM sign at the back of the restaurant. Dr. March studied Jerry's face.

"You sure now?"

Jerry grinned. "I'll only be a minute."

Dr. March liked to see Jerry smile. Normally Dr. March would accompany Jerry wherever he went for safety's sake, but he thought Jerry had had enough embarrassment for one night.

"Okay, don't get lost."

"I won't."

Dr. March watched his prized patient lope toward the restroom. He turned to Dr. Kapelman. "He's a good kid," he said, then took a sip of his drink. "Now, where were we?"

As Jerry aimed himself in the direction of the men's room, which cut a path across the kitchen traffic, he looked to see if Dr. March was keeping an eye on him. The two men, one balding, one with hair, were nodding and bobbing in apparent conversation. Jerry quickly turned away from the men's room and passed behind the partition that circumvented the restaurant. As he did so, he heard the kitchen doors swing open behind him, spilling the sounds of cooks, pots and pans, and a steamy dishwasher out into the restaurant. But Jerry's mind was elsewhere.

He thought about the woman.

He imagined sitting with her at that table instead of that evil man. With him, she wasn't crying. She was smiling, her eyes affectionately resting on his, like the couple he had seen earlier in the restaurant. Saying so much with just her eyes, there would be no need for words.

Feeling the warmth of her gaze... her tenderness. Jerry's heart began to burn in his chest.

He intended to approach them from the other side of their table, the side she was nearest, just walk up and stand alongside her as if he had known her all his life and confront the man with the scar... tell him that he knew what he was up to and to leave the lady alone if he knew what was good for him. He had seen it done so many times in the movies. It just had to work.

But when Jerry came around the partition by their table, all he found was her handkerchief lying on the floor beside her chair. He bent to pick it up, feeling the softness of its silk. The warmth in his heart surged.

He looked up and quickly scanned the restaurant. He spotted her over by the doorway, leaving, composing herself, squaring her shoulders, and lifting the collar on her coat before pushing the door to the exit. She disappeared in waves as she passed behind the rippled glass of the restaurant's foyer, gone.

The man she was with was nowhere in sight. Perhaps he left moments before. Perhaps taking the rear exit. It didn't matter now. Hanging his head, Jerry realized he did have to go to the bathroom after all.

He rubbed the handkerchief between his fingers as he walked toward the men's room, feeling her gentle presence within the fabric. When Jerry reached for the men's room door, the door suddenly flew inward, and a man walked out, bumping into him. Jerry looked up and saw the scar. "You," he heard the man's voice slither. Then Jerry felt himself being dragged forward into the brightly lit room.

"So, I see you've got a piece of her," the man said, spinning Jerry around and pinning him firmly against a stall. The sudden crash rebounded off the porcelain tiles, amplified. Jerry looked sidelong. The bathroom was empty.

"Oh, yeah, she's a honey pot, that one. All the young boys would like a piece of her. Only you seem to have your hands full with just her hanky." The man laughed insidiously. Jerry stared at the man's face; it was only inches away. Every hair, every pore, every bit of stubble on the man's chin stood out in a hideous bas relief. The man's scar took on gigantic proportions, cutting deeply into his cheek. His offset eye seemed to slide on his face, ever downward. Scenes from Tarantula and The Hunchback of Notre Dame unreeled before Jerry's eyes.

"I have a suggestion for you, kid. Whatever you think you saw or heard, you didn't. You got that!" The man's eyes suddenly went dark and piercing, making their point intimidatingly clear.

But Jerry swallowed and said, "I know what you're up to," in a voice that trembled on the edge of changing octaves, "and you better leave that lady alone if you know what's good for you."

The man's face returned to normal, its expression now sliding in reverse to one of utter amazement. For a moment, the man was completely without response, but then a crooked smile broke across his features. "I like you, kid. You've got guts." The smile cracked into toothy fragments. "But too bad those guts aren't going to be with you for very long. C'mon." The man slipped a knife from out of his pocket. "Let's go," he said.

The man grabbed Jerry by the shoulder and pushed him toward the exit. As he did so, the door opened and in walked one of the corporate types Jerry had seen earlier. Jerry could feel the knife behind him increase its pressure against his kidney, reminding him of his need to urinate.

"Excuse me, gentlemen," the businessman said, breathing alcohol into Jerry's face.

Jerry smiled haplessly as he was nudged from behind and out into the restaurant. "This way," the man commanded in Jerry's ear, steering him with the knife blade. To the right, at the end of the hallway was an emergency exit. They pushed through together, leaving the noisy restaurant behind.

They stepped out into a floodlit back parking lot. It was dark, just after dusk, and the orange glow from the overhead sodium lamps bathed the cars in a cold metallic light. The man kept close to Jerry, not taking any chances."I didn't plan this blackmailing scheme for months just to see some nerd ass, crazy kid from nowhere mess it all up," the man said, as if talking to himself. "Tomorrow is payday. Tomorrow, I'll be on a plane saying so long to all the suckers who ever crossed me in my life. Nope, not gonna happen."

Jerry reached into his pocket to make sure he still had the handkerchief. Who was she? What could she have done? An indiscreet love affair? An unwanted pregnancy? Jerry shook his head. Whatever it was, it didn't matter, he decided, as he craned his neck toward the night sky looking for the moon. Her secret was safe with him.

They approached a dark two-door sedan parked at the edge of the lot. The man pushed Jerry up against the car and fumbled keys out of his pocket. When he unlocked the door, he ordered Jerry into the back seat. "Now, be a good boy and put your seatbelt on tight!" Jerry did as he was told. "You wouldn't want me to get a ticket now, would you?" The man laughed the same sordid laughter as before, as he slid in behind the steering wheel.

None of this was real to Jerry. Nothing ever truly was. It wasn't real that he should be shuffled from doctor to doctor with promises of cures and therapies that didn't work, that would never work. Jerry knew this. It wasn't real that his parents should one day look at him as if he had just fallen out of the sky and landed in their living room. Only in the movies could it be real. Only in the movies could doctors find cures for impossible diseases, could parents love you, and understand you no matter what. Only in the movies could things really change. And this... this...

"What was that?" the man said, twisting his head around, a partial grin still ruining his features.

"This is just like in the movies," Jerry said.

"Yeah, right, kid." The man reached for the ignition key but froze. Because from behind, there came a sound like someone squeezing Jell O between their fingers. "Just like in the movies," Jerry repeated, only this time in a voice that sounded a lot like Lurch on The Addam's Family.

The man turned his head slowly, his ears suddenly pinned back, the whites of his eyes leading the way. The man had time enough to see what Jerry had become before a double row of serrated edged teeth ripped the scream right out of his throat.

"Ah, here he is," Dr. March said with a tone of relief as Jerry appeared from around the corner of the booth. "You had me worried there for a minute, Jerry."

"I'm okay," Jerry said, sliding his awkward frame into the booth. A smile assured Dr. March that there was nothing to worry about. But the smile quickly turned to nausea when Jerry looked down at his plate and saw what Dr. March had ordered for him: a T bone steak, rare and juicy. After all he'd been through this evening, he couldn't eat another bite.

WHERE AM I?

by Cole Jamison

I awoke enveloped in a feeling of overwhelming warmth. The warmth a child feels still in the womb. Comfortable. Safe. Like there's not a thing in the world that can cause it any harm. Just like a child in the womb suddenly thrust into the world, my minuscule moment of comfort was torn apart in what seemed like an instant.

I pulled my face out of what I believed to be sand, wiped the mess from my eyes and cast my gaze out onto an alien landscape. A seemingly endless expanse reached far past where my eyes could see. The sand that I dragged myself out of was the color of rust. It shared the taste as well. As I brushed it off of my body and spat the remnants out of my mouth I noticed that it was incredibly fine and seemed to melt when it touched moisture. Patches of it covered my body where I was sweating making it look like I was bleeding all over from unseen wounds. It was warm to the touch, which explains the feeling I had just experienced as I came to consciousness.

How did I end up buried in the sand?

I stood up and looked to the sky in an attempt to find my bearings, only to end up with more questions than I had when I was face down in the sand. The sky was as alien as the land; I'd never seen anything like it. Myriads of incomprehensible colored fractals painted the horizon. There was no sun. Light radiated from different patches of color. The brighter spots seemed to give off the illumination while the darker spots trapped all the light that came within its area. It stained the landscape in different colorful blots of luminescence and darkness.

I lost myself completely while I gazed deep into the sky. I felt so small, another insignificant speck of sand floating at the mercy of the wind. Before I could even try to grasp what the hell I was looking at, I heard an unearthly scream coming from behind me. I thought the sky resembling some fucked up kaleidoscope was a hard thing to grasp, but what my eyes fell upon next sucked the air from my lungs as if I were in the vacuum of space.

Something was pulling itself through the sand. At first I thought it was an animal, but as it pulled itself closer to me I realized in horror that this...thing...was human. The flesh that remained on the creature looked like it had been cooking in the sun for eons. The only way you could tell flesh from bone was the bleach white patches that stood out where the rotten skin had been stripped away. The hands resembled the talons of a bird, broken and warped into grotesque claws that it was using to pull itself along. Each bit of effort it expended was paired with a terrifying shriek caught somewhere between pain and rage. I couldn't take my eyes off of it.

There was an overwhelming feeling of dread as it came closer and closer. The fear robbed me of control of my limbs. The grotesque figure stopped about three feet from me. It was face down with its arms stretched forward, its claws dug securely into the sand. Its legs had long since rotted away. All that was left were two thigh bones that stuck out of its waist, both ground down over the course of time it had been dragging itself through the desert. Its face was still buried in the sand, with tufts of black hair coming out of parts of its head, spilling out onto the ground.

That's when the smell hit me.

There aren't enough words in the English language to describe how abhorrent the scent that entered my nostrils was. I immediately started retching. The only thing that stopped me from uncontrollable vomiting was the fact there seemed to be nothing in my stomach. All that came out was bile and spit. I tried to only breathe in from my mouth but it didn't matter, I could TASTE the stench. It tasted like a chunk of rotten flesh that had fermented in a pit of shit. I wanted to get as far away from this thing as possible. As soon as I started to move away from it, its head shot up from the sand and transfixed its gaze onto me.

The only thing left of its face that was recognizable was its eyes, and they were blood red. They were caked over with the sand, making it impossible to tell if its' eyes were bleeding or dyed red from its long time face down in the sand. There was no possible way this thing could still see yet there it was, staring directly into my eyes with unbridled purpose.

I looked at the rest of its face only to find that there wasn't a face left. Below its eyes remained only gore. From where its nose should have been down to its neck had been shaved down completely by the sand like someone had taken its face and pushed it down onto a belt grinder. Only part of its upper jaw remained, the white bone offset by the rotten flesh that surrounded it. Below that was an open hole choked with sand, trickling out like blood from the moisture that remained in its throat. Small chunks of its flesh remained in the sand it had pulled its face from and as I looked at the path from which it came, I could see a trail of decaying tissue following behind. Before I could inspect any further, the creature made a noise. This one wasn't a shriek so much as a whisper.

"oo...id...ssss"

Red sand blew out of the hole where its throat was. Each word was strained and broken, as if every utterance brought the creature great anguish. Through the coughing and tremors of pain, it never broke its gaze with me.

"yoouuu...idssssssssssss"

It was getting louder with each attempt, its' body was convulsing with pain as it desperately tried to push the words out. The noises is produced were garbled and inaudible. Its tongue had long since rotted away resulting in grunts that only vaguely resemble words. It shook violently and pushed itself up from the sand. Its front was completely stripped away, revealing bones and decrepit organs painted red from the ground. Entrails spilled out black with rot and crumbled apart across the sand.

How was it possible this thing was alive, yet alone moving?

Before I could contemplate it further, a blood-curdling scream ripped through the air at a volume no natural being could possibly create.

"YOOOOOOOUUUUUUUU DIIIIID THIIIIISSSSSSSSSSSSSS!!!!!!!!!"

With a final burst of energy, the creature lunged at me, trying desperately to grasp at my legs. Its body, which was held together only by thin scraps of old flesh, couldn't handle the sudden burst of movement and a sickening crack resounded through the air. The screaming stopped, and the creature fell silent into the sand, its lifeless eyes still fixated on me.

I did this? What did it mean? Did I cause this things demise? Did I shatter the world into this horrifying state? What did it mean, and what in the hell was happening to me?

I had to get out of there. I started running as fast as I could in the opposite direction. The image of its haunting eyes burned into mine and the sound of its painful last words embedded itself into my brain like a parasite.

You. Did. This.

Those words sent me back to another place. The ground here was red, but it wasn't sand. It was carpet. There was only one place with this kind of horrifying ground covering, and that was my shitty apartment. I found myself back in my old life, sitting in the same chair I always sat in with my eyes fixated on the television and a PBR in my hand. The air reeked of cigarette smoke and sweat. The air conditioner never worked because our landlord didn't give a single fuck about our level of comfort, just our level of money. It made living in that eight hundred square foot box of nightmares even worse. That's what led to the latest tantrum thrown by my fiancé Natalie.

"You did this you lazy prick. If you weren't such a god damn wimp you would go down to his office right now and tell him to fix the air conditioner, or you're going to knock his fucking teeth out. We pay him almost six hundred dollars a month for this trash heap, and he ought to..."

Her words trailed off into the void as I kicked in my selective hearing and focused back on the TV. Always for diplomacy, this one. Go down to the office and kick Jed's ass? That animal would put a hole in my chest with the shotgun he kept behind the counter before I could even clench a fist.

We stay in this dump because that's all we can afford after both of our lives went to shit. The only reason we're even still together was because we'd probably be homeless without the pathetic amount of money we both managed to scrounge together. It was all different when we first met. Before I lost my job and we lost the baby. All the love we had for each other dissipated as fast as the money did. Natalie did her best but after all of this she was just a shell of her former self. I tried not to resent her, but I did. It didn't matter how fair it was. Now we're both worthless and shattered things. I broke out in a fit of coughing hacking up dark phlegm with a hint of red in it. I was going to rot away in that fucking chair and no one would miss me.

A bolt of misery turned pain coursed through my chest. I snapped back to my current reality of sprinting through the sand. I never thought I would miss my pathetic life but all I wanted to do was go back to my dismal existence in my shitty apartment. To run up to Natalie and hug her as tightly as I possibly could. Even if I wasn't sprinting through an unknown desert hallucination I doubt that we would ever be happy together again.

Maybe I was dead? Maybe her life and the lives of everyone else I plagued with my existence would be better off. Suddenly I felt immense pain as the sand underneath my feet started to cut like glass. I fell onto my face and felt the same sensation pulse throughout my body. Each grain of sand felt like a blade slicing apart my flesh. I was screaming so loud the veins in my throat felt like they were popping. The pain numbed my mind, completely overwhelming me to the point where even my thoughts are screams. It was all my fault. I had treated the world with apathy and spite and this was the product, an eternity of pain.

I don't know how much time I spent lying on the ground writhing. Time became irrelevant. I began hallucinating from the pain; my life manifesting itself in this world. Warped versions of my friends and family appeared and began taunting me. My father called me a failure of a man and kicked me in the ribs. My mother quietly lurked behind him with bruised arms. I heard her frail voice tell me if I didn't open my mouth so much we wouldn't have been beaten and she wouldn't have killed herself. Natalie was behind them holding a small bundle and crying hysterically. There were no words from her, only choked sobs.

Bosses, co-workers, old flings, every person in my life I had ever slighted took their turn tearing apart my consciousness. It became one big clamor, but I could hear every single layer of it. It wasn't a dull pain one could manage to ignore; this agony tore at every fiber of my being. I had to get out of here. I couldn't take it anymore.

I rolled over onto my stomach and started pulling myself away, but there was no escape. The visions followed me with every agonizing movement. The sand cut through my flesh like glass as I crawled. I had to get away. All I could think about was pulling myself away from this torture. I felt my bones breaking from the repeated attacks of my personal demons. I felt the skin being ripped from the bone, but i had to keep pulling. I had to get away.

In the distance, I saw a lone figure. It wasn't like the rest of the hallucinations; it was just standing there staring at the sky. Maybe it could help. I WAS SAVED! Through all the torture my mind and body were suffering I focused on one single purpose: get to that figure. Keep pulling. Get out of here. My eyes were fixated only on him as the rest of my body fell apart.

I finally pulled myself close enough to make out details and let out a guttural scream. It wasn't a figure of salvation; it was one of only pain and misery. The person that was responsible for the life, and now eternity of pain which I had suffered. The hallucinations disappeared as all the hate and rage I could summon welled up inside of my chest. He would die for what he did to me.

"oo...id...ssss"

Killing Time

by Patrick Conlon

"I'm sorry, Mr. Tailor, but—"

"Call me Howard, please."

"I'm sorry, Howard, but the bank simply cannot extend your loan repayment any longer."

Howard wrung his hat in his hands and stared blankly at the bank manager across from him. The sharp edges of the man's suit only served to show how shabby his clothes were.

"I just need a little more time, Mr. Glenstone. I'll have the money, I promise."

"We have heard this before Mr. Tailor. You are six months behind; you're going to have to repay the loan in its entirety, or we will foreclose."

Howard's shoulders slumped. He reached into his pocket and pulled out a single crumpled hundred-dollar bill. It was all the money he had left after the gambling took everything.

"Here, how much time will this buy me?"

"This doesn't come close to covering your debts, Mr. Tailor."

"Call me Howard, please."

"I can give you the weekend, Howard, but no more. Either the loan is fully covered, or we'll have to take the house."

Howard nodded and rose immediately, leaving before Mr. Glenstone could change his mind. He trudged out of the building and onto the street. He started to raise his hand for a cab, then lowered it. He shoved his hands into empty pockets and started walking. Once he was far enough away from the bank to be noticed, he lowered his head and put his hands on the nearest telephone pole. A flier was attached that crinkled under his grip. He looked up and read the words in bold across the top of the page, "NEED MORE TIME? Interested in making some money? Currently looking for an assistant who would like more time on his hands. Come to 356 Fairhill Lane for an opportunity of a lifetime."

Howard ripped the flier from the pole and shoved it into his pocket.

"Howard, are you ready to test this?"

Dr. Stonewell stood at the control panel and twisted several knobs. Arcs of electricity shot from the tall coils and struck the silver bodysuit from all directions.

"You want me to put that on?" Howard flinched, as the arcs of lightning struck the suit repeatedly.

"It's perfectly safe, Howard."

"It doesn't look safe to me," Howard mumbled under his breath.

Howard pulled the gloves on. His hair was standing on end, and he felt the weird fabric still vibrating.

"Okay, now your right hand has the mechanism. You clench your fist to stop time."

Howard began to close his fist.

"Wait a minute," Dr. Stonewell grabbed his hand. "Time will stay frozen until you open your hand."

"Got it," Howard closed his hand, and the world around him slowed to a crawl. Dr. Stonewell's face lit up with pride.

"It was fitting," Howard thought. "The last few minutes of the old man's life should be good ones. After all, my life is just beginning. With this suit, my luck is going to turn around. I'm no longer a loser, a nobody. I'm going places." Howard looked at the happy face of the doctor, then at the staircase leading down to the basement.

"And you Doc, you are going places too."

"Prominent Doctor Dies in Household Accident. Dr. Sean Stonewell, noted physicist, was found dead after a nasty spill down his basement stairs."

Howard closed the newspaper and adjusted the collar on his new suit. It was a bit over-sized to compensate for the time stopper getup, but he couldn't walk around looking like a character from one of those cheap science fiction movies. He sprang up from the bench he was sitting on, grinning from ear to ear. He stuffed the newspaper into a bin and looked up at the building. The words "First National Bank and Trust" greeted him. With this score, he would never have to worry again. He clenched his fist. A pigeon taking flight slowed to a stop before him, wings stretched taut against the now nonexistent wind. Howard stepped around the bird and opened the large glass front door.

The polished marble floor of the bank was surprisingly dull, but for a few tiles that gleamed a hot brilliant white. Upon closer inspection, Howard found that the incandescence of these tiles was a result of the frozen spears of sunlight that sliced through the room. He waved his hand in one, and it disappeared into the shaft of light.

"This is incredible! Oh, Dr. Stonewell, it's almost a shame you aren't here to see this."

Howard crossed the busy lobby at a brisk pace, deftly dodging around the many customers. The statues of the living were all around him. Some were frozen mid-transaction, reaching for or handing over cash of varying denominations. He helped himself to some of the bills, sliding them from unsuspecting hands.

"Now, if I were Mr. Glenstone, where would I be?" Howard hopped over the counter. "He must be around here somewhere."

After searching all of the offices and the lobby, stopping here and there to rifle through the pockets of the more expensively dressed people, Howard decided that maybe he wasn't in today.

"Just my luck! All the time in the world and I have to come back!"

He glanced at the back of the bank, towards the bank vault.

"Unless of course, he's already in the vault!" Howard rubbed his hands together, practically skipping his way towards the vault.

He stepped around the large metal door. There was the bank manager, impeccably dressed in another of those three-piece suits. He was in the middle of pulling a safety deposit box from the insides of the vault. Howard removed the key from the lock of the deposit box and looped the chain around his hand. The man standing next to Mr. Glenstone was obviously wealthy. His clothing was immaculate, and his hair pristine.

Howard looked at the box in Mr. Glenstone's hands, then at the key in his own.

"Seeing as I've got time, let's be thorough."

Ignoring Mr. Glenstone for the moment, he moved to the far corner, he inserted the key into the topmost lock and turned it. It opened without resistance. The box slid out, and he opened it. It had several necklaces and rings, as well as a last will and testament. He tossed the will aside and placed the jewelry on an empty table in the middle of the room.

"This might take a while, but I've got some time to kill."

Howard looked over the scene. The customer laid out on the ground. Mr. Glenstone was holding the pistol with the hammer frozen just above the firing pin. He couldn't help himself. He needed him to know. He released his fist. The world began moving around him again, and the pistol fired. The customer's face was twisting into confusion as the bullet tore through it. Mr. Glenstone's face showed his bewilderment as well.

"What is going on?" The bank manager was splattered with blood, and his face contorted in horror.

"Why, you've just killed a very rich man Mr. Glenstone. I wouldn't be surprised if they gave you the chair for this."

At the sound of his voice, Mr. Glenstone spun around to face him.

"You did this! I don't know how, but you've killed this man."

"I doubt you'll prove that. I told you I needed more time, and you should have given it to me."

Mr. Glenstone raised the gun and fired at Howard. Howard closed his fist, and the bullet froze between the two men.

"Too easy." Howard smiled and walked out. He found the security guard at the other end of the lobby, running towards the sound of the gunshot. He dragged him to the door of the vault and positioned him just out of the path of the oncoming bullet. Drawing the guard's pistol, he placed it into his hand and aimed back at Mr. Glenstone. He then turned and walked out of the bank.

Once he had made it across the street, Howard unclenched his fist and waited. After several seconds, the front doors burst open, and people began racing from the bank, screaming and trampling over each other.

"This has been a perfect day." Howard clenched his fist, and the world froze again. "Time to make a deposit." The bank he had chosen was the Eastern Savings Bank, the next town over. Even with time frozen, it would take several days of his time to get there on foot, but that was a small price to pay for appearing miles away seconds after the robbery.

"I'll be able to pay off my house."

Howard rubbed at his jaw, and a wicked grin crossed his face.

"Or maybe it's time I got the respect I deserve."

Howard stood at the bedside of Vincent "Vinnie" DeMarco. Everyone knew the DeMarco family. They ran the underworld, and Vinnie ran the DeMarco family. Looking at the frozen man lying in bed, Howard couldn't help but think that he didn't look worthy of that respect. Howard restarted time and slapped his hand onto the pillow beside the sleeping man's head.

"What? Who the hell are you?"

"Me?" Howard smiled. "I'm the new boss around here. Thanks

for keeping the sheets warm for me."

"Mr. Funch!" Vinnie yelled. A moment later, the door opened quickly, and a mountain of a man dressed in an immaculate black suit stepped into the room.

"Mr. DeMarco?"

"Kill this upstart."

Mr. Funch's expression remained stoic as he stepped forward and reached for him.

"I think you'll find that harder than you imagine." Howard clenched his fist. The outstretched fingers froze inches from his neck. Howard moved around the frozen giant and left the room. He returned a moment later with a length of pipe in his free hand.

"Let's cut you down to size, shall we?" Howard swung the pipe into Mr. Funch's stomach as hard as he could. The pipe struck, and the impact radiated up his arms. He then grabbed the outstretched hand and pushed it up with all his might. It still took a full minute to move it.

Howard placed the pipe back outside of the room and moved into position. He lifted his arm, making it look like he had blocked the arm with his own. He then placed his fist against the stomach of the large man. He unclenched his fist.

A grunt escaped the lips of Mr. Funch as he collapsed in the middle and fell to his knees. The sharp intake of breath behind him confirmed Vinnie's shock.

"Now, as I was saying," Howard turned back to face Vinnie. "I am the new boss around here. I expect you to turn over all your holdings to me and get out of town." He balled his left hand into a fist and shook it.

"Go to hell." Vinnie pulled a short pistol from the drawer of his nightstand and took aim.

Howard clenched his right fist just as Vinnie pulled the trigger. The bullet stopped outside the barrel of the gun. Howard smiled again. He stepped slightly to the side and turned his body out of the path of the bullet. He restarted time. The bullet whizzed past him and impacted the wall. Vinnie blinked.

"How did you?" He looked at the gun, then raised it again. Howard stopped time again. He strode over and grabbed the gun. He stepped back and pointed the gun at Vinnie.

When time restarted, Vinnie's face went from rage to terror. He looked at the gun in Howard's hand, then down at his own.

"What is going on?"

"Nothing you need to concern yourself with. I believe you have some documents to sign." Howard walked over to the adjacent nightstand and pulled out the deed to the mansion and an ornate pen.

"How did you get that? What is going on?" Vinnie's eyes darted around the room, and he was sweating profusely.

"Don't worry, Vinnie; You can set up shop in another town and do very well for yourself." Howard pushed the pen in Vinnie's shaking hand. "And don't worry about your organization here. I'll make sure to give it plenty of my time."

"Mr. Tailor, is there anything else I can provide for you this evening?"

Howard looked at Mr. Funch, who was dressed in a butler's finest and smiled.

This man once inspired utter terror, but now he was the picture of passivity.

"No, I believe that will be all for tonight, Edward," Howard waved his hand dismissively.

"Very good, Mr. Hadon," The large man's fingers curled around the silver tray, and it bent under the strain. He stood there, unmoving for a long moment.

"Is there anything else you require, Edward?" Howard raised an eyebrow and made a show of flexing his fingers, still encased in the silvery gloves. The way that gesture made his new butler's eyes widen in visible fear sent a thrill through Howard. He watched as Mr. Funch shook his head and backed away from his chair, not turning away from him until he reached the door and let himself out.

"This is the life! This suit is amazing!" He raised his arms, then wrinkled his nose. He sniffed at himself, wincing at the smell. It had been over a week since he had put the suit on, and he hadn't removed it even for a second. He shrugged, it didn't matter how he smelled when he thought about it. When you have the money and power he had now, he could smell like a sewer, and no one would have the courage to tell him, let alone hold it against him.

Flipping open the newspaper, he glanced at the day's headlines. "Lion mysteriously vanishes from zoo" caught his eye. He chuckled and rubbed his feet along the brand-new fur rug that now lay in front of his chair.

"This is the perfect life! Nothing can get me down now." He took a long sip of brandy from his crystal snifter.

"Oh, I don't know about that, Mr. Tailor." A loud bang accompanied the voice. Howard felt the bullet enter his back just as he quickly clenched his fist. The world slowed to a crawl, but not before a blast of searing pain wracked his entire body. He tried to arch his back and move from the bullet's path, but he found himself frozen. He tried to get up, but he found that his legs wouldn't move.

Howard's mind raced. How had this happened? Had Mr. Funch decided it was worth the risk? No ,he thought, that voice was female and the accent foreign. He gritted his teeth.

"There must be a way out of this..."

"There is no way out of this, Mr. Tailor. That bullet severed your spine." The same female voice floated around the chair.

"Who's there, and how are you there?"

A young woman wearing a silvery bodysuit stepped around into his field of vision. It was the same type of suit, only much more patchwork. There was an odd insignia that Howard couldn't make out on the shoulder of the suit, and he could see that the woman was wearing a large backpack.

"Professor Stonewell thought that he had hidden well from us, but the obituary included his picture. It took a while to search his place and track down what actually happened to him, but I finally caught up to you."

Howard wasn't sure, but that accent could be Russian.

"Where did you get that suit?"

"The good professor used to work for us, or did you think that he funded this technology all by himself?"

"Who? How? Why?"

"Oh, nothing is impossible with this technology. However, this prototype is less than impressive." She kicked at his foot, but Howard felt nothing. The fingers of his right hand twitched slightly.

"Oh, you can open your hand any time you want. But as soon as you do, that bullet will finish its grisly work, and with no one left to help you, you'll bleed out on your luxurious carpet. Now, I'll be leaving you here."

"Wait. We, we can make a deal."

"You have nothing I want, Mr. Tailor. The only reason we are talking at all is as a courtesy. I just wanted you to know that your suit will be back in Russian hands soon."

"But how long are you willing to wait?"

"And don't worry about that, I won't have to wait at all. Once you open your fist, time will restart, and I'll claim your suit. For me, it will happen almost instantly." She opened her hand.

The last thing Howard heard before the mysterious woman vanished back into time was: "But I am wondering how long you'll spend in here, killing time."

OLD GROWTH

by Michael Fassbender

Helmuth Eggert gripped his musket as he surveyed the woods around him. Although it was only two in the afternoon, the ancient growth around him stifled most of the sunlight. A rebel sharpshooter—or worse, an entire regiment of New England militia—could lurk anywhere in these shadows. According to the Oberst, the rebels had fled the island three days before, yet someone had attacked a small team of Jäger passing through these woods last night.

One of those Jäger accompanied the Unteroffizier at the head of the detachment, guiding the team through winding paths to the site where the attack had happened. Twenty musketmen followed them in a column of twos, with an Offizier riding in the rear. Helmuth marched in the column's second rank and could hear every word that passed between the Jäger and his Unteroffizier. They talked freely, but their words did little to calm Helmuth's mind.

The Jäger fully supported the Oberst's decision to send twenty men to investigate. He had been part of a scouting party that numbered only six, and his team had been ambushed in an abandoned settlement in the midst of these woods. The enemy did not fire a shot in the engagement; either they did not have muskets, or they had too few to match a half dozen Jäger and resorted to knife-fighting instead. Either way, twenty trained musketmen should suffice to flush them out and eliminate them.

The Unteroffizier was troubled, however. A veteran of this insurgency since the first Hessian regiments were delivered to the British, he had seen what Indian auxiliaries could do. A single Indian could have killed three Jäger in rapid succession in the night woods; at the same time, it could have been a much larger war party, and if so, they might have limited their attack by design. By allowing three men to live and tell the tale, they gained the chance to kill twenty-three today.

To this, the Jäger had laughed. "I would indeed worry about that if the Indians had allied themselves to the rebels. Fortunately, they fight for us." Helmuth noted that he kept his voice low as he said it.

For his part, the Unteroffizier plied the Jäger for as much information about the attack, and the site where it had happened, as he could. The Jäger would not comment on his team's original mission, save to note that he was meant to confirm that the rebels had indeed left Aquidneck Island after the failed siege. Beyond that, he reported to General von Lossberg directly.

"We were passing through these woods," the Jäger continued, "and we happened upon a clearing with a small settlement in it. It was primitive, and probably could host no more than two dozen inhabitants, but at the time it seemed deserted. There was one dead man, lying against a grave marker in a small burying ground. He'd been shot, and recently too. Three days ago, this stretch of woods was in rebel hands. It would have been a New England militia regiment, either a local one from Rhode Island or neighboring Massachusetts."

The Unteroffizier took the news soberly. "A loyalist?"

The Jäger shrugged. "It could just as easily have been a robbery. Or it might have been a personal grudge, and the war provided the opportunity to take revenge without consequence. We may never know. It may be worth looking for a cause while we are there, but I should not be surprised if the answer eludes us."

"The only murders that concern us are those of your comrades." The Unteroffizier pointed ahead with his partisan. "How exactly did they happen?"

"When we found the body, we fanned out. We could not tell how fresh the body was, and if the killer were still nearby, we did not wish to present a target. We found cover for ourselves, and then we began to look for anyone who might be in the area with us. Whoever attacked us was stealthier yet. There was a sudden rustle of leaves as Johannes cried out. We all began to move toward his position, as quietly as we might, and I think Lothar reached it first. He fired off a shot, but he must have missed. He was the next to die. Bernhard was further away when he was attacked. That was the main reason we thought there could have been two or more attackers. If it were just one man, he moved fast as well as quietly."

"And he may have abandoned these woods as soon as the rest of you ran off to seek reinforcements."

"He might have done so. If he did, we shall confirm that he is gone and return to the garrison."

Helmuth scowled as he heard this. Part of him hoped that nothing would be found, and he could leave these confusing woods, but it would taste like failure if the detachment returned to the garrison with nothing to show for its efforts.

The Jäger continued. "You will, I trust, assist me in burying my comrades?"

This was a given, but even so, the Unteroffizier said, "Of course."

The conversation faltered. The detachment drew nearer to the site of the attack, and the Jäger walked a little further ahead of the column, issuing directions with gestures instead of words. Twenty soldiers made enough noise on the march; he did not wish to proclaim their presence any more obviously. At length, he raised his hand to halt the march and peered carefully around a bend in the path. Satisfied, he waved the men on, and the column passed into the clearing.

Helmuth sniffed as he walked into the clearing. The smell of decay hung heavily in the air. The forest floor might be open for a hundred feet in any direction, but the canopy above was tightly closed. Few rays of light made it to the ground below, and the humid air threatened to smother him. It was an unhealthy place.

The Unteroffizier began barking out orders. Helmuth, the man in front of him, and the two men in line behind him made a crisp turn left and advanced with muskets at ready. Helmuth was glad; he was facing most of the buildings in the clearing. If anything happened, he would see it. The men who had previously been to his right were now facing the other direction, while several other men hurried to cover the approaches on either side. Danger could come from any direction, but most of the investigation would take place before him.

The Offizier dismounted and left his reins in the hands of one of the musketmen. He strode confidently to the Jäger and Unteroffizier. Directing his attention to the former, he extended his left hand toward the buildings in the clearing and said, "Lead on."

Helmuth surveyed the abandoned settlement while waiting. Four dubious-looking shacks lurked amid the trees at the periphery of the clearing, continuing what seemed like several decades of decay in the shadows of the ancient trees. He might have mistaken this settlement for one that had been abandoned in the first half of the century, if not for the remains of a recent fire in a circle of rocks six feet in front of him. The embers had ceased to smolder for some days already, but leaves had not yet fallen upon the dead coals.

The Jäger was pointing at a thick oak to Helmuth's left. It stood at the back of a small cemetery of some sort, with crude wooden markers already fading. If Helmuth spoke the English language, he would still meet with considerable difficulty in deciphering their epitaphs. Behind the wooden markers, Helmuth could see a most impressive collection of shelf fungus growing at the lower end of the oak's trunk. Next to that was an unexpected color: a dull shade of blue.

The Jäger began his explanation of that very fact. "We might have thought this clearing long deserted, but for this body. Note the shovel in his hands; he was tending to the graves when the men who shot him approached. There is no way to know whether others dwelt here with him, but fled into the forest, or if he was indeed the last of those who lived here."

The Unteroffizier surveyed the body as the Offizier looked on. He glanced up to his superior officer and noted, "Then it is a murder. This man was performing common labor. He can have been no threat."

The Jäger said, "Perhaps, but it could have been an accident of some sort. This man might have surprised a squad of soldiers fanning out for reconnaissance. A shot fired at an unexpected sound can always result in tragedy during wartime."

The Offizier hesitated. "However it may have been, this man was cut down prematurely. It brings us no closer to finding the men who attacked our soldiers."

The Jäger fell silent and crouched down next to the body. The Offizier held his tongue as well, allowing the scout to ply his trade in peace. At length, the Jäger reached out for a small branch, and gingerly prodded at the dark brown stain on the dead man's lower torso. He frowned.

Without looking up, he asked, "How long would you say that this man has been dead?"

The Offizier cocked his head, and after a moment, said, "Three days, maybe four."

The Jäger nodded. "Perhaps as little as two days, in this accursed heat, but no more than four. But have you seen many corpses, sir?"

"I have served in my share of engagements. I have seen both friend and foe die."

The Jäger prodded at the wound with his branch. "This wound has rotted much more quickly than the rest of the body." He winced. "And the smell. Terrible."

The Offizier drew back half a step. "What of it? I have seen men lose legs from gangrene."

The Unteroffizier spoke up. "No, sir, he is right. There is some kind of fungus growing in the wound. It must have taken root shortly after the man was shot."

The Jäger looked up. "And it is growing very quickly."

"What of it?" The Offizier glared at the Jäger as he spoke. "We are not naturalists on an expedition. We are looking for lost men and those who attacked them."

The Jäger rose but spoke quietly. "And we would be wise to be aware of all possible dangers as we perform that mission. Any one of us might suffer a wound if we encounter the men responsible for these attacks. Should that wound be infected by this fungus, it might not go well for the prospects of that man's recovery."

That statement inspired nervous glances in most of the men. Helmuth, too, cast his gaze about him, looking for some obvious sign of danger. Suddenly, the oppressive odor of rot hanging over the clearing took on ominous overtones. Now his brain registered every sound ringing out in the distance: every creak of a limb, every beat of leaves in the wind, every mad rush of a squirrel or fox. A thousand warnings from his childhood in Hesse of the dangers in the deep woods echoed in his head. His British masters did not understand, could not understand what the Hessian mercenaries knew from generations of experience. The English had spent too much of their wilderness in the construction of ships. The Hessians respected the primal power of a large forest.

Helmuth would not have cared to admit it, but he feared it, too. The forests of home were powerful things in their own right, but here, on a new continent, God alone knew what might lurk in the deepest shadows of these trackless woods. And here in the north, in what they called New England, the settlers carried their own baggage of horrors and sin, with witchcraft and curses at every turn. Here, amid his comrades, he gave no sign of his fear, but he suspected that at least half of them shared it.

Even so, his head turned sharply right when he heard the crack of a branch in the distance.

Nearly every musket swung in that direction. The Jäger swung on his haunches, steadying himself with his left hand on the ground as he scanned the foliage. The Unteroffizier swept his right hand to the side in a needless gesture for silence. For his part, the Offizier merely turned to face the opposite way, seemingly unflappable in the face of a potential threat. All waited.

And yet, nothing seemed to happen. Helmuth expected an order to stand down at any second, and for a moment, he wondered how effective it might be. The men were spooked; bad things happened when frightened soldiers failed to relax. In particular, he knew Markus to be a superstitious man, constantly muttering dire predictions of what the soldiers would find in the shaded battlefields of the New World. Markus was the next man on Helmuth's left, and that made him nervous.

In the next moment, their roles were reversed. The Offizier turned sharply to his right and pointed at two men, Markus and Gebhard, before directing them with another brisk gesture into the brush beyond the buildings. Helmuth glanced at Markus and saw his stricken look, but the man was too well trained to give any further sign of his reluctance. The two soldiers advanced as swiftly as they could while maintaining stealth. Several seconds later, they were lost to sight.

These were soldiers of the line, not Jägers trained for forest reconnaissance. Their progress was easily marked in the form of breaking twigs and the slap of leaves, although not in a degree that might be considered excessive. Helmuth found the sound reassuring. For as long as the soldiers were free to advance into the woods unimpeded, no threat had been discovered. Perhaps, he thought, it was a squirrel after all.

The minutes stretched on, and finally, the soldiers returned to the clearing. Gebhard reported, "There is no one else nearby. We have found one of the missing Jägers."

The Offizier nodded. He pointed at Helmuth and said, "You. Stand guard while these two recover the body."

Helmuth clenched his fingers around his musket as he stepped forward. The only saving grace in his position was that he had been assigned to watch. He was free to be alert to any danger while his fellows attended to the body.

Still, his heart raced as he followed Markus and Gebhard into the dense growth beyond the clearing. His eyes sought out any potential threat, whether man or wolf or some peril in the ground itself. The ancient forest itself troubled him. He recoiled from a cluster of fungus he saw near his feet, and then jerked back when he realized how close he was to a broad, dead oak dappled with generous bands of lichen. This forest is sick, he thought. We should leave before we fall ill too.

It seemed like ten minutes before they reached the body, though he knew it was less than half the time. The man lay on his side, arms outstretched before him. His uniform was crusted with dried blood. The stench of death was palpable and mixed with something else, something earthy yet unwholesome.

Markus and Gebhard slung their muskets over their shoulders and knelt at either end of the body. They were veterans of too many campaigns to be squeamish about a corpse. They rolled the body onto its back, and a fresh wave of foul air erupted among them. Markus flinched at the smell; Gebhard turned and retched into the weeds.

Helmuth blinked several times to clear his eyes, then looked down at the body. Wide gashes marred his upper chest and belly. For a moment, he offered an internal salute to the fallen Jäger; the man had died fighting, not running. Then he noticed the gray matter poking out of the wounds. It looked as if a fungus had taken root in the body after death, but if so, it had grown at a phenomenal rate. He thought of the body by the tree in the clearing, and the fungus that filled its wound. With alarm, he thought, This is bigger.

Another thought rose unbidden: At least as far as I could see. In the end, he couldn't really know. The dead man's trunk might have been riddled with this rot, but only a small piece of it could be seen from without. Helmuth began to question the wisdom of the order to recover the bodies, and he was just glad that those orders did not include a recovery of the dead civilian.

He forced himself to look away from the body while his comrades sought to straighten it out. His role lay beyond their immediate circle. Even if these wounds had been caused by an impossible monster, it was his job to shoot the beast down if it should make another appearance today.

He cast his gaze out in every direction. These accursed trees offered so much cover. A threat might lie just thirty paces away, yet he would not know until it was too late. He held his musket at ready, questioning whether he'd even be able to aim and fire in time.

Gebhard was standing again. He searched in all directions, then evidently made his choice. He walked some fifteen paces off to Helmuth's right, then bent to pick up a fallen limb. It was fairly straight, and he plainly meant to fashion a crude stretcher if he could find another limb to match it.

Gebhard stood, leaning on his branch, and looked about for another. Helmuth glanced to his left and then slowly swept his gaze right. A sense of movement near Gebhard drew his attention back there prematurely. In that instant, he spied another figure behind his comrade, though he could make out only the silhouette of a head and a gnarled hand rising above Gebhard's shoulder. He shouted, "Down!" as he leveled the musket.

The warning came too late for Gebhard, who was raked across his back by the sinister hand Helmuth had seen. Gebhard arched backward in pain, blocking Helmuth's shot and his view of the assailant.

Markus suffered under no such interference. He unleashed an inarticulate cry; Helmuth could not discern if it was a challenge to the interloper or an expression of fear. To his credit, Markus scrambled for his musket and fired. With the attacker still obscured by Gebhard's writhing form, Helmuth could not discern whether the shot struck true or embedded itself in the tree beyond, but Helmuth did see a spray of solid fragments where it hit. It did not appear to be a spray of flesh and blood.

In the next moment, Markus gave another cry, this one clearly of pain. Another attacker had emerged behind him and struck him in the shoulder. Markus turned and engaged his attacker using his musket as a large club. Once again, Helmuth lacked a clear shot.

Unable to help Markus for the moment, he turned again to Gebhard, who was manifestly losing his engagement. Gebhard was falling to his knees, offering Helmuth a clear shot at the attacker's upper body. Helmuth sighted a telling blow to the chest and squeezed the trigger. The flint struck, the barrel thundered, and Helmuth could see a shudder pass through the assailant's body.

Under the circumstances, Helmuth dared to reload his musket. His satisfaction dwindled as he scoured the inside of his barrel. He expected his first target to fall after the hit he had delivered, but the attacker had not done so. Instead, he reached down and raked his fingers across Gebhard's throat. The splash of arterial blood that followed told Helmuth that Gebhard was lost.

As Helmuth tamped his next shot in the barrel, the first attacker began to approach. His gait was uneven, and he moved rather slower than a man in combat would normally choose. After a few paces, he stepped into a patch of light, giving Helmuth his first good look.

The figure was as tall as a man, and shaped largely like one, but was clearly something other. Such flesh as it had was gray and cancerous, with random lumps clustered here and naked bone there. Enough of the skull remained exposed for Helmuth to see that the figure had once been a man, but all of his flesh had been stripped away and replaced, haphazardly, with layers of a substance that reminded him of the mushrooms he had picked in the woods as a child. The connection to the fungus growing in the corpses he'd seen today was inescapable.

Whatever the creature before him might be, it was much hardier than a man. Helmuth could now see that both balls had struck their target: Markus had blown free much of the flesh that encased its right shoulder, while Helmuth had bared the ribs of its chest where the heart would have resided. One of those ribs had been shorn in two, with a piece the length of his thumb missing. Despite the blow, the creature pressed on, bound for Helmuth now. The most that Helmuth had accomplished was that the damage to its right shoulder limited the use of that arm. Indeed, it had killed Gebhard with its left.

Taking inspiration from this observation, Helmuth ran toward Markus. "Sweep the leg!" he shouted. "Break it!" Markus swung the butt of his musket down, striking the left leg just above the knee. It snapped, and the attacker tilted left. As it fell, its right hand raked Markus on the forearm.

Bolstered by his run, Helmuth brought the butt of his musket down on the creature's head, smashing the lower skull. "Run," he said. "I'll be right behind." Markus started for the clearing while Helmuth turned and leveled his musket. The first assailant pressed for his position. Helmuth took careful aim at its head, squeezed the trigger, and struck it squarely in the lower face. First, the lower jaw clattered to the ground, and then the skull itself swiveled back. For a brief moment, its unwholesome flesh threatened to keep the head with the body, and then it ripped, letting the skull fall freely to the ground.

Now Helmuth turned and ran. He did not need the skills of a Jäger to follow Markus' progress, and he kept to the same path, hoping to catch up with his wounded comrade before any more of these monsters appeared. The wounds may have been worse than Helmuth expected; Markus was winded when Helmuth intercepted him. Helmuth grabbed his arm and pulled it around his shoulder to take off some of the strain. Soon they reached the clearing.

Markus did not wait until they had reached a respectful distance to begin his rambling report, shouting phrases like "under attack!" and "can't stop them." The Offizier raised an eyebrow, while the Unteroffizier stepped forward to meet them.

At an appropriate distance, Helmuth began his own report. "We came under attack. Gebhard is dead, and Markus is wounded. We took one of them down, and by rights, the other should be dead." Helmuth was astonished by the calmness with which he spoke. "It is not, and I don't think there is any way to clean out this forest but fire."

By now, the Offizier had stepped forward. "Were you not assigned to keep the others safe?"

"Yes, Sir, and any man would have died from the wounds I gave them." He pointed at the shelf fungus on the large tree, and the infected corpse beneath it. "Their flesh is made of fungus. Somehow it gives them purpose and strength."

The Unteroffizer intervened. "Helmuth, this is lunacy. You must have seen men in some kind of disguise. They say the early rebels dressed as Indians when they attacked the tea shipments in Boston. What you saw must have been some mummer's trick."

Before Helmuth could make a reply, Markus spoke again. "They're coming."

All eyes turned to the treeline. At least a dozen figures approached through avenues in the foliage. With a wave, the Offizier signaled that the others should accompany him to the other side of the squad's firing line. Once they were no longer standing in the field of fire, the Unteroffizier took up the commands for an infantry engagement. Half of the team knelt and sighted the figures emerging from the woods; the other half stood behind for a second wave of fire.

Upon command, the lower row of muskets erupted with fire. Thick plumes of smoke obscured the village clearing before them, and all waited for several seconds until they could see their targets.

Helmuth could feel the dismay of his comrades when it was seen that no foe had fallen. The shadowy figures, manlike yet perceptibly misshapen, continued their inexorable march. The Unteroffizier began his commands for a second volley, and then Helmuth spotted a familiar shape.

One of the figures trudged on despite the absence of a head. Its right arm hung limp, while its left tensed at ready for combat. Seeing the two ball wounds in its trunk, Helmuth caught the attention of the Unteroffizier. "Look! That is the one that Markus and I shot. Musket balls do not stop them. I blew off its very head, yet still it comes."

The Unteroffizier blanched. He looked up to the Offizier, who had mounted his horse by then. The Offizier nodded, and the Unteroffizier changed his orders. The men who had already fired filtered between the standing men and formed an advance guard before the Offizier. As the front of the column commenced a hasty march, the rear guard discharged their muskets before falling into formation.

After fifteen minutes of uneventful marching, the men began to relax. The attack had not been pressed. Perhaps the second volley might have had some effect; a few dared to hope. Mainly, it was the men at the rear of the column who entertained this notion; significantly, this theory made them the heroes.

For his part, Helmuth thought the attack had been abandoned because its purpose had been fulfilled. The squad had quit the field. He did not care why that was necessary. Whether those creatures were protecting territory or hiding a secret, they were welcome to it. Helmuth was only grateful for surviving two assaults. He did not fancy his chances in a third.

The squad returned to barracks with orders to maintain strict secrecy on the subject of their mission. The Jäger returned to his outfit and said nothing more of the incident to the line infantry. Helmuth was called before the Oberst himself to report on what he had seen in the forest.

Helmuth withheld nothing as he recounted the story. He saw frank disbelief on the Oberst's face, but not shock or outrage. He had heard variations on the tale before that meeting.

In the end, Helmuth was released without further consequence, but with orders to say no more on the subject to anyone. Little was said about the fate of Markus, but he never recovered from his wounds. He had been delivered into the care of the regimental surgeon immediately upon the squad's return to barracks. Whatever the surgeon had tried was inadequate; Markus died two nights later. Much to the annoyance of the chaplain, the body was cremated in the morning. The official explanation was that Markus had contracted an awful disease, and they wished to prevent its spread.

Those who had not been on the mission speculated about diseases from typhus to the Black Death. Like the rest of his squad, Helmuth said nothing, but he had his own thoughts on the matter. He had seen these things up close and knew them for the bones of men encased in a new flesh of animate fungus. He had seen the bodies of those recently killed in that stretch of woods, their wounds infected with a colony of fungus. When he had seen the state of the dead Jäger, he had already begun to wonder how deeply the seemingly small cluster of fungus had penetrated the viscera of the dead civilian. The same would likely have befallen the body of Markus if all traces had not been burned away.

For the remainder of its time on the island, the regiment never again probed the deep forest. When at last its services were no longer required, he returned to Hesse gratefully. More than a few of his comrades chose to stay in the New World and build a new life in places like Pennsylvania, but Helmuth understood that the land was as old as any other, and filled with perils of its own. Having glimpsed one of them, he chose to return to more familiar risks.

A Lovely Evening

by Colin Anderson

Wholly inebriated by ale and smoke, Robbie swam through his jumbled thoughts and focused as best he could on his phone. With shaky fingers, he entered the name of his hotel into the app and pressed the button to summon a car. He pocketed his phone and rubbed his tired head with his hands. The humid summer night wore heavily on him and did no favors for his muddled condition, leaving his curly red hair matted and wet, and his face rosy and flushed. Soon though, he would be in his hotel bed for a few hours of rest before heading to the airport in the morning.

Robbie's phone chimed, and he clumsily grabbed it from his pocket and read the notification. "Casper will arrive in a black wagon. Three minutes."

"Casper." Robbie chuckled. Intrigued with the name of his twilight driver, he opened the taxi app and began reading Casper's profile.

Name: Casper

Fun Fact: Lovely.

Robbie laughed with unashamed volume on the curb of the quiet street. The nonsensical fun fact paired with the driver's name was too perfect. Lovely, Robbie thought, then said, "Casper. Lovely." The profile, perhaps a bit odd, was certainly more amusing with the benefit of intoxicants.

Robbie stumbled off the curb chortling as a long black wagon turned the corner, its dim headlights barely noticeable through the darkness. It seemed not to cast light onto the ground. As the wagon approached and passed under a street lamp, Robbie could discern it was an older model of which he was unfamiliar. The black paint did not shine, and the windows and windshield were darkened and dull. The wagon moved silently, unusual for a vintage for which rumbling exhaust or squeaks and creaks could be expected.

It came to a quiet stop next to Robbie. He composed himself as far as the ale would allow, then opened the rear passenger-side door using the button-handle and slid onto the black bench seat. He closed the door and heard a click a moment after.

A mild aroma of worn leather, cedar, and sweet smoke hung in the pitch-black interior. A welcomed chill embraced Robbie, contrasting with the moist summer evening. He had difficulty seeing Casper, a silhouette that would have gone unnoticed if not for the expectation that a driver would be in the driver's seat. There seemed to be a considerable distance from the rear bench seat to the driver, and Robbie could not determine if there was any seating or anything at all, in-between. Darkness shrouded the upholstery he sat on, and from his vantage point, Robbie could not see outside of the vehicle, even through the windshield in front. He could see nothing save the shadow aspect of his driver.

A cabin light turned on above the driver inaudibly and created a gentle orb of subtle illumination. No objects became visible with the introduction of the light. No reflections became noticeable. No light crept into the rear passenger area, still engulfed in shadow. Casper leaned just to the edge of the glowing orb, forging his silhouette into Robbie's vision. He pinched the brim of his top hat and pulled it into position, centered atop his head. He turned the right side of his face toward Robbie. Casper's features only appeared as shadows on the cusp of the soft radiance, yet the outline of his face and whiskers was very clear. His mustache hung as black drapery over his lips, bristling in waves as coarse whispers slipped through. "How are you this evening, sir?"

"Uh, I'm good, Casper. How about you?" Robbie answered tentatively, squinting and trying to orient himself with the swirling darkness while attempting to comprehend the driver's curious appearance and voice.

"I am lovely, sir," Casper replied with a rumbling whisper. "Shall we depart?"

"Yes... Yes, please," Robbie said noting, and welcoming, the levity Casper's response brought.

"Of course, sir."

The cabin light extinguished, and again all was black. The wagon accelerated into the evening without making a sound. Robbie could feel the car moving, but there were no vibrations, no bumps or jolts, only serenity. Sound was absent, aside from his breathing. The silence and darkness were peaceful and comfortable, although completely alien to car travel. He had ridden in taxis before with flamboyant and eccentric drivers who used corny decorations to support whatever theme they hoped to convey. Surely though, Casper was simply a night driver, ferrying weary travelers to and from hotels and airports. Presumably, he adorned his cab as such to accommodate his expected clientele. Feeling anxious in his situation, Robbie soothed himself with these explanations. Additionally, the journey to the hotel should take only ten or fifteen minutes. He would be ready for bed in no time.

The effects of drink subtly escalated further, churning uncomfortably in Robbie's head. As he rubbed his temples with his palms, he heard the unmistakable clink of glass. Surprised, he peered down into the darkness and saw the shadowy form of a high-lipped tray. He reached toward the tray with his left hand and felt unfinished dry wood. Intrigued, he explored over the lip of the tray with his fingers and felt two glasses. He leaned toward the tray, trying to get a better view and could detect another object in the cloudy black. It was a small glass decanter. His mood transitioned to exuberance.

"Woah," Robbie exclaimed boisterously. "Wat'cha got back here, Casper?"

"Bourbon, sir. Please, enjoy some. It..."

"...Will make me feel lovely." Interrupted Robbie, quite amused with his wit.

"Yes, sir, of course." Casper susurrated with raspy breath.

"Thank you, Casper!" Robbie said as he delightedly groped the darkness for the decanter. His wandering hand grasped the stopper, and he pulled it free and set it down in the tray. Locating one of the glasses and with a practiced hand, he poured a splash from the decanter blindly. He put the decanter back onto the high lipped tray and replaced the stopper. Robbie then held the libation close to his face and gave it a hard stare. The rigid diamond pattern on the glass felt familiar and natural. From what his fingers told him, he could envision the vessel in his mind, but could not see more than a gray wisp with his eyes. He could barely see his hand, which appeared as a shadow. He tilted the glass to his nose and inhaled deeply. A rich bouquet of charred oak, vanilla, and alcohol saturated Robbie's nostrils. He sighed with satisfaction and put the drink to his lips for a sip.

Pristine bourbon coated Robbie's tongue and cheeks. He tasted everything noted in the aroma plus luscious caramel. The burn was strong, yet the finish smooth. This was an exquisite spirit.

Robbie made his home in Kentucky some thirty years ago. He had sampled bourbons directly at distilleries throughout the state and from every style of watering hole from dive bars to the most affluent establishments. He drank bourbons in a hotel under which, long ago, Al Capone himself smuggled barrels of the prohibited pleasure. Never had he enjoyed any liquor as he enjoyed Casper's bourbon.

"Casper, man, where'd you get this stuff? I need to get some of this. It's fantastic. What is it?" Robbie pleaded, slurring softly as his intoxication increased.

"It is not for me to say, sir. We shall arrive at your destination, momentarily." The reply came from the darkness.

Robbie decided it prudent not to press his inquiry further regardless of his dissatisfaction. He smelled his glass one final time before swallowing the rest of the bourbon, savoring the burn and taste, and placing it back in the tray. As he ruminated on the spirit's flavor profile, the car decelerated imperceptibly and came to a halt. Robbie realized this when the door clicked.

"We have arrived. Have a lovely evening, sir."

Robbie chuckled then sighed. "You too, man, thanks for the ride," he slurred enough to notice, which earned a subsequent laugh.

Robbie ran his hand drunkenly against the door until he felt the handle. He opened the door and staggered out of the car. The faint lighting in the parking lot contrasted so much to the shadows he emerged from that his eyes felt pain. Before closing the door, Robbie rubbed his face and peered inside, hoping for a glimpse of anything. He saw the wooden tray and glassware, pale and olden, sitting on worn black leather bench seating. He leaned and gazed at the driver's seat for a glimpse of Casper. Although still shrouded in shadow, Casper's top hat, the shoulders of a black suit, and long black hair were visible to Robbie. Casper did not turn to face Robbie, nor did he move at all. Robbie shrugged, closed the door, collected himself, and began his unsteady walk to the hotel lobby doors as the black wagon silently rolled away.

Robbie swung the lobby door open and immediately felt the torment of bright lights. His mind swirled as he squinted to acclimate himself. Almost unable to look up from the floor, he painfully made his way to the elevators, where he waited in dismay for the doors to open. He pressed the elevator button and quickly glanced at his surroundings. Robbie was relieved that the lobby was empty, devoid of onlookers who would only make the situation more unpleasant and uncomfortable. Even the front desk was unattended.

DING!

The elevator's arrival notification was startlingly loud, surprising Robbie and nearly causing him to topple over. A fresh wave of pain took hold in his head as the doors slid open. He shuffled into the elevator, pressed the button for the second floor, and slumped against the wall with his head in his hands. He covered his ears in preparation as the elevator slowed to a halt.

Ding.

Robbie sighed with relief, successfully muffling the bell's assault. He exited the elevator and was pleased to find the lighting much lower in the guest room hallway. Feeling better in the subdued lighting, although still intoxicated, he shuffled to his room, pulled the keycard from his pocket, slid it into the locking mechanism, and entered.

Robbie's room was completely dark and welcoming. Concerned with inflaming his headache, he carefully felt along the wall for the dimmer switch and raised it just enough to illuminate the room so he could navigate it safely. He disrobed completely and stretched for a moment.

Before lying down for the few hours he was afforded, Robbie heeded the call of nature and opened the bathroom door. His room lighting was enough, so using the bathroom light was not required. He approached the toilet, concluded his business, and put on a hotel bathrobe he found hanging by the shower. Finally beginning to feel comfortable again and content to pass out for a few hours, he headed out of the bathroom, but something caught his eye and held him in place.

Robbie turned to the mirror and in it saw a reflection of pure shadow. He quickly looked away and stared directly at the dark wall. His thoughts raced, and his stomach churned with fear. His breathing sped, and he felt sweat beading on his brow. Forced to face the inevitable, he coaxed his paralyzed arm into reaching for the bathroom light switch. Robbie flicked the switch upward and immediately absorbed the punishment of the brightness. He turned to the mirror in terror, praying the light would provide a rebuttal to the darkness' lies.

Robbie exhaled a weak gurgle. He looked into his own eyes first, completely black. His hair hung straightened and utterly black. Darkened gray tattooed his face and chest, swirling slowly. Shock and anxiety immediately provoked retching. Through his graying teeth sprayed obsidian vomit, viscous and voluminous, which splattered across the sink and mirror. He collapsed to the soiled floor and crawled out of the bathroom.

Stricken with horror and panic, he frantically shuffled through his rumpled trousers looking for his phone. Unable to locate it, he stood and ran to his room phone, snatching it off the hook. He heard nothing from the handset. He dialed 9-1-1. Nothing. He pressed the hotel emergency button. Nothing. He threw the handset against the wall and ran out of his room. He burst through the emergency exit stairwell door and raced down the steps. Gasping, he swung open the door from the stairwell to the lobby and was blinded by the lights. With blurred vision, he felt his way along the wall to the front desk. He slammed his fist on the desk bell, unable to see if anyone was there, and fell to his knees, weeping tears of ink.

The front desk clerk, a young woman wearing the hotel uniform, emerged from the management office upon hearing the bell. She saw Robbie sobbing on the floor and rushed around the desk to his side.

"Sir, are you alright?"

"No!" Robbie wailed, "Help me! Please!"

"What's wrong, sir?"

"LOOK AT ME!" Robbie screamed. "LOOK AT ME! LOOK AT ME!"

The bewildered clerk put her hand on Robbie's shoulder in an attempt to provide solace. Robbie flinched at her touch, which felt frozen cold.

"I need help. Help me. Please. Help..." Robbie pleaded, his screaming fading into incoherent whispers. "Look at me. What's happening? What's happening to me?"

"Sir... I.. I don't know what to say," the confused clerk stammered, trying to calm Robbie. "You... You look lovely."

Burn After Writing

by Phil Giunta

Crackling flames leapt from the immense stone fireplace like the snapping claws of some ravenous monster. Or is that just my imagination? Shane Conrad took a step back as he stared at the blazing hearth in Adrian Halka's lakeside cabin. Behind him, multicolored file folders had been stacked atop a table by Halka's widow. Food for the beast.

It had been the great writer's final wish that they be burned—no exceptions.

While Shane understood Halka's reasons, he did not agree with them at all. To an editor and fellow fantasist, the very notion of destroying the unfinished works of one of the most awarded writers in history was abhorrent.

"I found two more." Robyn shuffled into the room and tossed a pair of blue file folders onto the table. Each one was easily an inch thick with pages held together by large binder clips.

Shane picked up the top folder and began flipping through it. "Is there a code behind these colors?"

"If I recall correctly, a blue folder indicates a story in progress. Yellow means that Adrian was still developing the idea and maybe had an outline, and the red folders have a page or two of notes he jotted down when inspiration struck. That's why the red ones are the thinnest."

Shane sighed as he fanned the pages. "I have to be honest with you, Robyn. I'm struggling with the idea of burning all this."

She joined him in front of the fire. "I know. I noticed your expression when the lawyer read that part of Adrian's will. I thought you were going to swallow your head."

"I can name a dozen capable writers, myself included, who would be honored to finish some of these—and we could do it in Adrian's style without sacrificing the integrity of his work."

Robyn chuckled as she sat against the table. It was probably the first time she had cracked a smile since her husband's death. "You remember Adrian's reaction years ago when that publisher turned one of his manuscripts over to a hack because Adrian refused to make the revisions they wanted?"

"He sent them a box of dead rats."

"By third-class mail in the middle of summer. Cost them thousands to fumigate."

"There will never be another like Adrian."

"To the relief of many in your business, I'm sure." Robyn placed a gentle hand on Shane's arm. "It wasn't that Adrian didn't trust you, but he was adamant that if his name was on it—"

"—it had to be entirely his work and no one else's, I know." Shane held up the folder. "Did you ever read any of these unfinished stories?"

Robyn shook her head. "I could barely keep up with the published ones—all two thousand over fifty-four years. Speaking of which, Adrian loved your stories. That's why he kept encouraging you to quit editing and get back to writing. What was it he used to say? There's a special place in Hell for editors. Present company excluded, of course."

Shane laughed. "As a matter of fact, I have three short stories coming out later this year and two novels in progress."

Robyn gave his arm a gentle squeeze. "Adrian would be proud." A slow melody began playing from elsewhere in the house. She pushed away from the table. "I left my phone in the kitchen. As much as it pains you, my dear, start feeding the fire. I'll be right back."

The moment she vanished from view, Shane gathered both of the blue folders and slipped them into his backpack beneath the table. By the time Robyn returned, he had burned through half of the remaining stack of folders. They finished the rest in silence.

Standing at the lectern in Ebba Mackie's Bookshop, Shane finished reading the opening chapter of his new fantasy novel before a small but appreciative audience. Ignoring the throbbing in his head, he smiled during their applause and began taking questions. A middle-aged woman in the second row raised her hand. "What inspired you to return to writing after so many years as an editor?"

Shane cleared his throat. "Last January, the world lost a brilliant writer in Adrian Halka. Some of you knew Adrian personally. He gave readings and signed books in this very store. I edited much of Adrian's later work for Cinderbox Press, and we became fast friends. Over time, I looked to him as a mentor. Years of exposure to his writing elevated the quality of mine until Adrian all but ordered me to quit meddling with other people's work and get back to creating my own." Shane held up the hardback copy of his book, "but it wasn't until his death that I finally took his advice."

He shot a sidelong glance at the back cover—and met the accusing gaze of Adrian Halka. *You took more than my advice, you son of a–!*

The book slipped from Shane's grasp and slammed onto the lectern. No one in the audience seemed to hear the disembodied voice, but they stared at him expectantly. Shane cleared his throat again as he straightened the book. "Sorry about that, folks." He pressed a hand to his chest. "Even after all this time, I still become... emotional when I think about Adrian. Any more questions?"

Two hours later, after scribbling his name in more than a dozen copies of his novel, Shane thanked the last customer before slumping back in his chair. He slipped off his glasses and massaged the bridge of his nose just as an older woman took the empty seat beside him. "You know, as I listened to your reading, I could definitely hear Adrian's influence. I look forward to reading the rest of it." She leaned forward, brow furrowed. "You feeling all right?"

Shane cast his weary gaze on shop owner Ebba Mackie. "I must be coming down with something. I woke up with a scratchy throat and a relentless headache."

Ebba pressed two gnarled fingers against his forehead. "You do seem a bit feverish, kiddo." She slid her chair a few inches away. "No offense. I can't afford to get sick. I'm a delicate old termagant. At least, that's what Adrian used to call me."

"Lady, you're about as delicate as Krakatoa."

"Are you implying I have a volcanic temper?"

"Remind me why you and Adrian got divorced?"

Ebba turned her gaze away and began straightening a stack of Shane's books. She flipped one over, and Shane was relieved to see his own smiling visage on the back cover. "Adrian was the unstoppable force to my immovable object. Writing was his mistress, and I couldn't compete. Of course, I didn't offer much support either. Ours was a brief and volatile marriage, but we became friends again after some time apart. I was happy for him when he found Robyn. She's a strong woman. What about you, handsome young stud? Any luck on the romantic front?"

Shane stifled a chill and began to suspect Ebba was right about the fever. He forced a wan smile. "Still looking for Ms. Right... but not today. Today, I'm going home, making chicken soup, and going to bed."

Despite the lively throng of well-wishers in his apartment, Shane couldn't stop shivering. As he walked through his living room, smiling faces blurred past on either side. Overlapping voices congratulated him on his recent success. He recognized most of them. His parents and sister, friends old and new, even ex-girlfriends had turned up to celebrate. Robyn was there, chatting with Ebba beside the familiar stone fireplace from Adrian's cabin.

How did this get here? Shane shouldered his way toward them and stood before the hearth, trembling uncontrollably. He crouched down and closed his eyes, relishing the warmth on his face and hands.

"How ya feelin', Shane?"

He turned to find a short, stout man in black cargo pants standing over him. His salt and pepper beard covered the top buttons of a disheveled blue and white plaid shirt. The room fell silent. Everyone else had vanished.

"Adrian. W-what–"

"Looks like you're running a fever, boy." Adrian's hands shot forward, clutching Shane's throat and pressing him backward toward the flames. "Better feed the fire!"

"Wait!" Shane awoke, thrashing and kicking in a tangle of sheets and blankets. When he'd finally extricated himself, he sat on the edge of the bed and glanced at the alarm clock. It was just after three in the morning. The TV was still on, casting the bedroom in a feeble blue glow.

He snatched the digital thermometer from the nightstand and slipped it under his tongue before wrapping himself in a blanket. Glancing at the TV, Shane instantly recognized an old talk show from the 1980s, though he couldn't recall the name of it.

"So what, if anything, do you dislike about writing?" the host asked.

"I don't dislike anything about writing," his guest shrugged, before turning in his chair to face the camera. "But I do hate people who steal my work!"

Shane tore the thermometer from his mouth. "Adrian..."

"Ain't no fever-induced dream this time, Conrad. You know, I don't even care that you lied to your publisher or to your readers, but you lied to my wife. Hell, you even lied to my ex-wife! You were like a son to me, boy."

Shane shot to his feet and started toward the TV, shivering either from fever or fear... or both. "Adrian, please, I'm sorry–"

"Screw your apology. You betrayed me. Why?"

Shane's vision blurred, and his knees buckled. He fell back against the bed. The digital thermometer in his hand began beeping, but he was too weak to lift his arm. "I... hadn't published a novel in eight years. I needed a fast comeback. Mine were taking too long."

"So, instead of respecting my final wishes, you stole my unpublished work. Of all people! You burn me up, Conrad, and now I'm returning the favor."

Shane slid to the floor, writhing under the furious scowl of Adrian Halka. What began as a tingling throughout his body erupted with the torture of a thousand bee stings, and the only sound louder than the electronic squeal of the thermometer was his own agonized shriek.

The police found Shane Conrad lying on the floor of his bedroom, loosely covered in the scorched tatters of a blanket. When the coroner arrived, the young sergeant was all too happy to give him a few minutes to perform his initial examination—any excuse to tear his gaze away from the body. "No sign of forced entry or struggle. We found no cigarettes or alcohol on him, and nothing else in the room appears to have been affected except for this." He held up an evidence bag containing the melted remains of a digital thermometer.

The coroner motioned for the body to be bagged. "Well, ruling out all that, it could have been a natural cause, but I won't know for sure until I perform an autopsy. You all right, sergeant?"

"It's his face. The neighbor who called said it sounded like the guy was screaming in terror. I've never seen anything like... that."

"I have, just not to this degree." The coroner stared at the body bag as the zipper closed over the charred, blackened corpse of Shane Conrad.

Not at this Time

by Colin Newton

No one expects a cold call, but Bill Wertham hardly expected phone calls from anyone. So, he was caught entirely off guard when he received—conveniently on his day off—a call from an unfamiliar voice that seemed quite familiar with him.

"I'm sorry, what did you say your name was?" he asked after a minute of spiel, interrupting the voice at the other end.

"Williams," came the reply.

"Right. And what is this about?"

"I'm a representative for a publishing firm, and we're always interested in new talent."

How did you get this number, Bill wondered. His mind drifted to a barely-used box of business cards lost somewhere in his apartment. Perhaps one had slipped from hand to hand until it reached this man.

"Look, I'm sorry. If this is some kind of a vanity press..."

"Oh no, no vanity, I assure you, Mr. Wertham. In fact, that's the wrong idea entirely. We are a firm that specializes in up and coming writers and artists, particularly those without any professionally showcased work. We buy unpublished works and hold them for a later date. And we do pay, as I think you will find, quite generously."

"Uh-huh."

"Mr. Wertham, our scouts have taken an interest in you, and I am happy to say I think you have great potential. I would love to set up a meeting with you to discuss our firm."

"Uh-huh." Bill was barely listening at this point. The whole thing was so unfamiliar that he was having trouble focusing on it.

"Look, again, I'm sorry, but I don't think I'm interested."

"Well, I am sorry to hear that, Mr. Wertham." There was a pause. "Let me give you my number, my personal line, in case you change your mind."

Well, what's one more phone number, Bill mused. "OK, hold on." He found a scrap of paper and an old pen. Its nib caked with dark gunk. He scribbled it to life and wrote the number down in clean blue ink before hanging up without bothering to say goodbye.

It was pitifully clichéd, but there can't be a cliché without there being a little bit of truth behind it. Bill Wertham was a struggling—and, to his way of thinking, unappreciated—writer. He probably wouldn't even have appreciated the cliché.

Bill worked two jobs—part-time at a Starbucks and part-time at a Barnes and Noble. Why he couldn't work full time at a Starbucks in a Barnes and Noble was beyond him, but the powers that be had decided he should work slightly more hours for slightly less pay than seemed fair, as well as spend an inordinate amount of time on the freeway.

It was a separate set of powers that decided he had to keep a Twitter account and a blog. Still, the best authorities said that half of being a writer in the 21st century was about maintaining a digital presence. Luckily, his bookstore job meant that he was always in touch with bestsellers and new arrivals, so he was always aware of what he should be reading and posting about when he was supposed to be working. In short, his business of being a writer was so time-consuming that he barely had time to write.

Perhaps it was unhelpful that he didn't always think of his online self and his literary self as the same person. On social media, which valued brevity, he was Bill Werth, but his authorial byline was William Wertham, and he relished the way the alliteration rolled off the page.

Unfortunately for Bill, it was a byline he hadn't seen all that often. His works had never graced a mainstream magazine or a literary journal, and he couldn't remember the last time he had been in an e-zine. Short stories rubbed shoulders with samples on the fallow pages of his blog, which never had the readership, subscriptions, or views he felt it should.

After his first rejection letter, he vowed to keep any that followed, feeling as if he had joined the ranks of other writers who had been unfairly passed over. At the top of each response, he knew his name, at least there, shared space with Vonnegut, Orwell, and Plath.

He had long since stopped keeping the letters.

Bill could not have said when the exact moment was—perhaps it was reading about the next author to have started in self-publishing get a TV series. Perhaps it was opening the latest statement for an overdrawn credit card. Perhaps it was simply seeing the scrap of paper with Williams's number make a triumphant rise to the top of the heap of kipple in his apartment—but Bill eventually gave the man on the other end of the phone a call.

In his head, he had rehearsed what he wanted to say, but with each ring of the phone, part of his speech jittered away. Still, when Williams picked up, he made his message clear.

"So glad to hear it, Mr. Wertham," Williams said, his tone changing from dim interest to true recognition. "Can you meet me today?"

Bill proposed they meet at a Starbucks—not the one where he worked, but one he frequented, both to write and take advantage of the employee discount. Bill arrived early, ordered a tall black coffee, and took a table at the back, effortlessly sinking into the background of uniform tans and greens, burnt smells, and low lighting.

Williams had asked him to bring some works he would consider selling, and Bill had collected them in an appropriately coffee-stained file folder. They were minor but not embarrassing pieces—character studies, creative meditations on contemporary life, even some sketch comedy thrown in to show media savvy—not his best but far from his worst. After all, if this was the real deal, he wanted to make an impression without letting go of his prize material.

It was only when Bill started thumbing through the pages he had brought that he realized he had not asked for nor been given a way to identify Williams when he appeared, but when he looked up, sensing an approach, he decided that wouldn't be an issue. The man heading smoothly toward his table had to be Williams. He was the most professionally dressed man in the room; his suit was the shade of navy that initially looks black but, once seen to be blue, cannot be seen as anything else.

"Mr. Wertham?"

"Well, yes," Bill replied. Williams extended a hand that had smoothed with age. Bill rose, clumsily took it, and sat back down, but Williams remained standing, leaning elegantly against the back of a chair. "How did you know?" Bill asked, looking up at the man.

"You're the only one here who's not working on a manuscript. Yours look quite complete. May I?" Bill placed the folder into Williams's hand. In an instant, the older man was leafing through it, a small smile spreading across his gaunt face as he read.

"This is quite nice," Williams said, and Bill couldn't help but feel a twinge of pride, despite the praise coming from such an odd source.

"Yes, I am quite pleased. And this isn't a vanity press?"

"Don't believe everything you hear," Williams cooed without looking up. "All is not vanity."

He set the folder back on the table and reached into his jacket, producing two stacks of paper separately stapled. He handed them to Bill, who saw they were identical contracts. Bill flipped through pages, hunting between "no less than but no great thans" and "until further notices" for a shred of sense. "What does all this mean?" he asked at last.

"I assure you, beneath all that legalese is a fairly straightforward deal," Williams answered. "You release all rights of the stories that we have outlined here, and we gain full publishing rights for the future, including reprints in magazines, anthologies, et cetera. In return, you will receive a rather handsome payment now, as well as the knowledge that you will continue to be published after you have achieved notoriety, keeping you in that all-important public eye."

Bill chuckled. "I'm sorry, man, I mean, I barely know you. How do I know you're not lying?"

Williams looked disappointed. "Oh, I wouldn't lie to you, Mr. Wertham. Not to you. You and I, we're going to embark on a great voyage. At least, I sincerely hope we are."

Bill shrugged and, with less a feeling of Odyssean camaraderie and more one of what-have-I-got-to-lose spontaneity, turned to the last page, wrote in his name and address, then dated and signed the contracts.

"Thank you, Mr. Wertham," Williams said, taking the first one of the contracts, then the folder. He tucked the contract inside. "I was quite serious about working in the future. Please retain my number for your records, as I shall retain yours." He placed the folder under his arm.

Bill imagined that, if he'd had a hat, he would have tipped it. "And remember a handsome payment." Williams bowed slightly and left.

A few weeks later, when a check came in the mail, Bill had to agree.

The most amazing quality of money is its ability to disappear. Bill was quick to pay off his credit cards, and he coasted on the remaining cash, sleepwalking his way through work and spending more time on writing. He felt as if a great weight had been lifted from his body, that he was propelled upward toward a vast, endless expanse of sky, and he worked appropriately with creative energy he swore he hadn't felt in years.

But it wasn't long before the check's presence was no longer felt. Bill could have gone on without the money except that his creative streak dried up.

One day, Bill found himself staring at his laptop screen, reading a rejection notice—an electronic rejection even worse for lacking the tangible dignity of a letter. He watched the screen dim from lack of activity and finally turn black. Staring at himself reflected in the dark surface, his thoughts turned to Williams.

Bill dug out the phone number, and Williams surprised him with the speed at which he picked up. Predictably, he was polite and professional, and it didn't take him long to venture a guess as to why Bill was calling.

"Of course, we can set up a meeting, Mr. Wertham. Are you available today?"

"Yeah, I mean, I can make some time."

"Would it be more convenient if I came to your address?"

"That would work."

Bill had a limited amount of time to cobble together a few stories. As he flipped through files on his laptop, a plan formed. Nothing second-tier this time. First-rate works only—although he was waiting on a few stories from this last burst of creativity, and he couldn't risk signing them over to Williams and his firm—and Williams would pay top dollar for them. Phase two would be to hurl himself into his work. He had treated the last cash infusion like an experiment. This time, he would be ready. A few printouts, a change of clothes and a quick tidying up later, and he was more than ready.

It was not long before Williams was at Bill's door. The older man seemed genuinely excited to see him. His face glowed with health, and his clean black jacket stylishly contrasted with a shiny cream tie.

"I must say, I am surprised, Mr. Wertham," he said. "After our last encounter, I thought you might be...reluctant to return to the firm. I can usually tell those who won't return, and I'm glad I was wrong with you."

"I'm happy to have been wrong about you too, Mr. Williams. I have some new stories I think you'll be interested in, and I," he paused to chuckle, "I am looking forward to seeing them in print."

"I think we all are. What helps you can only help us. Let me see what you have."

Bill tried his hand at bargaining and found that, although mostly unchanging, Williams delighted in the game. Given enough talking, he would alter some particulars, but only about price or the stories; ownership and reprint rights were strictly off the table. Soon, another pair of contracts were signed, and another grouping of Bill's work was placed in Williams's care.

"Thank you again, Mr. Wertham. You are becoming one of my favorite writers."

Williams drummed the folder with his fingers. "I would advise you to try your hand at placing some of your stories now. Maybe start that novel, eh? I think you're ready for it, and we expect great things. Best of luck."

With a slight bow, he was gone from Bill's apartment.

Bill almost immediately took Williams's advice, but first, he quit his job at Starbucks. He then paid for a massive overhaul on his blog, bought ads on Facebook, and began submitting stories to any paid journal and contest he could find. In theory, the time he bought by quitting at Starbucks was meant to be focused more on writing, and he did, but mostly tinkering away at a few unfinished short stories and an unfinishable novel.

Somehow, Bill expected a tumble into financial limbo would resemble a curtain crashing down when a show's run out of time, but it wasn't like that. Looking back, he couldn't say where it all began or how it progressed, just where it ended up. Credit card statements appeared faster than rejection notices from contests and journals. There was a missed payment here, a late fee there. These followed each other as naturally as the seconds on a clock face, and the next thing he knew, Bill was living in a storage unit north of town. It wasn't as if he'd obtained the storage unit to live in it. He was downsizing, restructuring. It was, again, a natural progression, one that happened to fit together all too well.

And it wasn't like he didn't try his options. Not at the first sign, but after the trouble started, he unsuccessfully asked for his job back at Starbucks. Later, when he was he was let go from Barnes and Noble, he reactivated a long-dormant Lyft account. He tried driving to fill some financial gaps, but his car became hopelessly mired in Kafka-esque paperwork when he tried to have it re-inspected. He called Williams more than once, but there was never any response. His surroundings deteriorated into a tightly circling wall of questions: Where are my stories going? When are they going to publish? Why isn't he answering me?

Bill was almost startled when Williams actually took one of his calls.

"Mr. Wertham." The familiar voice sounded different.

"Why haven't you been answering my calls?" His question surprised even him.

"I have just been busy. You aren't the only one under my care, you know, or the only one

who has signed a contract with this firm."

"Are you avoiding me?"

"I've been busy, nothing more."

"All right...all right." His answer surprised him even more. "I have some more stuff to sell. If you're interested."

"We're not buying at the moment, Mr. Wertham."

Bill's carefully wrought pitch disappeared.

"What do you mean?"

"I meant exactly what I said. I think it was plain enough."

"But I need this."

He could hear Williams sigh. "This doesn't work the way you think it works, Mr. Wertham."

"Stop calling me that," he snapped, shrinking a second later at himself. He softened his tone. "Can you at least look at some of what I've been working on? I have a few pieces I think you'd be interested in."

At first, there was the hum of empty space on the other end of the phone. "Very well," Williams said at last.

Bill stepped outside of the storage unit and lit a cigarette. It was a habit he hadn't indulged in since college. Along with an oddly diverse list of books he'd read, and a looming debt he could never quite pay off, it was the last vestige of an overpriced education.

Bill stared into the sun. It was late afternoon, twilight fast approaching, and the cracked asphalt of the parking lot and stucco units braided with age were stained appropriately in purple and orange. Bill took a final drag, crushed out his cigarette, and turned back into his unit. He pulled the door down and started looking for something to give Williams.

Not too much later, there was an echoing knock on the unit's door. Bill pulled it up and saw Williams, dressed impeccably as always in an ash-gray suit, framed by the setting sun. He smiled softly.

"All right. Shall we get down to business?"

Putting together something to sell had been harder than he'd thought. Some of his work was out making the rounds; some had already been sold to Williams; many of the others existed in that awful adolescence between a nascent idea and a fully-fledged story. What remained was either half-forgotten or just not very good.

"And this, this I wrote to be a TV pilot," Bill said finally, holding up a two-page treatment. That was a lie, but it was the most fleshed-out of the ideas he was trying to pass off as complete.

Williams looked at him, a smile poorly hiding his concern. "How did we get here?" he said at last.

Bill could not meet his gaze. "I don't know," he replied, surprised at his honesty.

Williams shuffled through the papers. "Mr. Wer...William. I'm sorry, but I don't know if we can take these," He flipped the same couple of pages back and forth a few times. Finally, he selected the TV pilot. "I can take this, but there's nothing more I can do."

"What about what you've already bought? Could you at least publish something out of that? Or sell something sideways?"

"You know our rules. We do not publish until authors have achieved some notoriety on their own."

"I know, but, I mean, I could use the exposure, and..." Bill finally looked at Williams. "It wasn't supposed to be like this."

"I know," Williams said calmly. "It never is."

"What is that supposed to mean?"

"Just that no one sets out to..." he looked into the setting sun. "It's supposed to be romantic, isn't it? A life lived for art." He turned back. "I'm not supposed to divulge this information, but we are going to publish a few of your stories. Not right away. In a couple of months."

It took Bill a minute to process the words.

"Well, well, that's great! When do I see it?"

Williams's eyes changed, but the smile didn't leave his face. "You won't. After some consideration, you've been picked up by our 'posthumous publishing' department." He smiled again, the smile of someone who doesn't want to admit they've regretted taking that last bite.

Bill could not respond. He had nothing to say. Williams looked at him with something like real sadness. "I'm sorry. I truly am."

Williams backed out of the storage unit, grabbed the chain, and pulled the door down. Bill sat for a few minutes in the unit before he realized the room had grown dark around him. He reached for the light switch with a numb hand.

OFFICE POLITICS

by Victoria Dalpe

The chicken screeched, trembled, and went slack in her hands. Hot blood spurted and sprayed upon the stones, filling the small clay pots and jars placed seemingly haphazard on the floor. To Peter, more blood landed on the floor, and on his damned shoes, then in the receptacles. He grimaced internally at wearing suede brogues to such an occasion but tried to keep the regret off his face. Must appear engaged and respectful, must be entranced by the ritual so few are privy to.

$300 shoes. Fuck.

The headless chicken jerked a few times, legs windmilling mechanically as the last bits of electricity coursed through it. Without ceremony, she dropped its body with a plop on the oil-stained concrete and knelt before the pots, gathering them up with the finesse of a diner waitress.

"And now?" He finally asked, the long silence stretching too tight between us.

"Now?" She smirked, passed by him, and walked a few paces to the altar. She set the various blood-catchers down amidst the myriad offerings: a plate with moldy bread, jars of honey, bags of strong-smelling herbs, broken shards of mirror, a vibrant bird feather, a small frog skeleton encased in acetate. Tall white pillar candles burned endlessly, their smell waxy and greasy like blown-out birthday candles.

"Now, nothing. You made your offer and your request. If he comes, he comes. If not," She shrugged, indifferent. "I got to get back to my customers." She turned and walked out, no goodbye, no show yourself out, nothing.

He stayed a little longer, looking at the ragged altar, tucked away in the corner next to an old rusty staff locker. The altar itself was just a small table with a muslin cloth over it. The table sagged with the weight of all the offerings, the air tinny and sour with the chicken's blood, and all the old dried up blood before it. And where the idol should be: An empty glass vase facing a small mirror.

The light outside was blinding, and he had to cover his eyes as he winded through the busy parking lot of the gas station. Once in his car, he looked back at the Speedy Gas, finding it strange that a "real" place of worship was tucked away in the old garage bay. Stranger still that he just participated in killing a damned chicken to a god.

Away from prying eyes, he squirted both hands liberally with a thick coating of antibacterial gel and let them air dry, welcoming the burn as the alcohol reached his nose and eyes, cleaning out all the grease and blood.

Peter took a sip of water from the bottle he bought inside, popped a piece of gum also purchased inside, and got on the road. Really a one-stop-shop, get your gas, grub, and god in one place. He grinned to himself as he got back on the highway. Talk radio filled the car, its monotone a relaxing counterpart to the gridlock morning rush hour traffic.

At the office later: sweat seeping through his shirt, just from walking from the car to the building. "A scorcher today?" Asked the security guard, Peter nodded, not bothering to even glance in the guard's direction. He was in the elevator, doors just about to close when a slender hand reached through and stopped them from shutting. Genevieve.

Genevieve was sexy and knew it. She worked in his department and was better at her job than he was. But she would never get the promotion because their boss was an old school chauvinist. Peter liked to consider himself a progressive guy, not like their boss, and hated to admit in this one instance he's relieved: he didn't want to lose his job or have Genevieve as his superior.

She was tall, close to 5'10", and was confident in her height enough to wear high heels. She stood at eye level with him, and he hated how threatening he found it. She was shapely, and wore a meticulously well-cut skirt suit that discreetly advertised all her best assets. Her perfume was musky, makeup impeccable, and gray eyes were hungry.

Or maybe he just imagined that her eyes were hungry and her outfit was sexy. Maybe the rampant cries of sexism in the office weren't as off the mark as he thought. She may just think she was wearing work clothes and lipstick, and he's reading into it because he's both infatuated with and terrified of her. The elevator doors had barely slid shut, and all of this had filled up his head. His face reddened with the shame of it.

"Hot out there, huh?" She said, not bothering to look at him. Instead, she faced forward, a few feet away arms crossed. Her nails gleamed blood red.

"Yeah," is all he replied, internally folding in on himself like a piece of origami.

As the doors opened to their floor, she turned to him, "Looks like you spilled something on your shoes, Peter." And then she strutted out of the elevator and down the main corridor of cubicles, like a supermodel, or a dominatrix. Her shoulders back, her head held high.

Or maybe she just walked as any other person would, and he had infused everything she did with a strange combination of sexuality and feminine dominance. Possibly, and most shamefully, it's the humiliation of her dominance that he found so alluring.

He slinked off the elevator, imagining himself her pitiful servant, trailing in her shadow as if carrying the train of her dress. Impotent and pathetic. He worried that no ritual at the Speedy Mart could save him from her.

Peter's desk was almost next to the window, save one other desk. Luckily, it's Johnson's, and he was out on a field assignment in the

Congo all week. He could pretend his desk was at the window, looking out at the meticulously manicured corporate lawns. The topiary and shrubs were arranged to show sigils from this high. Sigils to the worker Gods: Punctuality, Monotony, and Contentment. Like the three graces, only boring.

A memo sat on his desk; he squinted at it. He sweated, reread it, and swore to himself.

Before he could compose a better plan, he was on his feet and heading toward the Old Man's office. Not running, but close. He saw from across the room that Genevieve was also up and doing the same thing. They both held a sheet of paper in their hands.

He won the race and got to the door first, hand poised to knock just as it was yanked open. The old man was standing there, all rosy cheeks and big belly like a mall Santa in summer.

"Oh good, see you two got the memo. Come in, come in."

Peter saw a full cup of coffee on his boss' desk, and it reminded him of the blood bubbling at the altar, overflowing the little earthen pots, and smoke filling the empty vase. In his memory, the smoke took on a vaguely humanoid shape, like a Genie in a bottle.

His thoughts were interrupted by his phone, buzzing in his pocket. He pulled it out as quiet as he could. It was a text from an unknown number: **Come.**

He tucked the phone back in his pocket as discreetly as he could and looked back up at the Old Man and Genevieve. She was trying to assert herself, but also stay calm and cool because the Old Man had no tolerance for uppity women (his words). He assumed the Old Man had a mean, ball-busting mother, but that was just a guess based on how he flinched whenever a woman raised her voice.

"I don't think pairing us up is the best solution, Boss." She said carefully, and Peter nodded emphatically in agreement. He didn't want to be paired up with anyone, especially not her. "If he can't land the client, then just reassign him and give them to me." He stopped nodding and started to shake his head no, wanting to find the words to deny her claim. He can land the client on his own. He needs more time. For some reason, the words don't come, and he is left wagging his head, probably looks like one of those dashboard nodding dogs from the Old Man's perspective.

"Now hold on, I happen to have..." He finally said, fighting the urge to pull out his phone and prove to them he's onto something. He changed course. "I have some promising inroads. I just need a little more time."

"Now Pete, I have been hearing that for two weeks already." Old Man said with a sigh.

"Please." He said, not wanting to sound desperate, but knowing that he did.

"I am sorry son, your time is up. Genevieve is officially your partner on this, and I want it priority one. We got some big events coming down the pipeline, and we need this client on board. We need them, you understand?"

They both nodded and left the room.

"Just give me your files up to now, so I know what you have been working on." She said as they walked out together, and he bristled at the order. This was his case, and he was practically her boss. She waited for his response, and he was staring at her mouth, too angry to meet her eyes.

"Fine. I will email them to you. But there's no point. By tonight it will all be taken care of." Her eyes narrowed to slits. She didn't believe him.

"Confidence doesn't look good on you, Peter. Just email me the files." She turned and walked away before he could say anything.

The text in his pocket buzzed a reminder. He fished it out and stared at the message.

Come.

He emailed the files begrudgingly and headed for the elevator, phone in hand.

Back at the Speedy Gas station, Inverness was ringing out a long line of customers. Her eyes met his when the bell dinged. She nodded and went back to ringing up lotto tickets and gum. He was positively hopping foot to foot by the time the last person was out the door, and then he was face to face with the priestess/chicken killer/cashier.

"I got your text!" He said breathlessly, excitedly.

"Congratulations." She said deadpan and looked past him at the door ding. She smiled a greeting, and a waft of musky perfume alerted him before he turned. It was Genevieve.

"I got your text." She said, holding her phone up, ignoring him. He was breathless, confused, livid. He looked back at Inverness, and she merely shrugged. Like she didn't care. Like he wasn't there first. Bitch.

"Guess you both should go back then." She said dryly, eyes flicking between them.

"Wait, Wait! How did you know? Were you here earlier? Have you been following me?" He was tempted to jab a finger at her chest to drill the point home, but he stopped himself.

"I want this client, Peter, and I am not a moron. It was logical to come here and make an offering. Inverness is the best. Everyone knows that."

He looked at Inverness accusingly, wanting her to tell him why she hadn't mentioned another employee from Imago coming to her, making an offering, courting her god. Instead, she just flipped the sign at the door to closed and locked the deadbolt. Then she opened the back door to the garage. They followed her.

Was it fair to ask for loyalty from this priestess? Did he just not understand women at all?

"How's your doctorate going?" Genevieve asked as they passed through the doorway. Inverness laughs, a deep throaty laugh he'd certainly never heard, "Oh! A work in process. Nearly done my dissertation."

"Great, well, I would love to read it if you need any extra eyes."

Inverness nodded thanks, graciously.

"What the– How do you know any of this? How do you even know about her?" He asked, sputtering.

Genevieve raised a shaped eyebrow and looked at Inverness, both women chuckled, at his expense, no doubt. Bitches. Co-conspirators. But shit, she was the priestess, probably bad to think ill of her in a sacred space to her god. She'd warned him about negative energy earlier.

He tried to scrub his brain, tried to think of only clear, holy, minimalist thoughts. He failed as the two women chit-chatted with an intimacy that spoke of friendship. He felt jealous. And threatened. And scared.

Inverness's expression became more serious as they approached the altar. The space was very dark, save the dusty light from garage doors, and the flickering candles on the altar. At first, it looked like little had changed since he'd been there this morning, and yet something had, something hard to place.

Then he saw it. The blood was gone, and the food, and the honey. All the vessels were empty, scrubbed clean even. As if chicken blood hadn't rained all over it.

And the glass vase was now full.

Full with what was another question entirely. It looked like pink fleshy pudding, and the air smelled sweet, but foully so like spoiled fruit.

"Are you ready?" Inverness said, her voice vaguely threatening. Or maybe he was inferring that. The whole day had spun out of his control.

"Yes. I am." Genevieve said, confident, hungry, answering before he could get the words out. Lips in an angry line, he nodded, mouth dry. At that moment, he hated Genevieve.

Inverness began unbuttoning her top. The Speedy Gas button-down hit the floor. Then the bra, then the tan khakis. She was naked. He looked away, Genevieve notably did not.

Inverness walked over to the altar, dark skin golden in the candlelight. She had a beautiful body under any other situation. But the strangeness of the garage, the old equipment cluttering the corners, the sweet smells mingling with old grease, the stained concrete floors. His head swam.

She lifted the vase of pink and turned to them. "He is here." She smiled and raised the glass over her head. Peter called out to stop her, but it was too late. The thick slime, like pink mucus, slid from the vase and covered her hair and face, then crawled over her whole body, its mass multiplying before his eyes, coating her until every inch was enveloped. The smell was cloying. Bile rose in his throat. He glanced at Genevieve, but her eyes never moved from the goo.

The mass covering her body began to move and change. Shifting the form beneath, she grew taller, her face shape reformed, her entire physicality evolved as he bore witness. The most notable change was the flattening of her breasts and the unfurling, like a pupa from a cocoon, of a large pink penis.

And then, Inverness was gone entirely, and in her place stood a tall man, unnaturally pink. He was bald, hairless, and had the rubbery fleshiness of a newborn, or a preserved fetal pig. The pink man opened his eyes, which were entirely gold. Genevieve and Peter both gasped.

"You summoned me from beyond the realm of flesh, what is it that you seek?" The voice was male.

The golden eyes speared Peter in place, and he swallowed audibly. Struck dumb by an audience with a god, or the closest to such a thing he would probably get in his lifetime.

"I... uh... there is a client who we really need to move forward with this new program set for our calendar year. We need your help to convince him..." Peter stuttered.

The god almost sounded annoyed, "What is your request, and what is your offering?"

"My... offering. You mean beyond the chicken blood?" The god turned now to Genevieve and repeated the question. As if he'd merely dismissed him.

"The ability to bend the will of the Brenner corporation's CEO to me."

The god laughed, and Peter just stared open-mouthed at Genevieve. Bend the will?

"And your offering for such a large request?"

"The traditional one: My body, to use for your pleasure. I know you are a lonely formless God, after all, who loves women and the pleasures of the flesh. Which are now denied you."

"A tempting offer."

"And if you grant me the ability to bend the will of my current boss as well, Erle "Old Man" Wilson, then a human sacrifice, of course."

"Human sacrifice! Hold the phone. Are you telling me you are willing to fuck this thing and kill someone to get that client?!"

She met his eyes, with a slow smile on her face, "Yes, Peter, I am. I told you I wanted that job."

"It's just a job! You are a cold conniving bitch!"

Peter hadn't even heard him move, but suddenly, the pink god was right behind him, sweet-smelling and fever hot.

"The terms please us." The god said, breath like a desert wind on Peter's neck. His hands were suddenly on his shoulders. "Requests Granted."

Genevieve smiled, "Told you, Peter, I was going to get ahead of you, no matter what. And I am going to get Brenner, and then I am going after the Old Man. I've worked hard. Harder than you. Harder than any of you. But I've hit my glass ceiling. At least courting the god's favor is a little less icky then compromising my pristine work history. And if this is what I need to get by..." She shrugged. "I'll change it when I'm in charge.

And then the Pink God was on him. He didn't even have time to scream.

GRANDMA'S DEAD, ISN'T SHE?

by TS Alan

Mrs. Morrison was too busy to die. At 96 years old, she was the captain and star of her 4-person bocce team, the Weirton Knights. The team was sponsored by the Knights of Columbus Hall in the town she lived in since the time she had been born. She had so much life to live and so many more tournaments to win. Unfortunately, she was dead, but she was the only one that wasn't aware of it.

Amanda Morrison and her team had just won the West Virginia Italian Heritage Festival Tournament in Shinnston, West Virginia. It was the second year her team had participated in the event, and the first year they took home the coveted trophy. Amanda was very quiet on the two-hour drive back to Weirton, but her daughter Mendi attributed it to her being tired. After all, her mother may have been a spry senior, but bocce was a tough and demanding sport on her elderly mother, and today had been a very long day of competition.

Amanda did not rise and come to the kitchen by 7:15 am, as she did every morning for the past 22 years. Shortly after 7:30 am, Mendi became alarmed and went to check on her. She found Amanda still in bed with a smile on her face and the bocce tournament trophy lying in bed next to her. Mrs. Amanda Morrison was pronounced deceased at 8:42 am by paramedics, but Amanda wouldn't stay dead for long.

Emily Lynn and Jaime were heartbroken at the news that their beloved grandmother had passed away, and the entire family was aghast when Amanda strolled into the living room at 9:07 am, dressed and ready to take on a new day.

"Grandma's dead, isn't she?" Emily Lynn asked her mother,

seeing her grandmother step sprightly from the hall entry into the living room.

"Dead!" Amanda exclaimed. "Do I look dead, child? Come and give grandma her morning hugs, my little beauties," she requested, gesturing with open arms. However, Emily Lynn and Jaime were hesitant about hugging a dead person, even a grandmother who they loved dearly. The two girls had gone to their grandmother's bedroom and saw her pale, lifeless body. There was no doubt grandma was dead; even the death certificate declared grandma was deceased. Emily Lynn and Jaime grimaced at the thought of hugging a cadaver.

"What's gotten into yall?" Amanda asked, seeing the trepidation and fright in her family's faces.

"Mama," Mendi finally spoke up. "You're supposed to be dead."

"Dead? What's all this talk about me being dead? Do I look dead?"

In fact, Mrs. Morrison did look dead, or at least mostly dead. She was as pale as a corpse, even though she was chipper as a songbird.

"You died in your sleep last night," Mendi tactfully tried to explain. "The paramedics even declared you dead," Mendi informed and then held up the paper for her mother to see.

"Just cause I overslept a spell doesn't mean I'm dead. And that piece of paper in yore hand is nothin'. Fools!" Amanda pronounced. "Them paramedics are fools. I feel as fit as a fiddle. Now, what about breakfast?"

At 10:30 am, a hearse from the Griegs-Hartman Funeral Home arrived to pick up Amanda for preparation for burial, except Amanda wasn't home. She had put on her walking shoes and headed to the senior center to play checkers with some of her friends.

"Good morning. The transport attendant greeted Mendi. We're here to pick up your dearly departed, Mrs. Amanda Morrison," the man stated, and then handed Mendi a business card, identifying himself as the assistant funeral director. "And where is your loved one now?" he asked.

Mendi momentarily hemmed and hawed, not sure how to

explain that her deceased mother had got up, ate a huge breakfast, and then walked the mile and a half to the town senior center to "steal some quarters from the old farts," as Amanda called her business of fleecing her friends out of money they bet on their checker games.

"I understand how difficult this time can be, but I assure you, Griegs-Hartman Funeral Home has been serving the families in the tri-state area of West Virginia, Pennsylvania, and Ohio since 1922. And for three generations, we have prided ourselves on providing trustworthy, attentive services with compassion, care, and great attention to detail. I personally promise we will take the utmost care and show the due respect your loved one deserves throughout this difficult time or my name isn't John Calvin Griegs. Now, where may we find your loved one?"

Mendi could not tell the man that her dead mother was alive again; it was preposterous and impossible. The dead do not come back to life. She apologized to John Calvin Griegs and informed him there had been a terrible mistake in which her mother was mistakenly declared dead. Mr. Griegs bid her a farewell and the parting words that when the time was needed, he hoped she would call upon the services of Griegs-Hartman.

Many of Amanda's friends at the senior center took notice of her post mortem paleness and her purplish-red discoloration of her fingertips, commenting that she looked a bit peaked and needed to get a little sun. However, the state of her body didn't affect Amanda's ability to win at checkers. Though she was a little off her game, she had only won fourteen out of the twenty she had played, losing two more than she usually did. However, she still made six dollars for the day, which she would deposit into a 1950s wide mouth glass pickle jar that she used as a money jar to keep her weekly checker winnings. Amanda would use the money every year to buy her twin granddaughters something special on their birthday.

By day ten, Amanda began to show signs of rigor mortis and putrefaction. She had difficulty getting out of bed due to stiffness in her joints and muscles. Her fingers and toes were turning black, her skin was sloughing off, she was a bit gaseous and slightly bloated, and she began to have a distinct body odor. Although she barely perceived her noxious odor of rotten flesh, her family and friends had smelled an increasing stench of decay for the past several days.

Amanda knew by her poor complexion, her blackened fingers and toes, and the growing stiffness in her joints and achy muscles that she might have a condition, but it wasn't going to stand in her way. The third Thursday of every month was Bingo night at the Knights of Columbus Hall, and she never missed a Bingo night. It was the most lucrative day of the month to make more money for the pickle jar.

Amanda walked into the hall and paid for her cards, and immediately her "condition" got attention. As she passed and said hello to many of the regulars, she received many looks of disgust and a few people who seemed the most offended immediately withdrew handkerchiefs and put them to their faces. Amanda had no concept that she was offending everyone with her decaying appearance, her nasty stink, nor the flies that were buzzing around her. Amanda attributed the rejections to envious players because she always walked away a large winner when others didn't.

Amanda took her usual seat in the front table by the caller. But the usual participants that normally sat around her immediately departed after she took her seat. She paid them no mind; it was more room for her to spread out her bingo cards.

The Bingo Hall did not have air conditioning. On warm, muggy nights, the hall relied solely on large fans to circulate the air from the open doors and windows. Tonight was an extremely warm and muggy summer evening, and the fans were at their optimum setting. It took only a few minutes for the entire hall to be thoroughly circulated with Amanda's prodigious stench. Bingo for the evening was called off.

Mendi came and picked up her mother and kept the windows rolled down all the way home. Mendi was at her wit's end. If her mother didn't believe she was dead, then she would have to prove it to her. In the morning, she would call the paramedics again and have Amanda re-examined and declared deceased again.

"I'm confounded, Mrs. Antigo," the paramedic told Mendi. He had been the same paramedic who had declared Amanda dead just eleven days earlier. "I can't get a pulse, and I don't hear a heartbeat," he continued. "And if I didn't know better, I'd say the stiffness your mother is experiencing is the onset of rigor mortis, and her dead flesh and the rancid smell is putrefaction."

"You, young man, don't have the sense God gave a billy goat," Amanda interjected, taking offense to being talked about as if she was dead. "Rigor mortis my behind! It's just a touch of arthritis, that's all. Just need to get up and go for my walk. Then I'll be as fine as a fiddle again."

"Mrs. Morrison. With all due respect ma'am, you're clinically dead," the paramedic bluntly stated.

"He's about as confused as a fart in a fan factory," she announced. "Dead! Does a dead person talk? Cause I'm talking here."

The paramedic turned back to Mendi. "I simply don't have an explanation. By medical opinion, she's clinically deceased, but like she says, she talking. She needs to go to the hospital. Maybe they can figure out why she's decomposing."

"Dead, dead, dead," Amanda stated. Then looked at her daughter and said, "I ain't going to no hospital. I haven't seen the inside of a hospital since I gave you birth, and I have no plans on a second visit. Now let me be. I have gardening to do."

Amanda knelt in her flower garden, cultivating as the buzzing flies landed on her to lay their eggs, and the ants crawled onto her to feed off her dead flesh. Amanda was too occupied with thoughts of bocce practice on Saturday to notice the insects. Bocce meant the world to her and was the most important thing in her life outside of her family.

Emily Lynn and Jaime had been so traumatized at their grandmother's walking state of deterioration and toxic odor that Mendi had to send them to stay with her cousin Michelle in Ohio until Mendi could figure out how to get her mother to accept she was deceased.

After much thought, Mendi realized the more she tried to convince her mother she was dead, the more Amanda refused to believed she had passed away. Reverse psychology was in order. Mendi would treat her mother as the spry and intuitive person she had been before her sudden demise. Mendi was going to take her to bocce practice. Amanda's dead condition was well known throughout her circle of friends and the talk of the community and by day twelve, no one that knew her wanted to be anywhere near her. Her friends couldn't understand why Amanda refused to accept she was deceased, but Mendi had a plan. Mendi telephoned the members of Amanda's bocce team and explained.

With cotton stuck up their noses and generous portions of tiger balm placed above their upper lips, the Weirton Knights split into two, two-person teams and began their practice against each other. Bowl after bowl, Amanda could not seem to get the ball down the court to the jack to score. Game after game, her team lost. As morning drew to afternoon, the sun and heat began to take its effect on Amanda. Amanda began to bloat like a dead whale under the hot sun at the beach until she finally exploded, spewing rancid intestines onto the bocce court. However, Amanda was stubborn. The minor inconvenience of rotting intestines dangling from her stomach cavity was not going to get in the way. She was determined to win at least the final game.

With all her strength, Amanda bowled the ball, and as she did, her right arm tore from her shoulder and landed several feet in front of her. As she looked down at her detached bowling arm, she realized there was nothing left to live for. Amanda apologized to her teammates for her refusal to accept she was dead. Amanda did not speak another word that day. She picked up her arm and headed directly to Mendi's car and got into the passenger seat. Upon arriving home, she immediately went to her room and closed her door.

In the morning, Amanda did not rise early and come to the kitchen for breakfast as she had done for the past 22 years. When her daughter Mendi went to check on her mother, she found Amanda still in bed with a sad expression on her face and the bocce tournament trophy she had won over a week ago lying in bed next to her. Mrs. Amanda Morrison had died in her sleep, twelve days after she had been pronounced deceased.

WINTER PREY

by R.A. Goli

Sleet and rain sluiced from the windscreen as the wipers did their monotonous work. The tires momentarily lost traction, and the car's rear fishtailed slightly until Brent brought the vehicle under control.

"Crap."

He slowed down, leaning towards the windscreen for a better view of the road ahead. He'd need to pull over and put the chains on. He'd hoped to be home well before it'd started snowing, but luck nor the weather were on his side.

The road widened, and he saw the slip lane to turn off into the rest stop up ahead. He eased the sedan off the main road and pulled into a car space. He turned off the engine and scanned the area. There were no other vehicles around, but that didn't surprise him, given the lateness of the hour and the weather. The headlights punched beams of light through the dark, illuminating white flakes as they fell to the ground, adding to the slush. He had planned to leave the campsite no later than six p.m., but had gotten stuck helping a fellow hiker who had injured his leg and was struggling to pack up his gear. So, Brent hadn't left until almost eight, and his wife was pissed when he called. Being a nice guy didn't pay some days.

He needed to take a leak, so he left the relative warmth of the car and headed towards the dark concrete box that was the toilet. His feet sank into the snow, and he shivered at the icy chill. He clumped towards the building, his gaze eyeing the mysterious and ominous shapes amidst the nearby trees.

He thought he heard a snort and paused to peer into the woods.

The trees themselves sagged from the weight of their snow-laden branches, and shifting shadows made Brent's skin crawl.

"You're an idiot," he muttered to himself, then continued to the restroom.

A low growl from behind him froze him in place. He slowly turned his head. At the edge of the trees loomed the hulking mass of a large animal.

What the fuck is that? Is that a wolf? It was much larger than a wolf, but Brent couldn't imagine what other animals might be lurking in the woods. The area was not known for bears.

The creature shot out from the trees, loping on all fours, and Brent ran. He skidded through the toilet block's entrance and fell clumsily inside. He could hear the sound of crunching snow as the animal's feet galloped towards him. He scrambled up and rushed into the cubical, slamming the metal door and sliding the lock closed.

He stood to the rear of the stall waiting for the beast to come inside. His lungs threatened to seize with each cold breath of air he sucked in. His pulse pounded in his ears like he was slapping a hand against the sides of his head. He leaned against the brick wall, his breathing rapid. Then he heard it. The sound of nails tapping the concrete as the creature entered the building. Fear twisted his insides.

What the hell? Is it going to eat me?

Brent remained as still and silent as he could, knowing the animal could smell and hear him anyway.

"Go away, please go away, please go away" he mouthed.

Bang.

Brent jumped as the door was hit. Then there was a scraping sound, like metal on metal. Sweat poured down his face and stung his eyes. He fumbled into his pocket for his cell. For a moment, everything was quiet. Brent strained to listen. He turned on the phone and was relieved to see he had service and plenty of battery. In the light of the cell, he thought he could see a form under the door. Two dark shapes, as large as bear paws. He turned on the phone's flashlight and aimed it towards the door.

"Oh my God," he let out a shuddering breath. There were two paws visible under the door, but they didn't belong to wolf or bear. Each one was black as ink, and no fur covered them. Instead, they appeared hard, like the exoskeleton of a lobster or cockroach. The piss Brent had momentarily forgotten about flowed in a torrent down his leg. The beast screeched and thrust itself against the door, causing a sizable dent. Brent flinched and dropped the phone. It clattered to the floor and spun in a circle. He steeled himself, squatted and stretched his left arm towards it. The beast struck. Sharp claws raked through his hand, leaving loose flaps of skin and angry red gashes. A scream of agony erupted from his chest as pain radiated up his arm.

Large droplets of blood splashed onto the floor right next to the cell. Before he could do anything, a huge paw slid underneath the door, the middle of three clawed toes stretched forward and hooked the cell. Then the paw retreated back under the door, taking the phone with it. He saw the creature's foot slam down, breaking the cellphone into pieces.

"Holy fuck." A worm of fear spiraled through his gut. He had to get out of there. He tapped his pocket, his keys jingled reassuringly. He just needed to get back to the car. Then he'd drive off, fuck the snow and the chains! He grabbed the bottom of his t-shirt awkwardly in his injured hand and tore a large piece off, then wrapped it around his wound, using his mouth to tie the knot.

As though sensing Brent's plan, the creature bashed the door again. The metal screeched and bent towards him. Brent looked around. Above him was a small window, covered with old plastic slats. He was a lean man and felt confident he would be able to squeeze through. He climbed onto the toilet seat and punched his elbow through the plastic. It broke out easily and landed on the snow outside with barely a sound. He paused to listen, to ascertain if the creature knew what he had done. As it bashed the door again, Brent thrust his arm through the window, punching out the remaining slats. Once clear, he stood on the cistern and hoisted himself through the window. The brick was rough and scraped his palms. He winced but shimmied forward until his body was outside, and only his legs were in the window, pressed firmly against the sides to slow his descent. He relaxed them and fell headfirst into the snow. The landing was soft. He got to his feet and moved quietly to the side of the building. He could still hear the sound of the metal bending and weakening. He pulled his keys from his pocket once he reached the front of the building. The noise from inside had stopped. Brent's terror swelled as the massive black creature stepped into the night. It was bigger than a bear. It sat on its haunches, front legs firmly planted in the snow. Its misshapen body almost taller than the building. It turned its head in Brent's direction, and his heart stopped. But the creature didn't move. Instead, it looked forward again, towards the road.

It's toying with me. Brent calculated the distance to the car. Could he make it? He didn't have a choice. He had to try. He took a deep breath, then bolted. When he was close enough, he pressed the car's remote and unlocked it. He yanked the driver's door open and threw himself inside. His panting fogged up his window, and he had to rub his sleeve against it to see. The creature sat in the same spot, eyeing Brent with what looked like four large eyes. The things twisted spine transformed and stretched, and now Brent could see they were wings. It unfurled them until they blocked out the light of the toilet building. Then it disappeared into the black night.

A moment later, there was a massive thump on the roof of the car. The weight of the creature caused it to bend inwards. Brent fumbled with his keys, trying desperately to jam them into the ignition. Finally, he managed and started the engine. It spluttered to life, and Brent put it in gear and planted his foot on the accelerator. The creature flew up from the roof and landed with a crash on the hood, forcing the front of the car down into the snow. The engine squealed. Brent watched as the creature ripped through the metal. It flung pieces aside. Brent scurried into the back seat. He couldn't see what the thing was doing, but a moment later the engine died. Everything was quiet.

It stared at him through the windscreen as Brent cowered in the back. Then it pressed its face close to the glass, and Brent could see the rows of sharp, yellow teeth, dripping with viscous goo. It jumped onto the ground beside the car, moving on all fours now, the car windows meeting the height of its shoulder. When it reached the back window, it lowered its head to glare at him. Brent scurried back toward the opposite side, shifting as the creature moved to the car's rear. It leaned on the car, making the front come up out of the snow. The trunk. Brent slowly lowered one half of the back seat. If he could get to his pack, maybe he could do something. Staying in the car surely meant death. Eventually, the beast would become bored with its game and rip the vehicle apart.

He crouched through the gap, his arm extended, grasping for the backpack. He moved forward until he was half inside the cavernous storage space. The creature banged its huge paws down and the metal crumpled, like a discarded candy-bar wrapper. Brent felt a sharp scrape across his shoulder and sucked in a breath. He managed to hook his fingers around the strap and pulled, then shimmied backward just before the trunk's lid collapsed inward. He rifled through the contents of a side pocket until he felt the cold plastic of the flare gun.

The creature embedded its sickle-like claws into the metal and tore it loose. The rear window shattered, peppering Brent with cubes of glass. With shaking hands, he loaded a flare into the gun, aimed and fired. The flare burst forth like a firecracker into one of the creature's right eyes. It let out an anguished screech, gripped the sides of the car and flung it sideways. The vehicle rolled. Brent gripped the gun tightly. He bounced around the car's interior until it settled onto its roof. Adrenaline surged through him like water through a hose. Any bumps and bruises inflicted upon his body were worries for another time. He caught his breath and He fished out the remaining three flares and shoved them into his pocket.

The creature pawed at its face, stomping around, like a child having a tantrum. Brent crawled through the window, dragging his pack with him. He fished out the fuel bottle normally reserved for lighting his stove and hastily unscrewed the lid. The creature rushed him. Gas splashed across the thing's chest as it swung an arm at Brent. It's razor sharp claws sliced through Brent's clothing and into his stomach. Hot fluid soaked his jacket and pain spread through his abdomen and back.

He aimed the gun and fired. The beast's chest exploded in flames, and it took flight. Brent reloaded and shot, tearing a hole through its left wing. The creature dropped to the snow, its wings wrapping around it protectively. It writhed and squealed, rolling over, trying in vain to douse the flames. The blistering heat caused the creature's carapace to pop and sizzle, the surrounding snow to melt. Brent watched in horror and relief as the chitinous outer-shell melted away. The flesh underneath burned like pig fat, and he felt the urge to vomit.

Eventually, the alien creature stopped moving; its squeals reduced to whimpers. When the flames finally died down, they had consumed almost everything. All that remained was a charred lump of blackened flesh. Brent could no longer tell what it was. He wondered briefly if anyone would believe his story, then realized he didn't care. He loaded the last flare and aimed the gun high. The flare whizzed into the sky and shone like a beacon. He lay back, his hand clutching his bleeding belly and watched the bright blaze. He hoped someone would come in time.

THE LUSH WOODS

by Matthew M. Montelione

Ridge, Eastern Long Island, New York.
August 1900.

Helen Rains relished the sunshine as it drenched her skin and the lush grounds of her family's estate in bright yellow. "There's nothing like a hot summer's day," she thought as she patted down loose soil around the bell pepper plants in the garden. She loved the humid sea-soaked Long Island air. Summertime rendered her altogether happy and energetic. Still, she had been gardening for hours, and it was time to head inside. Her father, Dr. Walter Rains, told her earlier that a thunderstorm was expected in the late afternoon, and thick gray clouds already encroached on the sun.

Helen stood up and brushed the dirt off her knees. She was suddenly startled by the sight of something strange out of the corner of her left eye. For a brief moment, it looked like there were many pairs of large sunken eyes embedded in the thick oak trees that bordered the estate. She almost felt them staring at her. She rubbed her eyes and stared back at the woods. "Nothing. It must be in my head," she assured herself. "Too much sun."

Helen strolled towards her house and admired the beauty of the vast gardens. Her father was a dedicated botanist who spared no expense in growing the biggest and most diverse plants on all Long Island. He grew native and foreign plant species alike, which bloomed in brilliant colors in the spring and summer. She stopped next to the sunflower field and breathed in deep their scent. Somehow, she felt connected to the plants around her. She enjoyed their quiet company over people, who generally annoyed her. It was better off that way because her parents were overprotective and never let her venture outside of their rural town.

The sun disappeared behind a thick cloud as thunder rumbled above. Soft raindrops landed on Helen's head, and within seconds it started to downpour. She sprinted towards the front door. Whenever a storm hit, the family's housekeeper Mrs. Cotes had a habit of reminding her that thunder was God's way of letting humanity know that he was angered by their sins.

The family butler William Crawley opened the door and greeted her. He was a spritely young man with a long face. Mr. Crawley hardly ever missed answering someone's call at the front door, even if they hadn't yet called out to him. His family had served the Rains family for generations. "Just in time, Miss Rains," he said as he shut the door behind her. "Sir Walter warned us of the storm. He said it shall get worse before it is better. Shall I bring you some tea, Miss?"

"No, thank you, Crawley," Helen said with a smile as she shook her curly red hair dry. "Is father still in the greenhouse?" She didn't know why she asked the question because she already knew the answer. Dr. Rains was always in his greenhouse.

"Indeed, Miss Rains. He's been in there all day," Mr. Crawley replied.

"Not surprising," Helen said.

Like Helen, Dr. Rains preferred the company of plants over humans. But beyond their mutual passion for vegetation, the two weren't much alike. Helen was sensitive and had an overall cheerful disposition. She enjoyed living in the moment and the little things in life, like soaking up the sunshine. Dr. Rains showed love only for his work. He was a selfish and callous man who made little time for his family. His facial expressions were usually tense, and he seemed burdened by something dreadful – something he never spoke about. At least, not to Helen. Indeed, he hardly ever had much to say to her at all, except when it involved his projects. Her odd relationship with her father upset her, but she was used to it.

Helen made her way upstairs and into her room. It was large and quiet and decorated with various plants that reached towards the windows. She peered out of her western-facing window at the forest in the distance, where earlier she thought she saw those queer eyes. The woods looked dark and gloomy within as if the storm clouds had laid an ominous black pall over them, but there were no eyes to be seen. She thought about mentioning her strange vision to her parents, but she knew they'd call her mentally unstable. Perhaps she would tell Mrs. Cotes about it if it still bothered her later. Mrs. Cotes always made her feel comfortable and never judged her too harshly.

Helen laid down on her soft bed. She closed her eyes and listened to the soothing sounds of the wind and seemingly endless rain smacking against the roof. Her mind wandered wherever it wanted. She imagined the gusts of wind being blown by an exhaling giant outside and smiled at the thought. At that moment, a knock came at her door and interrupted her enjoyable quiet.

"Miss Rains," the familiar voice of Mr. Crawley rang out, "Lady Rains requests your presence in the drawing room."

"Ugh," Helen thought as she returned to reality. She looked at her clock and sighed. It was four o'clock in the afternoon, the usual time her mother, Lady Gladys Rains, forced her to play the harpsichord for her. In truth, Helen played the instrument beautifully, and she liked it. What she didn't care for was being demanded to play it for her mother's amusement nearly every afternoon.

Lady Rains was the exact opposite of her husband. She craved attention and conversation and much preferred the company of others over solitude, and certainly over plants. Indeed, she cared little for plants, although she pretended well when Dr. Rains rambled on about his work. She dutifully listened to his talks, but always admitted to Helen afterward that she couldn't wait until the subject was changed. She found the entire topic dull.

Helen's mother enjoyed local gossip - who was marrying who, which families feuded with one another, who was becoming destitute, and the like. She entertained many prominent women each week, and they talked for hours about such trivial matters. Much to Helen's chagrin, Lady Rains always invited her to join them. Helen obeyed out of respect, but couldn't wait to break away from the humdrum of the conversation. She oftentimes had to fight the urge to fall asleep in her chair. She certainly did not contribute much to the gossip and took to conversing with herself in her head while tortured by such discussions.

A shared love of music was one of the only things Helen and her mother bonded over, so even though it felt like a chore, she dragged herself out of her room and ventured downstairs to the drawing room. Lady Rains was waiting for her on the sofa, dressed in ruby and sipping red wine.

"There you are, darling," Lady Rains said cheerfully as she rubbed her slender index finger around the rim of her wine glass. "Will you play me some Vivaldi tonight?"

"Sure, mother," Helen unenthusiastically said as she sat down at the harpsichord. "At least Vivaldi is my favorite composer," she thought. She set her slim fingers to the keys and started to play. She fell into a state of pensiveness, just like she had moments before while she listened to the storm, taken away by the sweet sounds of her instrument. For a few moments, she forgot all about her attention-starved mother sipping her drink on the sofa. Although Helen loved her mother perhaps more than her father, she admitted to herself that it was a good feeling.

Suddenly they heard the opening of the front door. Dr. Rains came into the house and effectively ended Helen's tranquility and Lady Rain's enjoyment. Mr. Crawley ran over to him and helped take off his rain-soaked lab coat. Dr. Rains was muttering things under his breath that Helen couldn't understand from the drawing room, but she gathered that he was frustrated. As usual.

"Come in, dear," Lady Rains called out to her husband, "Helen was just entertaining me with such beauteous tones. She gets better every day."

Dr. Rains ignored her comment and made his way to the drawing room. "Has Sir Brewer prepared dinner? I am starved."

Lady Rains sighed. "How would I know? As I said, I have been listening to Helen play." Lady Rains shot an appreciative smile at her daughter, which was quickly reciprocated.

"Good afternoon, father," Helen started, "or shall I say good evening? I've always thought the delineation between the two was rather up for debate." Helen smirked as Lady Rains let out a slight chuckle.

"Hello, Helen," her father dryly said. And that was it.

"I tried. Yet again," Helen thought.

There were some seconds of quiet, save for the sounds of Lady Rains sipping her wine. Finally, Mrs. Cotes entered the room and announced that dinner was set for them in the dining room. Helen enjoyed the tasty meat and vegetable soup, but dinner was no different than any other night. The family sat in silence, and once Dr. Rains was finished, he got up and went upstairs to his study. He shut the door behind him and, like every night, would remain there until the late hours. Dr. Rains wrote profusely, filling notebooks with daily details about his experiments. A few times in the past, Helen snuck into the room and tried to read his papers. She had difficulty understanding her father's sloppy handwriting and learned little from them.

After dinner, Helen went to the drawing room and sat on the sofa. She leaned over to the end table and picked up her book, Charles Darwin's On the Origin of Species. It was one of her favorite works, even though she had only read about half of it so far. Darwin's theory of natural selection fascinated her. For about an hour, she explored the world of natural science through Darwin's words. She loved reading after dinner because then she was usually undisturbed by her mother. Her eyelids soon grew heavy, and she retired to bed.

Helen didn't stay asleep long. Although she had brushed it aside while awake, her slumbering mind led her to the dreadful eyes in the forest. She had a horrible nightmare where she found herself unable to speak in the middle of the dark wood. Then she saw them. The sunken yellow eyes embedded in the thick oak trees. Bloodshot eyeballs darted in every direction, until, all at once, they leered at her. She tried to scream but found that she couldn't. She felt paralyzed and couldn't run away. Columns of dirt shot up around her ankles and pulled her downward. Just before her head was swallowed underground, she awoke in a sweat.

A dark figure was shaking her. "Wake up, Miss Rains! Wake up!" Mrs. Cote's familiar voice rang out to her.

Helen's heart was beating fast. Her body slowly adjusted from the dream world to the real world. "Mrs. Cotes..." she answered in a haze.

"Yes, dear, it's me. You were having a nightmare. I heard your screams from beyond the hall," she said as she propped Helen up in bed.

"Thank goodness for you," Helen said as she smiled, glad that the nightmare was just that. "It was horrible. I dreamt that... well..." Helen paused. She suddenly wasn't sure if she wanted to blurt out what she saw in the woods earlier. "Nevermind. You're going to think that I'm crazy."

Mrs. Cotes chuckled and rubbed her back. "Oh, go on, dear."

"In my dream, I saw something that I spotted earlier in the forest. There were great yellow eyes in the trees. I'm sure it was a figment of my imagination, but this dream felt so real, and now I'm second-guessing myself. This was real... real and scary." Helen put her face in the palms of her hands.

Mrs. Cotes stopped rubbing Helen's back. "You saw... what?"

"Eyes in the forest," Helen replied. "I know it sounds mad."

Mrs. Cotes brushed Helen's hair out of her face and flashed a smile. It seemed like a fake smile, but there was no reason for Mrs. Cotes to be fake. Not to Helen. "A teenage mind is a wild place, dear," Mrs. Cotes said. "You're growing up so fast that sometimes it's hard to truly understand what's around you. Rest assured, you saw no such thing. No eyes. Indeed, stay away from that forest, dear. It's no place for a proper lady."

Helen wasn't completely satisfied with Mrs. Cotes's words of comfort, but that was that. No point in fishing for words of solace at three o'clock in the morning.

Mrs. Cotes rose from Helen's bedside. "I brought you some water. It's on your nightstand."

Helen grabbed the water and drank it down. "Thank you, Mrs. Cotes. Another glass, please."

"Of course, dear," the housekeeper kindly said and left the room to fetch another glass of water. After she brought it and took her leave, Helen forced herself to return to sleep. It was an uneasy rest.

Helen awoke around seven o'clock in the morning. She was exhausted but got out of bed and drew the curtains. The warm light perked her up and bathed the room in yellow. She got dressed, went downstairs, and had breakfast with her mother. Dr. Rains had missed breakfast and was already in his greenhouse. Helen wondered if he ever slept. She went out into the garden, just as she had the day before.

Helen felt energetic again after a few hours of gardening. She loved dirtying her hands with loose ground. She had almost forgotten all about the eyes in the woods until she heard it.

A blood-curdling scream.

It was loud, drawn-out, and ended in a sort of gargled moan. It was a moan of pain. There was no doubt about it. It came from the forest.

Helen's heart skipped a beat as she looked to the trees and saw the eyes. Those wretched, staring eyes! Her mind raced. She couldn't keep it from her parents anymore. In a panic, Helen ran over to her father's greenhouse.

"Father! Father!" she yelled as she dashed across the lawn.

She came to her father's greenhouse and, despite her fears, marveled at the ornate beauty of the iron and glass structure. She loved the greenhouse but was hardly ever allowed in it. She recently snuck in when Dr. Rains wasn't home and admired the growing plants in all their summer majesty: vibrant hollyhocks, ivy-leaf geraniums, violets, and more grew among young trees consisting of white and red oaks, red maples, and various spruces and elms. Soil was everywhere, in buckets, in bags, or heaped in piles. Burners, test tubes, racks of filled and unfilled vials and beakers, a microscope, and other apparatus were set on tables amid the botanic splendor.

Dr. Rains emerged from the greenhouse. He looked frustrated. "What madness plagues you, Helen?" he coldly asked. His wavy brown hair was wet with sweat that dripped over his dirtied face. He had an empty beaker in his hand that was stained with the remnants of some sort of thick green liquid. His lab coat was blotched with green and brown.

"Screaming eyes!" was all that Helen could initially muster. The strange eyes, her nightmare, and now the screams were too much for her to handle. She was anxious and confused. She took a deep breath. "I saw screaming eyes in the forest!"

Her father squinted and looked peculiarly at her. Helen wasn't in the mood.

"Father, I am not daft. I know what I saw! There were big eyes in the forest, and they just wailed. Did you not hear it?!" Helen put her hands crossly on her hips. She waited with wide eyes for her father's answer.

Dr. Rains sighed. "No, daughter, I did not," he said as he shook his head and rubbed the bridge of his nose. "I suggest you go inside and rest. Mrs. Cotes informed me that you didn't sleep well last night."

As usual, Dr. Rains didn't take Helen seriously and dismissed her concerns. "Why did I think it would have been any different this time?" she thought as she fumed, unsure of what to say next. She knew that he wouldn't care if she told him she couldn't sleep well because of a nightmare about the eyes, so she stayed silent.

Dr. Rains grew impatient. "I have work to do. Go inside, young lady. That's not a request."

Helen fumed. "Ugh! I'm sixteen years old for goodness' sake. He cannot demand me anymore!" she thought. She wanted to speak her mind to her father, to tell him how she really felt about his insensitive ways. But her hands were shaking, and her mind was still processing that god-awful scream. She knew that her quest for information wasn't over, but instead of putting up a fight, Helen just put her head down and consented to go inside.

Dr. Rains flashed her an awkward sort of half-smile for her obedience and returned to the greenhouse.

Helen pushed through the front door. She was sick of feeling emotionally rejected by her father. Mr. Crawley greeted her as she trampled through the house, but she ignored him. She wasn't in the mood for chit-chat and felt truly alone, like she had nobody to talk to. She went into her room and shut the door behind her.

"I *know* what I heard. The forest screamed. My nightmare. The eyes. What if the forest is alive?" She sat on the edge of her bed and stared at the wall. There, in silence, she remained until she was called down for dinner. Although she wasn't in the mood anyway, she thought it odd that her mother hadn't called her down to play the harpsichord. That was the first night in weeks that Lady Rains didn't request music. "Oh well," Helen thought, relieved that she didn't have to entertain her mother in such a fragile emotional state.

Dinner was more unpleasant than usual. The silence was truly deafening. Lady Rains, who tried to keep some resemblance of a conversation flowing, looked down at her wine, heartily sipped it, and repeated the process. She started to wobble in her seat. Dr. Rains ate slowly and was very grim. The servants looked troubled, especially Mr. Crawley and Mrs. Cotes. Helen felt numb, dealing with her internal struggles while trying to figure out what had the entire house lost in a black cloud. She ate well but didn't enjoy her food. At last, her father broke the uncomfortable quiet. She wished that he hadn't.

"You are no longer permitted to leave this house, Helen. Your mother and I have talked it over, and we have deemed that it is for the best."

Helen's heart skipped a beat. "What?" she instinctively asked. It was like someone just shattered a glass vase on the table. She knew what he had said, but she didn't understand why he said it. "What did I do that was so wrong?!" Her mind started racing.

"Mrs. Cotes told us about your nightmare," her father started.

"Oh, so you do care? You have a horrible way of showing it," Helen thought.

"Eyes in the forest? Really, Helen? And today, you run like a lunatic to my greenhouse, spewing nonsense about screaming trees. Perhaps you've had too much sun lately. You need to rest until we deem you're fit to return outside to your daily routine."

Lady Rains looked at her almost sympathetically but more mindlessly. "I'm sorry, dear, but your father is right," was all she said. Her tone was one of a defeated person.

Helen's eyes welled up with tears as she stood up from the table. Nobody was on her side. Nobody understood her or truly supported her. She ran upstairs, slammed her door shut, and wept.

Helen spent the rest of the night in her room feeling sorry for herself. Of course, her parents didn't bother to see how she was doing, but even Mr. Crawley and Mrs. Cotes stayed away. She tried to cheer herself up by reminding herself that she was the daughter of a wealthy family and didn't have to want for food and shelter. She knew of people in the village that were far worse off than she was. She heard her mother talk about those kinds of people often. Still, this recent verdict from her parents felt different. It felt final.

Around midnight, Helen tried to soothe herself to sleep, but her mind resisted. She tossed and turned, pulled the covers up to her chin, threw them down again. Nothing worked. She repeatedly snapped out of sleep at the last moment, just as the realms of waking and sleeping became blurred. Every time she awoke, she thought of the eyes in the trees. At three-thirty in the morning, at one such juncture between waking and sleeping, Helen was jolted out of bed by the sound of an anguished wail. She drew her curtains and stared outside towards the forest. "They're hiding something from me," she muttered. She knew what she had to do, and she would have no rest until she did it. She had to find out what lived in the woods that bordered her estate, and her parents' new rule wasn't going to stop her.

She slipped on her shoes and a jacket. She quietly made her way downstairs, being careful not to make the stairs creak too much. One of the servants would certainly hear her if she were too loud. She made it downstairs and secured a kerosene lamp to light her way. She slowly opened the front door. A gust of warm air rushed into the house; messy red tangles blew about her face. Helen took a deep breath and gently closed the door behind her.

Her light shoes got wet on the damp grass, but she didn't care. "Enough lies! Whatever my punishment will be for disobeying my parents, it's worth it." She was rather proud of herself, not only for breaking her parents' rule but also for having the courage to venture outside in the dark at such a late hour.

She stopped short at the border between the estate and the lush woods. The trees sighed as high winds ripped through leaves and branches. She held the lamp up in front of her; the forest was utterly black within. Pesky mosquitoes stirred all around her. She continuously swatted at them as they buzzed near her face.

"You can do this," she said, taking a deep breath. She stepped over the borderline and stood firmly in the woodland.

A strange voice bellowed from somewhere in the darkness. "Helen," the eerie voice said. "Helen, come to us."

"Who... who are you?!" Helen yelled out.

"Helen, help us," a higher voice rang out.

Then another. "Help us, Helen. We will not harm you."

"We are a part of you, Helen. Help us."

Helen followed the voices deeper into the wood. Wet summertime branches soaked her arms as she brushed past them. With every step, she grew more anxious, and her desire to abandon this insane mission altogether crossed her mind more than once. If she just turned around and headed back to bed, she could force herself to sleep. But then her parents would win. No. Why had they forbade her from leaving the house? She had to continue.

"Follow, Helen. Help us!" they called out in chilling unison.

She pursued the voices until, at last, she came to a large circular clearing. Staggered thick oaks lined the outer rim of the circle. Helen squinted in the faint light of the lamp. The black soil at the bottom of the trees looked somewhat fresh; their trunks were wrapped with colored strings .

"These trees did not naturally sprout here." Helen's eyes raced around. A person had planted them.

Suddenly, the bulbous oaks opened their eyes all at once. Yellow pupils, tinted with red, embedded in the very bark. The lamplight danced in their deep and sorrowful eyes.

Helen screamed. She tried to control her fear. "What are you?!"

The eyes stared at her.

A voice rang clearer now, but the voice was in her head. The trees had no mouths. They telepathically spoke to her! "We are your blood, Helen. Run. Run, while you still can."

"What are you talking about?" Helen started to ask aloud, but at that very moment, the oaks let out a tortured scream. It was that same heart-wrenching scream she had already heard twice, only now there were many voices screaming at her in unison.

"He comes!" the voices yelled.

Helen yelled in fright and dropped the lamp. She had had enough of this hellish place. She turned to run but tripped on a thick root that jutted out of the ground. Her body hit the dirt with a thud, she cut her right knee on a sharp rock. "Ouch!" She couldn't see how bad it was, but she felt the blood oozing down her leg. The trees stopped screaming, but their eyes still stared at her. As she sat up, she caught a glimpse of her wounded knee. "No. It couldn't be," she thought. She grabbed the lamp and pulled it closer to her wounded flesh. Her blood was viscous like oatmeal, but that wasn't the most disturbing part. Her blood was green!

Helen's heart raced. "This must be a nightmare," she said as she tried to convince herself to wake up. She pinched herself, but to no avail. This was no dream. She let out a horrified scream, and as she did, the trees joined her in unison. The darkness around her seemed to engulf her. She had no idea what to think or what to do. She just knew that she had to get out of this forsaken forest.

A shadowy man approached her. Fear gripped her as he came closer.

"Helen!" the sharp voice of her father rang out.

Although she wasn't happy with her father, she felt relieved. "I'm here!" she yelled in dismay. "Help me, father!"

The doctor made his way into the circle and kneeled next to Helen. "You're hurt," he said, but his voice was void of any sense of urgency, and he didn't say a word about the color of her blood. He took out a washcloth from his back pocket.

"Father, something is wrong with my blood," Helen said in a panic.

"Hush, child," he said as he put a moist washcloth over her wound and gently rubbed it over her cut. It burned. "I know."

"You know?" Helen asked.

Helen felt woozy and sleepy. "But... I... don't..."

"Rest now, Helen. Hush, hush. You'll be well soon," Dr. Rains said as he continued to pat her cut with the wet rag. He smiled.

She blacked out.

Helen awoke in a haze to the sound of her father's and mother's voices. She couldn't make out what they said. Her body was numb, and her vision was blurred, but judging by the wet heat around her, she could tell that she was in the greenhouse. In her daze, she couldn't recollect what had happened.

Her parents' voices gradually became clearer. She struggled to break free from her condition. Her mother was sobbing.

"I wish it hadn't come to this, Walter," Lady Rains said. "She was such a wonderful harpsichord player, and kept me company when my friends were unavailable."

"I know, Gladys. But we knew the risks of growing a teenager. They are too stubborn and inquisitive, too aware of their surroundings. She would never have stopped until she blew the lid off of my entire operation, and I'd be ruined," Dr. Rains replied with a tinge of sadness in his tone.

Lady Rains gently rested her hand on the trunk of a freshly

planted oak tree. "I suppose you'll have to try a younger child next time," she said in between her sobs.

Helen felt a hand resting on her, as if in sympathy. She tried to yell, but no words came out. She tried to squirm but found that she could not move. She was as stiff as a tree.

"How could I have foreseen that her siblings would manifest eyes and voices after I planted them?" her father asked. "It's an unfortunate yet fascinating consequence. No doubt, Helen will grow the same features soon enough."

Suddenly, a blood-curdling scream shot out from the young oak tree. Helen's parents jumped, but Dr. Rains quickly composed himself and chuckled.

"See that, dear?! Helen is already using her voice, and she hasn't even been planted a month yet! I think I'll keep her in the greenhouse for a few more weeks until moving her into the forest with the other failed experiments."

"The forest?" Lady Rains worriedly asked. "No, Walter, not there. Helen was special, and I'd like to visit her. Can't she stay in the greenhouse?"

"Well, alright, dear," Dr. Rains said as he ushered his wife towards the door. "We'll keep her in here until she grows too tall."

Helen hopelessly screamed again and again.

GIN, NEAT

by Jacob Jones-Goldstein

I was working as a truck driver back then. Usually local deliveries, but occasionally longer hauls. It wasn't great, but it felt like honest work, and it paid the bills. I was living by myself, so the hours didn't get in the way of anything. During the downtime, I liked to write. Usually short stories, but I firmly believed that I was destined to write a novel someday. I started a few but never managed to get very far.

The afternoon I met Max I was sitting in a bar on the southern shore of Boston. I had driven a delivery up from Sarasota and didn't have to be back on the road until the next morning. I'd bought a notebook and some pencils from the store next to the bar, and was indulging my love of whiskey and trying to write something. Your mind wanders during those long drives, and mine usually found its way to half-formed and half baked story ideas.

It was a miserable October day, and the place was mostly empty. A few people had come and gone since I'd staked out my real estate at the bar. When the man I would come to know as Max walked in, a gust of wind came with him, flipping the pages of my notebook. If I had been writing, I would barely have noticed, but I hadn't touched the pencil in half an hour. I was mostly staring at the handful of sentences I'd written and nursing my drink. The novel idea that seemed so perfect yesterday on the highway seemed thin and boring today.

The new guy came over to the bar and sat down a couple of stools over. Lorna, the bartender, had gone out back for a smoke, but the guy didn't seem to care. He stared at the mirror behind the bar with a haunted look that should have been enough for me to keep to myself, but the previous three or four drinks had loosened my tongue some.

"Bartender will be back in a minute," I said in my slightly southern accent.

"Thanks," he said and went back to staring at the mirror.

A few minutes passed before Lorna came back. She was a cheerful British woman who seemed too bright of spirit for a grim bar near the docks.

"What can I get ya, friend?" she asked.

"Gin, neat, please," he responded.

I raised my eyebrow at that. I'm not sure I had ever heard someone order gin neat in my entire life. In all honesty, it had never occurred to me that people drank it that way.

Lorna asked him if he had a preference, and he shrugged. She nodded and grabbed a tumbler and a mid-range bottle and poured him half a glass. He drank it in two gulps and then tapped the glass.

"Want me to leave the bottle?"

"Yes, thanks."

She poured him another two fingers and placed the bottle on the counter, "Let me know if I can get you anything else."

He nodded as she walked over to me.

"How about a refill, handsome?"

"Sure, beautiful," I responded with a smile.

She topped me off and told me to holler if I needed anything else. She grabbed a book from next to the register and went and sat in a booth along the wall. There were a couple of TVs in the place, but the sound was down on all of them, and no one seemed to have much inclination to turn it up. The radio was tuned to a jazz station.

I flipped the wind-blown pages back over and re-read the paragraph I'd written for the tenth time. The whiskey wasn't making it better.

After a few minutes, the man said to me in a flat Boston accent, "What're you writing?"

"Crap," I said. He didn't laugh.

"You a writer?"

"Truck driver, mostly, but maybe someday."

"What do you write?"

"Short stories. I've tried to write a novel a couple of times, but..." I shrugged at him.

He was silent for a minute as he finished his second drink, poured himself another, and picked up the glass. He twirled the gin around in it a little as if he was deep in thought. Finally, he slugged that back and turned to me, "I've got a story."

"Yeah?"

"Yeah. But it's not a nice one."

"Ahh."

"Want to hear it? Maybe you could write it down. Probably not gonna make a million dollars off it, though."

I looked around the bar. Everyone there was in their own quiet world, reading books or the newspaper. I had nothing else planned today, so I shrugged. "Sure, why not?"

He nodded gravely, put his drink down, and extended his hand, "My name is Max."

"Sam," I responded, shaking his hand.

Max began his story.

My parents died when I was a teenager. My uncle took me in, and I lived with him till I was 18. He worked as an oil surveyor, so he wasn't around much, but when he was, he was a good guy. When I was old enough, I went to work on an oil tanker, and eventually ended up working to build oil platforms out at sea.

It's a hard and lonely life, but I don't have many attachments, so I never minded much. Spending years at sea changes you a bit. You stop being able to function right on land or around people who aren't used to solitude.

After a few years, I got a call from my uncle. He'd been working for one of the bigger oil companies and had a little pull. He got me a job maintaining pipelines. It paid a lot better, although it wasn't any less lonely. You just end up in remote places on dry land rather than the sea.

I lost touch with my uncle. We're the same kind of guy, mostly keep to ourselves, so I didn't think much of it. Two years ago, I got a call from a person in the company to let me know that he had gone missing while doing some work in Turkmenistan. There wasn't much else to say. After a while, they declared him dead, and I got a little settlement.

I asked the company for more info, and they didn't have much information. He was working a surveying job in the desert, and one night just disappeared. That seemed weird to me, but apparently, it's not that unusual.

Anyway, last year I got sent to Turkmenistan to help work on a new pipeline. I figured while I was there I could take a day or two and ask after my uncle. I thought I owed him at least that much after he took me in and got me a job.

Max paused for a moment to pour himself another drink. He raised it and gestured to the bar mirror like he was toasting himself and downed it in one gulp. Then he continued.

I ended up in a place called Serdar, which is where my uncle's base of operations was while he was in the country. It's not much of a place—a little something surrounded by an awful lot of nothing. In the city, it's nothing but plain uninteresting buildings that look like they were built yesterday. Outside of the city is hardscrabble leading into desert. After getting acclimated, I started asking around about him. A few people who worked at the hotel and some of the bars remembered him, but mostly I was met with shrugs.

A month or so after I arrived, I was approached in a bar by a man wearing a weird combination of modern and traditional clothing. I'd seen a few people in similar dress, but not many. I got the feeling the locals didn't like them much. A co-worker who'd been in the country longer said that a lot of people resented the folks who held closer to older traditions. They thought they made them look backward around westerners.

He introduced himself as Gulsen and asked if I was the one looking for the man who disappeared. I said I was and mentioned my uncle's name. He nodded and said that he knew him and could take me to people who could help. He offered to bring me to them the next morning. This all seemed very dubious to me, but I told him I would meet him all the same. He gave me the time and place to meet and left the bar. I didn't really plan to keep the appointment. My company has drilled it into us that people would try and rob us or kidnap us and that the corporation wouldn't pay to have us released.

The barkeeper came over to me after the man had left and refilled my drink. He paused and looked around to make sure no one else was in earshot and said, "That man, he's not a criminal, but be careful around him."

This caught me off guard. I'd talked to the bartender before, but he'd never gone out of his way to talk to me, or any westerners that frequented the place.

"Why?" I asked.

"He's from out in the desert." He shrugged as if that told me everything I needed to know.

That night I had a dream about my uncle. I was flying around the desert like a bird. Soaring at high speeds and swooping up and down, scaring goats and camels. After a while, I began to gain speed, and the edges of my vision started to blur. The sand turned black, and in the distance, I could see a red glow, like a fire in the earth. I got closer and closer as the glow got brighter and brighter until a voice next to me screamed 'MAX!' I turned and saw my uncle standing in the black sand dressed in the same garb as Gulsen had been wearing. "HELP!" he shouted and then screamed as he erupted in flames.

I woke up drenched in sweat.

The next morning I went to the place Gulsen told me to meet him. He was waiting in a jeep, wearing the same clothes as the night before.

"Come," he said. "We have a long journey."

As I got into the jeep, he handed me a large bottle of water.

"It will be warm today."

"Where are we going?"

"Darvaza" was his reply. He said nothing else as he started the car and drove us out of Serdar.

We drove for a couple of hours, eventually approaching Ashgabat, the capital. It's an oddly futuristic looking city in the middle of a country where everything else seems worn out.

I asked him if that's where we were going. He said it wasn't and didn't say anything else. We skirted the city and eventually turned north and into the desert.

The road we took was different than the highway we were on before. There were no lights or buildings. We'd see the occasional structure in the distance, but it felt remote and getting remoter. I wondered if I had made a mistake. No one knew where I was, myself included.

After a few hours of driving and me getting increasingly worried, he said, "Almost there."

There was no 'there' anywhere that I could see, but after 20 minutes or so, a few buildings appeared on the horizon.

As we got closer, I saw that it was a small town, barely more than a village. It was late afternoon, but still bright enough out for me to be able to see the shabby state of things. A few people in similar dress to Gulsen milled about and watched as he pulled onto what passed for the main street.

"Darvaza," he said.

"Not much here."

"Maybe answers."

There wasn't much I could say to that.

He drove the length of the street and came to a stop at a long building that looked older than the pre-fab houses that made up most of the town. It looked like someone had built it here rather than dropped it off.

Gulsen got out of the jeep and walked over to the door, motioning for me to come with him. With some hesitation, I followed him into the building.

The temperature dropped 20 degrees inside, and the lights were dim. It looked like some kind of church or town hall. There were rows of seats and a thing that looked like an altar or a desk beyond them. There was an older man sitting there and a cardboard box on top.

"Wait here," Gulsen said and walked over to the old man. They talked quietly for a few moments and then waved me over.

"You are the nephew of Frank?" the old man said in a voice that was barely above a whisper. Up close, he looked ancient.

"Yes, he's my uncle...was. Do you know what happened to him?"

The old man gestured towards the box. I hesitated for a moment and then opened it. Inside was some clothes, a battered old hat, some well-worn boots, and a leather wallet. I picked up the wallet and flipped through it. It held my uncle's drivers license, some business cards, some cash, and other things.

I don't think I had really accepted that my uncle was dead. Seeing what appeared to be his personal effects drove it home that he was gone. I guess I had hoped that he had just decided he'd had enough and skipped out on his life.

"What happened to him?"

The old man simply said, "The desert."

"What does that mean? He just died out in the desert?"

"No," he replied. "The desert took him."

Gulsen interjected, "It's dangerous out here in the desert. Lots of ways to die."

"No," the old man said more harshly. "He did not die. The desert took him."

"I don't know what you're talking about."

"I will show you."

He got up and waved his hand towards a side door. He walked over, opened it, and went out. We followed him.

Outside, the sky had darkened considerably. The old man told us to wait and pointed towards the horizon to the north. I couldn't say how long we stood there in silence, staring out into the gloom until I started to notice a glow in the distance. It looked like what I saw in my dream the night before.

Max paused again, shook his head, and took a deep breath. He looked like a man who wasn't all that interested in remembering something.

"You sure you want to hear the rest of this?"

I nodded in response. I don't know that I believed much of what he was saying, but I had nowhere to be and still had whiskey in my glass.

He glanced at the mirror again and then continued.

"What...what is it?" I asked.

"Will show you."

"I'm not sure I want to go out there."

"You come this far, don't you want to know what happened to your uncle?"

I'm not easily spooked, but I admit that I thought about hopping in the jeep and driving back to civilization. If something happened to my uncle out here, maybe it was better just to let it lie. I couldn't though. He was the only person who ever really cared about me. The least I could do was put him to rest.

"Ok, let's go."

The old man walked around to the front of the building and climbed into the jeep. We drove out of town into the darkness along a track that could barely be called a road. After a while, I wouldn't even call it a track.

We drove through a night that was black as pitch and nearly silent. Usually, there is some sound in the desert, but out here, there was nothing. I saw no sheep, or goats, or birds. There was nothing but the red glow getting closer.

Soon the glow turned into a blaze. We crested a rise, and I saw the cause. Before us was a giant crater that was on fire. I couldn't tell how deep it was as we approached, but it was a furious red, licks of fire flickering inside and coals glowing brightly as the sun. The air felt so hot that I thought I might burst into flames the closer we got.

Gulsen parked the jeep and refused to get out. The old man exited the vehicle and began walking towards the hole. He turned once and looked me dead in the eyes. His gaze seemed different now. At the village, he seemed like a benign old man. Now, something was different. I didn't want to, but felt somehow compelled to follow him. My body began to move slowly, almost of its own accord.

I walked over to where the old man waited, and he pointed to the inferno. I could hear the fire burning, not the warm crackle of a campfire, but a hellish hum that sounded like a shriek, an unholy vibration. I wanted to scream but couldn't. All I could do was put one foot in front of the other as I got closer and closer. Behind me, I heard the sound of the jeep driving away.

Sweat was pouring from my forehead, but I couldn't move my arms to wipe it away. I shut my eyes tight and tried to blink it away. When I opened them, there were people in front of me. Maybe a dozen. All wearing clothing that looked older than old and hoods that obscured their faces. They stood on either side of me, lining my path to the pit.

I couldn't scream.

Then I was at the edge and stopped walking. The heat was unbearable. I could barely see. The sound coming from the crater was nearly deafening, then I felt a voice in my head, louder than anything I've ever heard cry, "LOOK!"

My eyes opened, and all the sweat dried away. I saw my uncle, but it wasn't my uncle, not really.

I blacked out.

Max skipped pouring the gin into the glass and took a long pull from the bottle. He then stared blankly into the mirror for a long moment.

I realized my heart was racing.

"What happened?"

He turned and stared at me, or more accurately looked clean through me before blinking, shaking his head like he just remembered where he was. He went on, "I woke up in my room in Serdar."

I woke up drenched in sweat with my head pounding. My mouth was so parched I could barely remember what moisture felt like. I got up and stumbled to the bathroom, turned on the water, and shoved my head under the tap. I lapped up the water greedily like a dog, drank too much, and immediately threw up half of it. I was utterly dehydrated and repeated the cycle of chugging the water and throwing up until I could feel my tongue again.

I crashed onto the cool tile of the bathroom floor and tried to remember. Whatever had happened after looking into the fire was gone from my memory. I didn't even know what day it was. My whole body hurt, and when I looked down at my hands and saw they were burned and red. My arms and legs were as well as if I was standing too close to a fire for a long time.

I was able to get myself to my feet and went to the mirror. I looked to see if my face was burned, and this time I did scream.

My face was reddened, and my beard singed and black, but that wasn't why I screamed. In the mirror, standing behind me was my uncle. But he looked wrong. His mouth was opened in a grin, but it was too large. He had fangs rather than teeth, hundreds of them. Everything about his features was wrong, but the worst was his eyes. They were large, too large to be human, and I could see the fire of the pit reflected in them. The thing that was and wasn't my uncle met my gaze and began to laugh. I spun around, but there was nothing behind me.

I could still hear it laugh. I looked back to the mirror, and there he was, laughing at me. Then it started talking, and the things it says to me...

He stopped there.

I was struck dumb. I'd heard some ghost stories in my day, but that one beat them all.

"Maybe you should write all that down," he said, gesturing to my notebook. "I bet people would eat it up."

I laughed. "Yeah, I bet they would."

He shook the bottle and poured some into the glass and slid it over to me. "You can have the story, just have a drink with me."

I nodded and picked up the glass. He clinked it with the bottle and took the last sip; I drank what was in the glass. It tasted better than gin usually does. My mouth was dry after listening to his tale.

He stood up from the stool and stretched his arms. He looked into the mirror again, and this time smiled.

"I have to go, but thanks for sharing a drink and an afternoon with me. Good luck to you," he said and turned towards the door. He caught himself quickly and said, "Oh, right, forgot to pay." He dug into his pocket and tossed three coins onto the bar and walked off.

I started to say something then looked at the coins; they looked gold and ancient. I turned and called over to him, "Hey, are these gold?" but he didn't respond. He just walked out the front door.

Lorna came over and asked, "Did he pay?"

"Yeah," I said, pointing at the coins.

"What the hell are these?" she asked, holding one up.

"I think they're solid gold."

She whistled.

I settled up and headed out. I had to head back to Florida the next morning and wanted to get some sleep. I went back to my room and passed out.

That night I had a dream that I was flying in the desert. I was soaring over the landscape, diving down and brushing past terrified sheep. It was dark, but in the distance, I could see a bright red glow. I turned towards it and began to pick up speed. Faster and faster, I flew towards the glow until the ground below me began to turn black as if it was scorched, and I could see flames rising ahead of me. The air whistled past me, and just as I was about to fly into the fire, I bolted awake.

I was drenched, my heart was pounding, and there was an awful noise blaring. It took me a moment to realize it was my alarm. I was late. I threw on my clothes, grabbed my bag, and ran out the door. The truck depot was a block away, and halfway through running there, I stopped and threw up in the street.

I mentally promised never to drink gin and let oil men tell me stories again.

The dispatcher was angry at my lateness, but still pointed me to the truck I would be driving. He also told me I stank. I'd have to take a shower at a truck stop.

I finally got in the truck, tossed my bag to the side, started it up, and pulled out. There was a place I could stop down the road on 95 once I was away from the city. As long as the truck was on the road, the company would be happy, and I could make up some time past Virginia.

After a while, I flipped down the visor to see how bad I looked and froze. Behind me in the mirror was Max, but not Max. His dimensions were all wrong, his mouth too big, his nose in the wrong place, and his eyes. His eyes...

And then I heard his voice, and I screamed and screamed and screamed.

"That's some story!" the guy in the blazer with the gold rugby patch on it said. "Were you ever able to sell it?"

"That's why I'm in town, meeting with a publisher," I said.

I looked at the bottle of gin. There was just enough for two.

"Well, congratulations, I look forward to seeing your book!"

"Thanks!" I said with some enthusiasm. "I should probably head out. One for the road?"

He nodded. I poured us each a drink, emptying the bottle. I slid his across the table.

"To new friends!" the man said. We both drained our glasses. I shook his hand and headed out into the cold October sun.

I avoided looking at the bar mirror on the way out.

Meet the Authors

TS ALAN is an American author of horror, supernatural fiction, and suspense, but also frequently incorporates elements of fantasy, science fiction, mystery, and satire. He is most known for his zombie stories. His first published novel was *The Romero Strain* (2014), which was originally published by Books of the Dead Press. In 2018, it was re-released with an unpublished chapter. His sequel, *The Romero Strain: The Dead, the Damned, and the Darkness* was independently released in November 2017. His third novel, *World War Dead*, will be released October 31, 2019. As influences on his writing, Alan lists Clive Barker, Dean Koontz, Stephen King, Edgar Allen Poe, and O. Henry, among others. www.tsalan.com. Facebook.com/TSAlan1. Twitter/Instagram: @tsalan1.

COLIN ANDERSON drifts through life under the oppression of the City of Newark and writes short stories every now and then.

DONALD J. BINGLE is the author of six books and more than fifty shorter works in the horror, thriller, science fiction, mystery, fantasy, steampunk, romance, comedy, and memoir genres, including *Frame Shop*, a murder mystery set in a suburban writers' group, and (with Jean Rabe) *The Love-Haight Case Files*, an paranormal urban fantasy about two lawyers who represent the legal rights of supernatural creatures in a magic-filled San Francisco. He also edited *Familiar Spirits*, an anthology of ghost stories. More on Don and his writing can be found at www.donaldjbingle.com.

LYNNE CONRAD currently lives in Cookeville, Tennessee with her family and works in the medical field. She enjoys reading, playing piano, traveling and writing. She has had stories included in *Under the Bed Magazine*, *Heater Magazine*, *Fictional Cafe*, *Sanitarium Magazine*, *Endless Night*, an anthology, and most recent, in *Bewildering Stories*. She has a facebook page at Lynne Conrad/Midnight Writer or you may send her an email at lmc.read@yahoo.com if you would like to contact her with questions or comments.

VICTORIA DALPE is a writer and artist. To date, her dark short fiction has appeared in over twenty anthologies. Her novel *Parasite Life*, came out in 2018 with *ChiZine Publications*. She also co-edited *The Necronomicon 2019 Memento Book* with Justin Steele. Victoria makes her home in Providence, RI where she lives with her husband, writer, and filmmaker Philip Gelatt and their young son.

MICHAEL FASSBENDER is a part-time writer in the Chicago area whose first literary love is supernatural horror. Poe and Lovecraft inspired him to begin writing in high school, but 2016 marked his first appearance in print media apart from a few college journals. His story "Inmate" appeared in *Sanitarium Magazine*, and "The Cold Girl" appeared in *Hypnos Magazine*. On his website, michaeltfassbender.com, there is also a short story in the tradition of Poe on the fiction page.

PHIL GIUNTA'S novels include *Testing the Prisoner*, *By Your Side*, and *Like Mother, Like Daughters*. His short stories appear in *A Plague of Shadows*, *Beach Nights*, *Beach Pulp*, the *ReDeus* mythology series, and the *Middle of Eternity* speculative fiction series. As a member of the Greater Lehigh Valley Writers Group, Phil penned stories and essays for *Write Here, Write Now*, *The Write Connections*, and *Rewriting the Past*, three of the group's annual anthologies. Phil is currently working on a science fiction novel while plotting his triumphant escape from corporate America where he has been imprisoned for over twenty-five years. www.philgiunta.com.

R.A. GOLI is an Australian writer of horror, fantasy, and speculative short stories. In addition to writing, her interests include reading, gaming, the occasional walk, and annoying her dog, two cats, and husband. Check out her numerous publications including her fantasy novella, *The Eighth Dwarf*, and her collection of short stories, *Unfettered*, at ragoliauthor.wordpress.com or stalk her on Facebook.com/RAGoliAuthor.

JOHNNY GUZMAN was born on July 1st in Los Angeles, California. Raised in Delaware, has lived in Texas, Illinois, and Maryland. A first time writer, he enjoys the works of Edgar Allan Poe and Victor Hugo. He is a huge DC Comics fan and enjoys anything that involves the Batman family. He is a self-described Pro Wrestling "mark". Born to a wonderful mother, and a proud Mexican-American citizen.

COLE JAMISON is a Real Estate agent, bartender and general rabble-rouser from the state of Delaware. While this is his first foray into professional writing, he has always been a lover of world-building and storytelling. He is an avid player of games like Dungeons and Dragons, World of Warcraft and a lover of all fantasy TV shows, movies and books (especially Mark Lawrence novels). Moving forward Cole will be writing more, special thanks to his friends at Oddity Prodigy for giving a little push and a great opportunity! Maybe someday he'll learn how to write in the correct tense.

CLOVER S. LAUREL is a Gothic fantasy and horror writer, currently residing in Delaware. Clover developed her love for literature at an early age and began writing when she was eight years old. Now twenty-five, she has self-published three books and has worked with several clients through freelance editing. When she isn't working on her own projects, she writes for a collaborative comic book series entitled *Freeloader*. Though she takes inspiration from large, epic fantasy worlds, her works tend to be more character-focused and psychological.

SCOTT MCGREGOR is a Canadian Writer residing in Calgary, as well a student at Mount Royal University, currently studying English and Sociology. His interests in the realms of fiction range from psychological horror, black comedy and dystopian science fiction. He is also a board game and caffeine addict, and has a natural ability for making people uncomfortable. Sarcastically appealing and unapologetic, Scott is either drinking tea or sassing the ones he deems as friends in the off time he isn't living and breathing stories. You can find him on Twitter at @ScottMSays

JACQUELINE MORAN MEYER is a writer, artist and small business owner living in New York. She received her master's degree from Teacher's College, Columbia University. Jacqueline has had stories published in *Yellow Mama Webzine, Bewildering Stories, Teach. Write. A Writing Teachers' Literary Journal* and *Black Hare Press Dark Drabble Anthologies: Monsters, Beyond, Unravel, Apocalypse*, and *Hate*. She also loves her family, hiking, and watching scary movies. Jacqueline's mantra: "The only time it's too late to try something new is when you're dead." jmoranmeyer.net

MATTHEW M. MONTELIONE is a horror writer born and raised on Long Island in New York. His stories have been published in *Quoth the Raven: A Contemporary Reimagining of the Works of Edgar Allan Poe, Thuggish Itch: Devilish, MONSTERS: A Horror Microfiction Anthology, Eerie Christmas*, and other titles. Matthew is also an American Revolution historian who focuses on the local experiences of Loyalists on Long Island. His work on the subject has been published in Long Island History Journal and Journal of the American Revolution. Matthew lives with his wife in New York. maybeevils.com. Twitter: @maybeevils.

MIKE MURPHY has had over 150 audio plays produced in the U.S. and overseas. He's won a dozen Moondance International Film Festival awards in their TV pilot, audio play, short screenplay, and short story categories. His prose work has appeared in several magazines and anthologies. In 2015, his script "The Candy Man" was produced as a short film under the title DARK CHOCOLATE. In 2013, he won the inaugural Marion Thauer Brown Audio Drama Scriptwriting Competition. Mike keeps a blog at audioauthor.blogspot.com.

COLIN NEWTON is a writer from Los Angeles whose fantastic fiction has appeared in *The Ignatian Literary Magazine* and the horror anthology *Crypt Gnats*. He's also been a freelance journalist in LA and an artist-in-residence at Oregon State University's Shotpouch Cabin, but don't hold that against him. He blogs irregularly about media, monsters and metaphysics at IdolsandRealities.wordpress.com.

KURT NEWTON'S stories have appeared in numerous magazines and anthologies over the years, including *Weird Tales, Dark Discoveries, Weirdbook* and *Hinnom Magazine*. He is the author of two novels, *THE WISHNIK* and *POWERLINES*. He lives in Connecticut.

JUDE REID lives in Glasgow, Scotland, and writes horror to fill the gaps between full time work, chasing her kids and trying to wear out a border collie. She likes to run away from zombies, studies ITF Tae Kwon Do and drinks a powerful load of coffee.

M.C. ST. JOHN is the author of the short story collection *Other Music* and the novella *FewBlox*. His stories have appeared, as if by luck or magic, in *Aphelion, Bronzeville Bee, Coffin Bell, Ghostlight, Quail Bell Magazine, Transmundane Press,* and *Word Branch*. Aside from the worlds he's dreamed up, he can be found in Chicago, where he teaches students how to break the rules of writing and attempts to beat his partner Jamie and their cat Queso at book bingo. See what he's writing next on www.mcstjohn.com or follow him on Instagram under the handle @MC_StJohn.

THE ODDITY PRODIGY TEAM

MARCELLA HARTE CONLON has been fascinated with art and illustration since childhood. The same passion and attention to detail that won her school a sizable arts scholarship followed her to the University of the Arts, where she earned her bachelor of fine arts in illustration. She is currently working on a children's literature project. Her publishing credits include the anthology *The Stories in Between* by Fantasist Press, a collection of science fiction and fantasy stories published in 2009; cover art for the *All-Out Monster Revolt Online Magazine* in 2015; and most notably *The Mermaid in Rehoboth Bay*, a national award winning children's book published in 2016.

J. PATRICK CONLON is a genre fiction author currently living in Bear, Delaware. He is a member of the Written Remains Writer's Guild as well as a fellow Oddity in Oddity Prodigy Productions. His writing focuses on fantasy and speculative history themes. He has appeared in anthologies and magazines, most notably as Associate Editor for *Beach Pulp*, a collection of pulp fiction put out by Cat and Mouse Press.

JACOB JONES-GOLDSTEIN is an internationally published author, journalist, and editor. His short stories have appeared in anthologies such as *A Plague of Shadows* from Smart Rhino Press and *Beach Pulp* from Cat & Mouse Press. Beyond fiction, Jacob has covered the Philadelphia 76ers for a variety of online publications. He also writes about music for his personal site, ShoutingStreet.com. Beyond writing, he hosts popular podcasts "The Scary Stuff Podcast" and "The Mix Is In." You can find him on twitter @shoutingstreet and @jakeonsixers. He loves comic books, movies, cities, cats, family, friends, Joel Embiid, and his wife [who he suspiciously put last, very much noticed by said wife, who is doing the layout on this book.]

NICHOLAS LEAMY is a well-known miscreant who has lived in Northern Delaware all his life. Working as a supervisor for a web hosting data center, with a B.S. in Computer Science, he is well outside his wheelhouse when it comes to writing fiction. He has decided, however, that his minor in philosophy makes him interesting enough to pull it off. He also happens to be a lover of board games, horror movies, his wife, his kids and anything bizarre. Nicholas has been published once before in Oh Snap it's Oddity Prodigy. Having avoided being committed to an asylum, he plans to release several more stories while on the run from police.

JENNIFER MARANG loves werewolves. What else needs to be said? Yes, fine, she also did the cover of this book, and the interior layout; she's a graphic designer by trade. She spends most of her spare time writing in the third person (like now), and broke into the industry in grade 6 with the award-winning illustrated story *Indiana Jones and the Last Banana*, released by her own printing press (handwritten on construction paper), distributed at the local library, and published in the newspaper of her tiny outback town in Australia. Look out for her next published work in 2021, *The Flame's Heart*—a non-sweeping fantasy about a complete dick trapped in a sword. Jennifer lives in Delaware, by way of Montana and Australia, with five ridiculous cats, and a husband she adores but purposely put last because that's where he put her; looking at you, Jacob.

STEVE MYERS is an award-winning cartoonist and graphic designer who lives in Bear, Delaware. He spends his days working as a Search Engine Optimization professional, and his evenings running a hyperlocal news website in Lower Merion Township, PA. In between all of that, he draws comics and cartoons, including *The Adventures of Superchum*.

SHASTA SCHATZ is an eager reader, occasional writer, and lifelong fan girl, the latter of which translated into a costuming obsession in her adult life. Her B.A. in English laid the groundwork for Shasta to become an addicted hobbyist with professional leanings. Between HEAs, TPBs, and NDAs, Shasta is a hot mess wife and mother with a penchant for coffee and organized clutter. While she prefers not to be associated with these people, their links can be found on her costuming blog, <u>GreenLinenShirt.com</u>.